'You want to be kissed again. Immediately and more thoroughly.'

'The question of whether or not I want to be kissed by you is inappropriate.' She crossed her arms over her breasts and tried to ignore the way they felt. 'Completely and utterly inappropriate.'

'But you do want to be kissed.' Kit cupped her cheek with firm fingers.

She fought against the impulse to turn her face into his palm.

'It is in your eyes.' His thumb traced the outline of her mouth. 'And your lips.'

He lowered his head. This time his kiss was slow and coaxing.

Hattie brought her hands up and rested them on the solid broad cloth of his coat. His hand moulded her body to his. At the insistent pressure her lips parted slightly and she tasted the cool interior of his mouth. Nothing in her life had prepared her for the sensation rippling through her.

She allowed herself one more heartbeat of pleasure. She felt ridiculously feminine and pretty—someone to b̶ ̶

AUTHOR NOTE

On a cold and windswept day in March 2011, I travelled to the University of Birmingham with my daughter. We were early for her visitors' day, so we went to the Barber Institute of Fine Arts. There in the foyer was a portrait of one of its main benefactors, Martha Constance Hattie Barber, with her dogs.

Instantly and most inconveniently—because I was trying to finish another manuscript—the heroine of this novel, Harriet Wilkinson, popped into my brain and refused to leave. Her appearance was swiftly followed by the hero, who took to whispering in my mind that I really needed to write their story rather than writing the other one. Luckily I have dealt with such characters before, and I promised—as long as I finished the other manuscript first.

They agreed, and I kept my promise. However, immediately I started to turn my attention to them they became coy and refused to tell me their story. I saw the days start to tick by towards my deadline. Was I going to have to abandon them?

Luckily the *Hexham Courant* happened to run a story about a long-ago incident at the Stagshaw Bank Fair, and I was intrigued to learn that the fair was once the largest one-day fair in Britain and took place every year on 4th July. The fair has since been replaced by the Northumberland County Show, and now takes place on the late May Bank Holiday. But once I had read about the fair I knew I had my story, and thankfully my hero and heroine agreed.

I do hope you enjoy it as much as I enjoyed writing it— once my two stubborn and self-willed characters began speaking to me!

As ever, I love hearing from readers. You can contact me either by post to Harlequin Mills & Boon, via my website, www.michellestyles.co.uk, or my blog: www.michellestyles.blogspot.com. I am also on Twitter @michelleLstyles, and maintain a Facebook page.

HATTIE WILKINSON
MEETS HER MATCH

Michelle Styles

First published in Great Britain 2012
by Mills & Boon, an imprint of Harlequin (UK) Limited.
Harlequin (UK) Limited, Eton House, 18-24 Paradise Road,
Richmond, Surrey TW9 1SR

© Michelle Styles 2012

ISBN: 978 0 263 89277 2

Harlequin (UK) policy is to use papers that are natural, renewable and recyclable products and made from wood grown in sustainable forests. The logging and manufacturing process conform to the legal environmental regulations of the country of origin.

Printed and bound in Spain
by Blackprint CPI, Barcelona

Born and raised near San Francisco, California, **Michelle Styles** currently lives a few miles south of Hadrian's Wall, with her husband, three children, two dogs, cats, assorted ducks, hens and beehives.

An avid reader, she became hooked on historical romance when she discovered Georgette Heyer, Anya Seton and Victoria Holt one rainy lunchtime at school. And, for her, a historical romance still represents the perfect way to escape.

Although Michelle loves reading about history, she also enjoys a more hands-on approach to her research. She has experimented with a variety of old recipes and cookery methods (some more successfully than others), climbed down Roman sewers, and fallen off horses in Iceland—all in the name of discovering more about how people went about their daily lives. When she is not writing, reading or doing research, Michelle tends her rather overgrown garden or does needlework—in particular counted cross-stitch.

Michelle maintains a website, www.michellestyles.co.uk, and a blog: www.michellestyles.blogspot.com. She would be delighted to hear from you.

Previous novels by the same author:

Did you know that some of the novels
are also available as eBooks?
Visit www.millsandboon.co.uk

For Victoria Parker, whose support and enthusiasm
for this story helped so much.

Chapter One

End of June 1816—the Tyne Valley, Northumberland

A stifled noise, halfway between a giggle and an excited gasp, caused the Honourable Harriet Wilkinson to halt in her march back to the ballroom. Her entire being tensed. She knew what that sound signalled—in Summerfield's small card room, someone flirted with ruin.

'None of your business, Hattie Wilkinson,' she muttered. When had she become a censorious busybody poking her nose into other people's lives, rather than someone who understood a ball held the possibility of romance? Today was no time to start, and particularly not at a ball to celebrate the first anniversary of Waterloo.

Another trill of laughter sounded. 'That is highly amusing. Why should I ever feel in danger with you?'

Hattie sighed. Turning her back on an unknown couple was one thing. Turning her back on her high-spirited niece during her first foray into polite society was quite another. Far too much was at stake. Livvy with her clear blonde looks, graceful manner and more than adequate dowry had the potential to be a huge success in the London marriage market...if she was allowed to make it that far.

Hattie leant forwards and rattled the door handle.

'I wonder,' Hattie declared in a voice loud enough to wake the dead, 'where on earth have my gloves gone? I suspect I left them in the card room earlier. I had better check.'

She placed her lace gloves in her reticule, counted to ten slowly and flung open the door. The snug room with its artfully arranged tables, high-backed sofa and small fire in the marble fireplace was the sort of room that could offer privacy, especially as there was an unseasonable chill in the June air. In the centre of the room, her sixteen-year-old niece stood closer than strictly proper to a gentleman in evening dress.

Hattie pointedly cleared her throat. 'Excuse me, but I have mislaid my gloves.'

The couple sprang apart. Hattie noted Livvy's bright pink cheeks and mussed lace. Silently she thanked her guardian angel that it was she who had happened on the couple rather than one of the old cats who prowled the corridors searching for the latest tittle-tattle.

'This is Mr Hook, Aunt Harriet. He and I...' Livvy flushed scarlet. 'That is—he's a visitor to Northumberland and...'

'I'm looking for my gloves. Have you seen them, Livvy dear?' she asked brightly, ignoring the way Livvy quickly attempted to straighten her bodice and how young but dangerous Mr Hook appeared with his London-cut frock-coat and tousled Corinthian-styled hair. The time for a lecture on propriety, the necessity of maintaining one's spotless reputation and not settling for the first man who pays you a bit of attention was due later after Hattie had extracted Livvy from this tangle.

'You must know the ones I mean, Olivia,' she continued. 'The lace ones which your dear mama gave me for my birthday.'

'Your gloves, Aunt Harriet?' Livvy did an impression of a trout, repeatedly opening and closing her mouth.

'I think they might be in here. I was…' Hattie paused, trying to think up a reason why she might have been in the card room earlier. Her mind refused to yield the excuse. She opted for a brilliant smile. 'Olivia dear, would you mind helping me to search?'

Livvy behaved like any sixteen-year-old and rolled her eyes. 'If I must, Aunt Harriet, but honestly…'

'I positively insist. I am all sixes and sevens. Balls and me…well, the least said about my nerves the better.' Hattie waved a vague hand, well aware that Livvy had no idea about her normal behaviour at balls and quite probably considered a twenty-seven-year-old aunt bordered on senility in the general course of events.

A crease formed between Olivia's brows and Hattie could see the desire to appear older warring with her natural inclination to stay with her new swain. 'Yes, you are always like this at balls. When did you last have them? Think carefully now.'

Hattie's shoulders relaxed. Livvy had taken the bait, even down to spouting the exact words she always used with her nieces. The next stage of operation commenced now—gently guiding Livvy back to the ballroom with no moonlit detours.

'And you will do the usual and help me to look. Your sharp eyes are so much better at finding things than my ageing ones.'

Hattie waited for Livvy's agreement. Slowly and steadily she would prise Mr Hook from Livvy's life before he did any lasting damage. Unlike Livvy, she knew precisely the pitfalls of London gentlemen who made extravagant promises. Whilst she had avoided ruin seven years ago, she had been unable to avoid the heartbreak that goes with discovering one's beloved had, in fact, been another woman's beloved at the same time. Livvy would not suffer that fate. None of her nieces would. Silently Hattie renewed her determination.

'Perhaps your aunt left them in the garden,' Mr Hook said in a falsely concerned voice. 'We could investigate, Miss Parteger.'

'What a splendid idea.' Hattie clapped her hands and fixed Livvy's would-be seducer with a stern eye. 'You may search the garden, Mr Hook, while dear Olivia and I search the library, drawing room and the card room. Make sure you leave no stone unturned in your quest to find my gloves.'

Mr Hook gulped twice and scampered out of the card room faster than a fox with the sound of a hunting horn ringing in his ears.

The sound of slow clapping filled the room.

Someone is here! Livvy mouthed, turning redder than a beetroot. A cold shudder snaked down Hattie's back. She'd once been a carefree girl like Livvy. But after succumbing to the advances of a dashing soldier, she had been hustled into a quick marriage, a marriage she had considered romantic beyond her wildest dreams until she had discovered the sordid truth after his death. Even now the humiliation of her discovery caused the bile to rise in her throat. Livvy deserved better.

'Bravo! Bravo!' a rich masculine voice called out. 'A truly stunning performance.'

'What are you doing here, sirrah?' Hattie demanded, brandishing her reticule like a sword towards the sofa. 'Listening into others' private conversations? Show yourself.'

The man rose from the sofa with a book in his hand. Hattie swallowed hard. He was the sort of man to make the pulse beat faster—crisp black hair with brooding dark grey eyes combined with broad shoulders and a lean frame. His face was saved from utter perfection by the presence of a nose which had obviously been broken several times in the past. 'One could hardly help overhearing. You are the one who should be apologising for interrupting my reading and sending my godson on a pointless game of Hunt the Gloves, but I shall forgive you if you beg prettily.'

'Aunt Hattie?' Olivia tugged at Hattie's hand as she started to back out of the room. 'It's Sir Christopher Foxton.'

Christopher Foxton. The name thudded through Hattie. The entire village had been gossiping about him for weeks, ever since it became known that he'd finally decided to visit Southview Lodge. About how he'd beat a man near to death over a game of cards and while the man lay recuperating had stolen his mistress and his fortune. How he was unbeaten in the ring, daring to fight bare-knuckled with the best of them. But mostly how because of his breeding, good looks and personal charm, every door in London was open to him and how various mamas predicted that they would capture him for this or that daughter, even though his mistresses were reputed to be some of the most sought-after courtesans in London.

The amount of sighing and speculation over him had reached such epidemic proportions that it seemed all anyone in the village could speak about was Sir Christopher and his exploits.

Hattie raised her chin a notch and met his intense gaze head-on. He had another think coming if he expected her to beg his forgiveness, prettily or not. She was immune from such men and their superficial charm.

'Where are my gloves, then, if I have sent your godson on a pointless game?' Hattie cried, exasperated. Confessing her rescue mission was out of the question. She'd rather face a gaggle of gossips dressed only in her chemise and petticoat than reveal her true purpose to this…this rake!

'Your gloves are in your reticule.' Sir Christopher held out an uncompromising hand. 'Allow me to demonstrate, my dear lady.'

'There is no need. And you will call me Mrs Wilkinson. I am not your dear or anyone else's dear or any other endearment you care to mention.' Hattie clutched the reticule to her chest. Panic clawed at her stomach. The gloves! How could he know? How would he twist the discovery?

'There is every need, *Mrs Wilkinson*.' Sir Christopher's tone hardened to well-tempered steel. 'Your reticule.'

Silently Hattie passed the beaded reticule over to him. Their fingers brushed and a single tremor of warmth ran up her arm. Ruthlessly, she suppressed it. A delayed reaction to all the gossip about his private life, that was all.

He weighed the reticule in his well-manicured hand as if trying to decide what to do. She prayed for a miracle and that he might suddenly reveal a handkerchief. He opened it and withdrew a pair of lace gloves with mulberry bows tacked to the cuffs.

'Very pretty they are, too. Or perhaps you have another pair and keep these for emergencies.'

'They are mine,' Hattie ground out, silently wishing him, his dark brooding eyes and his infuriatingly superior expression to the devil. 'I obviously forgot where I had placed them. I thank you for your assistance.'

'Always happy to oblige a lady.' He made an ironic bow. 'But you owe me a forfeit for finding them.'

'A forfeit?'

'The next dance.' Kit Foxton concentrated on Mrs Wilkinson. The woman with her carefully coiffured crown of blonde braids and severe dress needed to learn a light romance at a ball was something to be desired rather than condemned.

'Olivia, close your mouth,' the overbearing Mrs Wilkinson declared. Her skirts swirled as she turned, revealing surprisingly shapely ankles. 'Sir Christopher found my gloves. We shall be returning to the ballroom. Behave as if nothing has happened. Say nothing about this incident. Ever.'

'Such a simple stratagem, but I found your gloves.' Kit clenched and unclenched his fists. Mrs Wilkinson appeared to believe that she had the right to pass judgement on others' behaviour and to fashion the world how she wanted. He looked forward to proving her wrong. 'You may have them back once the forfeit is properly paid.'

Mrs Wilkinson gave a pointed cough. 'Olivia, the ballroom! Now!'

'What are you afraid of, Mrs Wilkinson? Why are you running when it is you who started this game?' he called out. 'Your reputation being ruined? It takes more than a few moments of pleasant conversation to sully a reputation as you must know.'

She froze, slipper dangling in mid-air. 'My reputation has never been in danger. Ever.'

'I'm pleased to hear it.'

She slowly turned to face him with her hands balled on her hips, blue-green eyes flashing with barely suppressed fury. 'It never will be. I would thank you to remember that.'

'You want to dance with my aunt? But she is a widow of seven years!' Miss Parteger clapped her hands together.

'Dancing is not forbidden to widows,' Kit said.

A widow. Why did the knowledge not surprise him? The only shock was that she must have once experienced romance.

Kit frowned as Mrs Wilkinson turned her head to glare at her niece and he saw her long swanlike neck. The curious dead part of his soul that had been part of his existence for a year stirred and moved. Mrs Wilkinson had possibilities.

'We appear to be in a bit of a tangle here,' Mrs Wilkinson said, putting her hand on her hip. 'You will cease your funning this instant, Sir Christopher, and return my gloves.'

'They are safe in my care until the forfeit is paid. To the victor, the spoils.'

'Just wait until Mama hears about this,' Miss Parteger said, clapping her hands together. 'She will be at sixes and sevens with excitement. Aunt Harriet has a beau. Finally.'

'I would suggest, young lady, that you hold your tongue about this adventure.' Kit gave a cold nod. Mrs Wilkinson had lost. He knew it and, more importantly, she knew it. She would yield to his suggestion.

Miss Parteger blinked rapidly. 'Why?'

'Because if you don't, it will reveal you were somewhere where you shouldn't have been and your trip to London might become a distant dream,' Mrs Wilkinson replied without missing a beat. The colour drained from her niece's face. 'And, yes, Sir Christopher, I will dance with you, but it must be the next dance. I want this fanciful forfeit finished and this entire episode an unwelcome memory as soon as possible.'

Kit resisted the temptation to crow. There was no point in grinding one's opponent into the floor like his father used to. Kit didn't require abject humiliation, just total surrender.

Kit held out his arm and smiled at the overly confident Mrs Wilkinson. A waltz in this backwater would be too much to hope for. A simple quadrille which would allow him to put his hands on her waist was all he desired. Mrs Wilkinson needed this. She would thank him for it…later. 'Our dance awaits.'

As Hattie set foot in the ballroom, flanked by Livvy and Sir Christopher, the music ceased and the mass of humanity seethed around the dance floor as people exchanged greetings and partners.

Hattie breathed deeply and released Sir Christopher's arm. Tonight's adventure was finished. A solitary quadrille with Sir Christopher to prove her point, and she'd be finished. The dance would prove useful if Livvy was unable to resist confiding her adventure. She would merely claim that Sir Christopher had requested a dance and she'd agreed. No one needed to know the precise circumstances.

'Shall we?' She gestured with her fan towards the middle of the dance floor, well away from the chandelier and its dripping wax.

'This dance? Don't you want to know which one it is?'

'Why wait? Or are you a coward?' she called out. 'I wish to get this forfeit over.'

She was halfway across the dance floor when the master of ceremonies announced that the next dance would a German waltz. Hattie halted. A waltz? The next dance couldn't be a waltz. They never waltzed at Summerfield. A waltz would mean being in Sir Christopher's arms, looking up into his dark grey eyes. Impossible!

'It would appear I was wrong. It isn't a quadrille, but a waltz.' Hattie shrugged a shoulder and attempted to ignore the ice-cold pit opening in her stomach. 'Fancy that.'

'Is a waltz problematic?' he asked, lifting a quizzical brow, but his eyes gleamed with hidden lights.

'Such a shame. We agreed to a quadrille.' Hattie gave a falsely contrite smile. Escape. All she needed to do was to escape. He wouldn't come after her. He wouldn't create a scene. 'It has been a pleasure, Sir Christopher.'

She dropped a quick curtsy and prepared to move towards where Stephanie sat, surrounded by the other matrons, surveying the dance floor.

Sir Christopher reached out and grasped her elbow, pulling her close to his hard frame. 'Not so fast. We have an altogether different agreement.'

She tugged slightly, but he failed to release her.

'Have you gone mad? What in the name of everything holy are you doing?' she said in a furious undertone. 'All I wanted to do was to rescue Livvy from your godson. Nothing more.'

'You promised me the next dance, Mrs Wilkinson. A German waltz is the next dance.' He tightened his grip, sliding it down her arm until her hand was captured. He raised it to his lips. 'I hope you are the sort of woman who keeps her promises.'

Hattie hated the way his velvet voice slid over her skin, tempting her to flirt with him. Her traitorous body wanted to be held in his arms. But that would lead to heartbreak. She'd sworn off such men for ever. She concentrated on all the gossip about him—the women, the duels and the gaming—but her body stubbornly remained aware of him and the way his fingers held her wrist.

'I implied, rather than specifically promised. There is a difference,' she said, looking him directly in the eyes. 'You of all people should know the difference.'

'An implied promise remains a promise.' His full lips turned upwards. 'Consider what might have been, Mrs Wilkinson, before you reject me entirely.'

Hattie studied the wooden floor, scuffed with the marks of a hundred dancing slippers, and concentrated on breathing steadily. Her entire being longed to say *yes*. Charm, that's all it was, just as it had been with Charles. Once she allowed herself to be swayed, she'd lose everything.

'I suspect you say that to everyone.' She gave a light laugh and her pulse started beating normally again. 'You've never seen me waltz.'

'Ah, you don't know how to waltz. You should have said rather than stooping to subterfuge.'

'Waltzing reached Northumberland several years ago.' Hattie put her hand on her hip. Talk about assumptions. Did she really look like a frumpy wallflower? When had that happened? 'I can and do waltz when the occasion demands. I simply prefer not to waltz right now.'

'Unfortunately, we can't always get what we want, Mrs Wilkinson. Here all I had intended to do was to dance with you. However, if you insist, we shall have a flirtation in the garden. My late uncle always said that northern women were bold, but until I met you, I had no idea.'

'Do such remarks cause the ladies in London to swoon at your feet? Up here, you are more likely to get a slapped face.'

'It is one of my more endearing traits. Impossible, but with a modicum of wit,' he said, giving her a hooded look. 'But will the lady waltz? Or is she a coward with two left feet?'

'I'll waltz with you, if only to prove you wrong about my dancing ability,' Hattie ground out.

'Hand on my shoulder now and we shall begin.' His tone became rich velvet which slid over her skin. 'I promise you a dance to remember.'

'Are you a dancing master now? Is there no end to your many talents?'

'I endeavour to give satisfaction, particularly to the ladies.'

'Proprieties will be observed, Sir Christopher.'

'Did I suggest otherwise?' Kit stopped. The instant his hand had encountered hers, he'd felt an unexpected and searing tug of attraction. For over a year, he hadn't felt any attraction and suddenly this. Why her? Why this widow with an over-developed sense of propriety and hideous hairstyle? He had made it a policy not to be attracted to respectable women ever since Brighton.

'I'm pleased we hold the same view.'

'What can I ever have done to result in your censure?' he murmured, slightly adjusting his hand so it fit more snugly on her slender waist. Kit gave an inward smile as they circled the room. Mrs Wilkinson's lesson was proving more enjoyable than he first considered. He inched his hand lower. She gave him a freezing look and he returned to the proper hold.

'Your reputation preceded you, Sir Christopher.'

Kit could easily imagine what the village gossips were saying about him and his wicked past. There had been a time when he hadn't cared or appreciated what life could offer. He had gambled and whored with the best of them. He fought bad men with his bare hands. All that had ended a year ago when his best friend gave up his life for him and he'd become one of the walking dead.

'You have been listening to common tittle-tattle. That should be beneath you,' he said.

She tilted her head to one side and gave an unrepentant smile. 'When someone as notorious as you comes from London, his antecedents are discussed. It is the way of the world. Mr Hook is your protégé. He follows your methods, but fortunately for my niece, I happened along rather than one of the Tyne Valley gossips. Olivia will not suffer the fate of so many of your women.'

A blaze of anger went through Kit. She'd judged not only him, but also Rupert, on the basis of a few pieces of tittle-tattle. He renewed his determination to ensure that a full and complete flirtation happened. 'I'm no saint, Mrs Wilkinson, but neither am I a black-hearted villain. I have never ruined a débutante or indeed participated in the ruining of a débutante. Neither have I ever seduced a woman from her children or her husband. It is against my creed.'

'But they said…I'm sure…the stories…'

'Yes, I know the stories, but more importantly I know the truth. Do you? Have you ever been misjudged?'

She dipped her head, showing her intricately braided hair. Only the smallest curl dared escape. 'Perhaps I have been over-hasty in my judgement. I will accept your word that you would have said something if I had failed to come into the card room. And I'm wrong to punish you for another's actions.'

'Apology accepted. Shall we start again and endeavour to enjoy the dance?'

He pulled her waist closer to his body so that her skirt brushed his legs. Her hand tightened about his. His breath caressed the delicate curve of her shell-like ear. Her shoulder trembled under his fingers. He smiled inwardly. A little romance always brightened everyone's life. He looked forward to discovering Mrs Wilkinson's hidden depths.

'Will you give me a chance to prove the gossips wrong?' Kit asked quietly. 'Will you dance with me again or, better still, take a turn about the garden where I can plead my case?'

He waited for her breathless agreement.

'This is where the dance ends,' she said in a voice that left no room for dissent. She gave a small curtsy. 'We would hardly wish to cause a scandal. We are only strangers after all.'

'I must become a friend and discover what sort of scandal you have in mind,' Kit murmured. 'Be reckless. Further our acquaintance. You intrigue me.'

'One dance will have to satisfy you, Sir Christopher.' She stepped out of his arms. 'I bid you goodnight.'

She strode away, her hips agreeably swaying and her back twitching. Kit frowned. He had nearly begged for her favour. He never begged. His skills were rusty.

He patted his pocket where he'd placed the gloves. Their little romance was not over until he decided. Mrs Wilkinson had a lesson to learn and she would learn it…thoroughly. 'Until the next time, Mrs Wilkinson. Sweet dreams.'

Mrs Wilkinson paused, half-turned, then, appearing to think better of a retort, she resumed her march in double-quick time as if the devil himself was after her.

Chapter Two

'You left Sir Christopher Foxton standing on the dance floor even though the dance hadn't finished!' Mrs Reynaud said with a stifled gasp as Hattie reached the end of her highly edited tale the next morning. The sunlit parlour with its dimity lace curtains and artfully arranged ornaments was a world away from last night's splendours of the ballroom.

'It was the right thing to do.' Hattie reached for her teacup. There was little point in telling Mrs Reynaud about how her legs had trembled and how close she'd been to agreeing to his outlandish suggestion of a turn about the garden. She knew what he was, why she couldn't take a chance with him and still the temptation to give in to his charm had been there. Even after all she'd been through with Charles and his unreliability, a part of her had wanted to believe in romance and she refused to allow it to happen.

'Do you know you were the only lady he danced with all night?'

Hattie set the cup down with an unsteady hand. She could hardly confess to have been aware of Sir Christopher in that fashion. 'How do you know that *on dit*?'

'My maid had the news from the butcher's boy this morning,' the elderly woman said. 'Your waltz is the talk of the village. I've been in a quiver of anticipation. Thank you for telling me what truly happened, my dear. It makes my mind rest easier.'

Hattie kept her gaze focused on the way her papillon dog, Moth, was delicately finishing her biscuit, rather than meeting Mrs Reynaud's interested gaze. The whole point of the story was to enlist Mrs Reynaud's advice about Livvy's behaviour and how best to approach the talk she knew she'd have to give, rather than discuss her near-flirtation with the village's current most notorious resident.

Why was it that women lost their minds as soon as Sir Christopher's name was mentioned? Her sister had gone fluttery when Hattie returned from the dance floor, demanding to know how Hattie was acquainted with Sir Christopher. Hattie glossed over the card-room incident and Stephanie appeared satisfied.

'It was a waltz, nothing more,' Hattie said finally, seeking to close the matter. 'We had a brief verbal-sparring match. He dislikes being bested, but the game has ended. Honours to me.'

'Do you know how long Sir Christopher will be in the neighbourhood?' Mrs Reynaud handed Moth another biscuit. The little brown-and-white dog tilted her head to one side, waiting, but after Hattie nodded gobbled the biscuit up.

'He failed to confide his intentions.' Hattie stroked Moth's silky ears. Moth had come into her life just after Charles's death and for many months was the only bright spot. 'It has taken him over a year to visit his inheritance. Our paths won't cross again.'

'Predicting the future is always fraught with danger, my dear.' Mrs Reynaud brushed the crumbs into a pile for Moth. 'It does my heart good to hear news of him after such a long time, even if it's only for a short while.'

'Are you acquainted with him, then?' Hattie stared at the woman.

'I knew the family years ago. His late uncle arranged for me to have the lease on this house.'

'Perhaps he will call on you once he realises you are here.'

The colour faded from Mrs Reynaud's face, making the pockmarks stand out even more. 'My dear, I…I have changed a great deal since we last encountered each other.'

Instantly Hattie regretted her words. Over the last two years since Mrs Reynaud had taken up residency in the tiny cottage, she'd become accustomed to Mrs Reynaud's ruined features. 'An old friend never looks at faces. They are pleased to renew the friendship.'

'I doubt that he will remember me, whatever the state of his manners,' Mrs Reynaud said, raising a handkerchief to her face. 'Pray do not bother him with an old woman's remembrance of a past acquaintance. I was wrong to mention it. Ever so wrong.'

'Very well, I won't insist.' Hattie buried her face in Moth's fur. What was she doing, clutching at straws, searching for a way to encounter Sir Christopher again? Had her experience with Charles taught her nothing? A few minutes waltzing with a confirmed rake and she behaved worse than Livvy. 'It is a moot point as our paths are unlikely to cross.'

'Are you that ignorant of men? He forced a forfeit and waltzed with you and only you.'

'He did that for…for his own purposes,' Hattie explained. 'They say his mistresses are the most beautiful women London can offer. Why would he be interested in someone like me and my few charms?'

'You underestimate yourself, my dear, and that borders on foolishness.' Mrs Reynaud held out her hand. 'I merely wanted to point out that having done your duty to your fallen hero and mourned him properly, you can start to live again. But if your heart is for ever buried with your husband and you are one of the walking dead, then so be it. A pity with you being so young.'

Hattie swirled the remains of her coffee. Living again. She thanked God that Mrs Reynaud didn't know what her husband was truly like. The extent of his perfidy and hypocrisy had only emerged after his death.

Before then she had considered that she had a blissful marriage with someone utterly reliable and steadfast. She'd had no idea about his other family or the debts he'd run up. Thankfully, the woman in question had been discreet and she'd managed to scrape together the required amount. But no one else knew. She had her pride.

Sometimes she felt as if she was still living a lie, but she couldn't confess the full horror. Not now, not ever. It remained her problem and she didn't want false sympathy.

She opted for a bland, 'I hardly know what to say.'

'A light-hearted flirtation never did anyone any harm. Allow a little romance into your life. You're a handsome woman and should be aware of your power! You should celebrate being alive, rather than running from it.'

Hattie focused on the tips of Moth's ears as Moth snuffled crumbs. Flirtations could harm people, if they believed in romance. That lesson was etched on her heart. 'I'll bear that in mind, should ever the question arise.'

'Oh dear, I fear I've shocked you. It's what comes from living abroad for such a long period.' The corners of Mrs Reynaud's mouth quirked upwards. 'You'll get over it in time and forgive me, I hope. I do so look forward to your visits. They are always the highlight of my day.'

'I should go to Highfield and see how Livvy fares before I go back home,' Hattie said, plopping Moth into the now-empty basket. Moth gave a sharp bark and placed her paws on the rim.

Although she loved her sister and nieces and nephews, Hattie maintained her own establishment—the Highfield Dower House at the edge of the Highfield estate. Her old nurse Mrs Hampstead served as her housekeeper. Close enough to be on hand if there was a crisis, but far enough to maintain her own life.

She had come to Northumberland shortly after Charles's death was confirmed. Her mother had died of a fever a few months before and her father of a broken heart, a week before Charles's things arrived.

She'd always been grateful neither of them knew of Charles's perfidy. She couldn't have hidden the truth from her mother.

When Stephanie's plea for help came, Hattie had considered it better than staying in London with her brother, the new viscount, and his wife. She had discovered a peace in Northumberland that she hadn't considered possible.

'You spend far too much time running around after your sister and her brood. She uses you as an unpaid lackey.'

'There may be flowers or notes,' Hattie said at Mrs Reynaud's look. 'And don't worry, I will tell you everything about Livvy's progress when I next visit. I think you are right, a quiet word and then tales about the wonders of a London Season should suffice.'

'Come tomorrow. I will regale you with tales about how I escaped from the harem. Lots of danger and excitement.'

A great longing to see far-flung places and experience life swamped Hattie. When she was a little girl, she used to watch the ships on the Thames and swear she'd go abroad some day. But the furthest she'd travelled was to Northumberland and now that had become home.

Now that Stephanie's children were nearly grown, she could start thinking about travelling. Doing things for herself rather than for others, but she still had to be aware of how her actions could affect the family. Outward appearances were everything. 'Did you really escape?'

'I feel the sheikh desired me more than I desired him. I was a great beauty once, you know.'

'You still have a beautiful soul, Mrs Reynaud.' Hattie covered Mrs Reynaud's hand and ignored the tear that trickled down Mrs Reynaud's face.

'You have no idea the mistakes I have made and how I've paid for them.' Mrs Reynaud's gnarled hands fumbled for a handkerchief. 'Sir Christopher… Remember, I specifically want to know when he departs from the neighbourhood.'

Hattie firmed her mouth. She wouldn't enquire into Mrs Reynaud's reasons, but she suspected they would both be relieved when he went. 'If I learn any more news about Sir Christopher, I'll tell you. I promise.'

* * *

The gravel crunched under Hattie's feet as she marched towards Highfield's rose garden. Despite the pile of unopened cards and several bouquets littering the drawing room, her sister and nieces were entertaining gentlemen callers in the rose garden.

Hattie knew she should have come earlier, but she had wanted to visit Mrs Reynaud and get her opinion before she acted. Surely Stephanie could cope with Livvy's high spirits for a few minutes? When the time was right, she intended to have a quiet word with Livvy. Romance at a ball was all well and good, but some day, you had to wake up and face the harsh reality of the morning after when the evening prince turned out to be an unreliable toad.

Moth gave a sharp bark, indicating she wanted out of the basket. Hattie set the basket down. Moth gave Hattie a quizzical look and wandered off to investigate the garden, but came racing back almost instantly and sat at Hattie's feet. Straight behind her strode Sir Christopher, his black coat and tan breeches gleaming in the sun. A gentleman caller with a difference.

'Ah, I had wondered if you were going to grace us with your presence, Mrs Wilkinson, before I managed to wear out my welcome.'

'Sir Christopher.' Hattie hoped any high colour would be attributed to her walk, rather than his nearness. Mrs Reynaud had put ideas in her head about flirtations. Not precisely true. Her sleep had been filled with dreams of them dancing where Sir Christopher spun her round and round as Charles stood in the shadows.

'Is the miscreant dog yours?' he asked. 'I caught her attempting to dig a hole in the borders. She is hardly bigger than a cat.'

'Yes, Moth is mine. She is a papillon.'

'A trained killer, rather than a butterfly.' Sir Christopher bent down and tickled Moth under the chin. Moth lifted her chin a notch higher before rolling over and exposing her belly. Moth gave a little whimper of pleasure as Sir Christopher obligingly stroked her belly.

Hattie belatedly realised she was staring and turned towards a stand of deep-blue delphiniums. 'An unexpected pleasure.'

'My godson was anxious to call on Miss Parteger, but my true purpose involves you.'

'Me?'

'The return of your gloves.'

Hattie winced. The gloves. How had she forgotten he had retained them until the blasted forfeit was over? 'Where are they?'

'Your sister has taken possession. She expressed surprise that you were so careless with her birthday gift.'

'It was good of you to return them.' Hattie kept her gaze carefully on the gravel path, rather than meeting his intense grey eyes. 'I'm sure my sister will hand them to me. She is very trustworthy in that regard.'

'I assumed they were precious to you. You were very concerned when you mislaid them earlier in the evening.'

'That had a different purpose, as you rapidly guessed.'

'I know, but you neglected to finish your forfeit and collect your gloves. What does this say about you?'

Hattie winced, knowing she'd been the one to make the mistake and leave the dance floor so abruptly. She'd been foolish to give in to her anger and to forget that he held the gloves hostage last evening. It wasn't his fault that she'd once believed a night's romance at a ball would last for ever. All Sir Christopher had required was light conversation during the dance and a polite goodbye, something seven years ago she'd have done without considering the consequences. Instead she had behaved like the worst maiden aunt, storming off as if he had attempted to make love to her on the dance floor. 'The dance was over.'

'We shall have to examine another forfeit for leaving me bereft on the dance floor.'

'Have you spoken with your godson about his behaviour?' she said more tartly than she intended as she tried to banish the sudden image of Sir Christopher kissing her. She would not be agreeing to any sort of renewed forfeit.

'Rupert now understands the necessity of behaving properly if he desires to further his acquaintance with your niece. Your niece is very adept at the use of her fan. He had considered that she was older.'

A cold shiver went down Hattie's spine. She could just imagine. She knew all about Livvy's fascination with fan language for flirtation purposes. She'd warned Stephanie about it weeks ago. Obviously nothing had been done. The problem was how to discuss Livvy's use of the fan without revealing where she had been. 'Livvy is impetuous, but innocent. It was a game to her, to see if she could. Nothing more.'

His shadowy grey eyes locked on to hers. 'And was it a game for you, bursting in on them? Attempting to find evidence of a flirtatious game gone too far? Or is any flirtation too far for you?'

'My niece's reputation is paramount.' Hattie

hugged her arms about her waist and tried to control the shiver. 'And anyway, why are you wandering about the grounds on your own?'

'Your sister is playing the chaperon while I attempt to find the cedar of Lebanon. As Rupert has decided he wants to do more than play infantile fan games with your niece, he needs to make a favourable impression on your sister.'

'Have you found the tree?' she asked brightly.

'I was on my way when your dog discovered me.' He checked his fob watch. 'A quarter of an hour to make a good impression is all Rupert requires.'

'You need to find the tree before your time is up. Truth in all things.'

'We reach complete understanding at last, Mrs Wilkinson.' A smile tugged at his features. 'It is part of my creed.'

Hattie shook her head. His charm was lethal. She was certain most women discounted his words and only focused on the seductive warmth in his voice. Listening to him, it was easy to understand why he enjoyed such a reputation with ladies. But she knew the trick—the words, not the tone, were important.

'You're going in the wrong direction,' she called as he started going towards the boating lake.

'Am I? How remiss of me.' A dimple shone in his cheek. 'Perhaps you will be kind enough to show me the proper way, Mrs Wilkinson? Getting hopelessly lost could ruin the entire matter. Consider it a fair exchange for leaving me on the dance floor.'

'When you put it that way, how can I refuse? Find the tree and all obligation will end.'

'Something like that,' Sir Christopher murmured.

Hattie placed her gloved hand on his arm. Every inch of her being hummed with awareness of him and the tantalising sandalwood scent he used. A pleasant conversation would not harm anyone, particularly as she remained in control. Mrs Reynaud was right. It was about time she started living, rather than hiding behind her widowhood.

'We should take the left-hand fork here,' he said.

She glanced at him under her lashes. His entire being radiated smugness. 'You engineered this walk! You know precisely where the tree is. Stephanie gave you directions.'

'Walks are more pleasant if there are two people, even if one of them has tendencies to be sharp-tongued.'

'I'm not. What is the point of having a mind if I can't speak it?'

'Never apologise. Women fall over themselves to falsely compliment me. You make a change.'

'Why were you in the card room?' she asked to keep her mind away from the potential rocky subject of comparing her to other women. 'You hardly seem to be the shy and retiring type. Were you waiting for a lady to appear? One of those who fall over at your compliments? Surely you can confess all to a sharp-tongued widow like me.'

He stopped abruptly in front of a spreading oak. All humour vanished from his countenance. 'You continue to do me a disservice, Mrs Wilkinson. I only ever pursue one lady at a time.'

The butterflies started beating inside her. *One lady at a time.* He had sought her out after the dance when he could have sent the gloves.

The news made her blood fizz and tingle.

She removed her hand from his arm and took a gulp of life-giving air. She was not going to start to believe in the illusion of romance again. Charles Wilkinson had for ever cured her of that. Sir Christopher had an ulterior motive, but he would be disappointed. She would show him that at least one woman would not tumble into his bed with the merest crook of his finger or a seductive laugh. Two could play this game. He would learn a lesson.

'Is that the only explanation I will get?' She forced her voice to sound playful. You'll trap more flies with honey than vinegar, she reminded herself.

'You require more?'

'The mystery intrigues me. Did you see the fan play between Mr Hook and my niece and know where the proposed liaison would happen?'

'I was not playing an errant knight. Alas.' Kit stopped and stared out into the garden with its low hum of bees and faint birdsong rather than at the soberly dressed woman who stood next to him. The scene contrasted so much with the thick mud and scent of gunpowder that had filled his nostrils a year ago. The feeling of being truly alive washed over him again.

The circumstances, rather than the company. Kit forced the brief panic down his throat. After his mother's departure when he was four and his later experience in Brighton, he'd vowed never to care about a woman. In any case, Mrs Wilkinson was far too severe for his taste. She wanted an explanation, she would get it. That would be an end of the matter.

'A year ago last Thursday, I attended a ball in Brussels. It was all gaiety, but like many other men I had to leave early. We went from the Duchess of Richmond's ballroom to the mud and stink of war. I returned, but many of my comrades didn't.' He waited for her to take the hint and politely change the subject.

'You were at Waterloo? As a soldier?' she asked, her eyes growing wide and luminous under her bonnet.

'I was at Waterloo,' he confirmed.

'No one ever mentioned you being in the Army. Not a single word.' She turned her head and all he could see was the crown of her impossible bonnet and the back of her shoulder.

'Does it bother you?'

'It is unexpected. I have heard stories…'

Kit could well imagine what was said of him. And for the vast majority of his life, he hadn't cared. It was far better to be thought heartless than to be ridiculed as someone whose mother couldn't love him, who had left his father because of him.

After Waterloo, it had changed. Brendan Hook had thought him a good enough friend to die for. London and his former pleasures lost their allure.

'It doesn't matter what others think. It has never mattered,' he said. 'The battle only occupied a few hours of my life. Being in the Army lasted a few short weeks and then I went back to my usual haunts.'

'You are wrong to minimise it,' she said, turning back towards him. 'Very wrong. You played a part in a great victory. People will be celebrating Waterloo for years and you can say that you were there.'

Kit regarded her earnest face with its English-rose complexion, gazing up at him. She possessed a delicate beauty, he realised with a start. He wondered how he'd overlooked it before. But the highly conventional widow was also not his type.

Kit was very strict about the women in his life and his rules surrounding them. They asked for no more than he was prepared to give. They were experienced and knew the rules without them being clearly stated. He always ended it before emotions were involved.

Mrs Wilkinson was trouble, but he was also loath to leave before this lesson in mild flirtation finished.

He turned the conversation to more mundane subjects as they continued towards the tree. To his surprise, the conversation about gardens was far more enjoyable than he had considered possible at the start of the journey.

'Behold the tree. We can turn back now,' Mrs Wilkinson said as they rounded a bend.

'Yes, the tree. It is a magnificent sight.'

A gentle breeze moulded her skirt to her remarkably fine legs. Mrs Wilkinson possessed a far better figure than he'd first imagined. Kit struggled to keep his gaze on her face and not wonder why she had failed to remarry. None of his business.

'You keep changing the subject.' She laid a gloved hand on his arm. 'Why keep your service a secret? Weren't you supposed to be there?'

'I rapidly acquired a lieutenant's commission in the Life Guards once I heard of Boney's escape and was lucky to get that. Everything was snapped up in days. The whole of London society seemed to be in Brussels last year. A number of friends couldn't even get a commission, but they came anyway. They got out when the fighting got too hot and left it to the proper soldiers.'

The green in her eyes deepened. 'But you stayed until the end. You didn't run, even though you are determined that I should think the worst of you. If you had run, it would have been the first thing you said.'

'I know how to be a soldier.' Kit's shoulders became light. Even without his saying it, she believed he'd done the right thing. He hated to think how few people ever believed that of him. It mattered. 'Eton prepares one for it.'

The memory of those long-ago days swept over him. Back then, he'd thought himself capable of anything. In his final year, he'd believed himself in love and that Constance Stanley would marry him once he asked her.

His illusions were shattered when he'd arrived at her house unexpectedly with the engagement ring in his pocket. He'd overheard her assessment of him as the son of two wicked people and how her family needed his money and how she'd feared that she would have to marry a devil. He had stepped out of the shadows. Constance's shocked face had said it all. All of his father's warnings thudded into him. He bid her and her companion good day and gave the ring to the first beggar woman with a baby at her breast that he saw.

Never again had he allowed himself to contemplate marriage. Never again had he allowed a woman to get close, preferring to end the thing before it happened. Kit had a variety of presents he'd send—a bouquet to end a flirtation, a strand of pearls to end a brief but hugely enjoyable weekend, sapphires to end something longer.

Mrs Wilkinson turned her back on him and walked with quick steps over to the cedar. She stood there, unmoving for a moment, her brows drawn together in a frown. He waited for her to make a remark about the weather or society.

'Why aren't you down in London? With Rupert's father?' she asked.

He turned from her and stared towards where the great cedar towered over the garden. Everything was so peaceful and still, except for the distant cooing of a dove, calling to its mate. No danger here. This was the England he'd fought for, not the bright lights of London. He wanted that peace that had eluded him. He wanted to show that he had changed and that he did deserve a future, a future that he did not intend to squander. 'Rupert's father died.'

'I didn't know. I'm sorry for you and for Mr Hook.'

'False sympathy fails to matter. You never knew him.'

'You're wrong. Any man's death should be remarked on and he was your friend. You must miss him,' she said with an intense earnestness. 'When did you decide to come up to Northumberland?'

'When I was on the battlefield, surrounded by men dying on either side, I swore that next year I would be somewhere which epitomised what I was fighting for.' The words came from deep within him. He wanted her to understand that on the battlefield he'd decided what was important and how his life needed to change. She, of all the people he'd met recently, might understand and the very thought unnerved him. 'I thought of the fair, the Stagshaw Bank Fair, and how it is held every year on the fourth of July.'

Her dusky-rose lips turned up into an incredulous smile. 'You are asking me to believe that you decided to come to Northumberland when you were at Waterloo? I can think of a dozen other more likely places that should have sprung to mind.'

'It seemed as good a place as any to my fevered mind. When I was a lad, my uncle brought me here. The day has long stood in my memory. He bought me a wooden jumping-jack.' He shook his head.

There was no need to explain that it had been the first time since his mother's departure that he'd received a gift or anyone had taken notice of him beyond cuffing him on the ear. He'd kept that jumping-jack for years, hidden in his handkerchiefs so that his father would not stumble across it and destroy it.

'It seemed like a place worth fighting to see again. I said as much to Brendan, who was on my right—*there will be time enough to reminisce as the years go by, but next year I would be up in Northumberland and would go to the fair.* He agreed to go with me.'

'And that is why you and Mr Hook are here,' she breathed. 'To honour your vow.'

Kit closed his eyes and said a prayer for Brendan's soul. He had said enough. She didn't need to know the rest. He'd asked Brendan to exchange places with him because he thought he'd get a better shot. Brendan had agreed with a laugh and a clap on his back. The next thing he'd heard was the soft thud of a bullet hitting Brendan in the chest. Brendan's last words were about his son and his hopes for Rupert's future. Kit had promised and he intended to keep that promise.

'But he would have been here. We made a vow together.'

'Is it why Rupert is with you? To fulfil his father's vow?' She tilted her head to one side. 'It would appear that I misjudged Mr Hook. There are not many men who would have done that.'

'His mother died soon after he was born.' Kit stared at the grass. There was no need to explain that Rupert's mother had been a courtesan and they had only married on her deathbed, at Brendan's insistence. Seventeen and a widower with a baby. Brendan always claimed his heart had died with the woman. Kit tended to counter that at least he had a heart. 'Rupert's grandmother took charge of the boy, but she died shortly after hearing of her son's death. I promised her that I'd make sure her grandson would become the fine man that his father wanted him to be.'

He willed her to understand his reasoning.

'I hope the fair lives up to your expectations.'

He forced a smile. 'I'm sure it shall. Anyway, I was invited along with Rupert to the ball, but I found I needed time alone to reflect, particularly as they had played a reel that I remember from the Duchess of Richmond's ball. I went to the card room for a few moments and found a book. You know what happened next.'

'I'm sorry for not believing you.' She took a step closer to him. Her dark-red lips softly parted.

'It doesn't matter.' He knew he lied. It mattered more than he wanted it to. 'It is in the past. I rarely think about the past.'

'It was my fault. I rushed away from the dance floor,' she whispered, putting her hand on his arm. 'We should have had the second dance. I would have if…if I'd realised about your past.'

'Never do something because you feel sorry for a person.' He covered her hand with his. Their breath laced. He knew that all he had to do was to lean forwards a few inches and her mouth would yield. He was surprised that he wanted to. But for the lesson in flirtation to be complete, the movement needed to come from her. He'd be magnanimous in the lecture which he gave her later.

'Aunt Hattie, Aunt Hattie! I know you are here. Moth found me. We have visitors! You will never guess. Livvy has an admirer!' a young voice called.

Mrs Wilkinson jumped back and her cheeks flamed bright red. 'I need to see my niece. You do understand the propriety of the thing.'

Kit forced his hands to his sides. His little lesson in flirtation was proving more enjoyable than he'd considered. He would see where the game led. 'No one is preventing you.'

Chapter Three

Hattie picked up her skirts and ran to the rose garden, not daring to look behind her and see if Sir Christopher was following. If Portia hadn't shouted, she would have kissed him. Her lips ached with longing. It went against everything she had promised herself and yet she didn't feel ashamed, only disappointed. The next time… Hattie stopped and pressed her fingers to her temples. There would be no next time. Sir Christopher had explained why he was in the card room. The matter was finished. She'd survived. Hattie picked up speed as if the devil himself was after her.

As she reached the rose garden, Portia hurtled into her, throwing her arms about her. 'You will never guess who is here!'

Hattie disentangled herself from the hug and

regarded her favourite niece who was four years younger than her sister, Livvy, and still far more interested in four-legged creatures than young men. Her pinafore had a series of smudges and a solitary wisp of hay clinging to the hem. Hattie knew despite her mother's orders Portia had spent time in the stables, helping out.

She always kept a tit-bit in her pocket when Moth came to call. It was no surprise to Hattie that Moth had gone wandering off to find her treat, but a small part of Hattie wished she hadn't and that she and Sir Christopher had remained under the cedar tree. Alone.

'Sir Christopher and Mr Hook,' Hattie answered, putting away all thoughts of kisses from Sir Christopher. It wasn't going to start.

If she ever was attracted to any man again, it would be to someone who was steady, sober and scandal free, someone who was completely different from Charles Wilkinson. Not someone who lived and breathed sin. If Charles Wilkinson had a dark wild side which no one knew about until it was too late, then Sir Christopher was midnight-black wild through and through. She forgot that at her peril. Sir Christopher was not a man to be relied on. A man whose wit and conversation were to be enjoyed rather than to be thought of as a life's partner.

'Sir Christopher wanted to return my gloves from last night and Mr Hook came along for accompaniment.'

Portia's plump face fell. 'You knew? How!'

'Aunts know these sorts of things. Little birds.'

'I've the honour of being the little bird,' Sir Christopher said, coming to stand by her, a bit closer than strictly proper. His stock was ever-so-slightly undone and she glimpsed the strong column of his throat. Hattie hurriedly pretended an interest in the roses. 'Your aunt met me, Miss Portia, and kindly showed me the cedar of Lebanon's location.'

Portia beamed back at Sir Christopher, her entire countenance lighting up under his voice's spell.

'There, you see,' Hattie said, putting an arm about her niece's shoulders and turning her away from Sir Christopher. 'All is explained.'

'How did you find the cedar tree, Sir Christopher? Does it approach the magnificence of your boyhood home or surpass it?' her sister, Stephanie, called out from where she sat in the rose garden with a silver teapot by her side. On her other side perched Mr Hook, looking much like an overgrown schoolboy. Livvy appeared all young innocence in her light-blue muslin gown, but the tips of her ears glowed pink. Hattie hated to think how quickly that sort of innocence vanished.

'I found what I was looking for, yes.' Sir Christopher gave Hattie a searing look.

Hattie resisted the temptation to explore the renewed aching in her lips. No one could brand with just a look. She clenched her fists. She was not going to behave like a fool again. Heady romance was an illusion that she could ill afford.

'I discovered Sir Christopher and kept him on the right path.' Her voice squeaked on the word path. Hattie cleared her throat. 'It was the charitable thing to do.'

Stephanie, who looked like an older and plumper version of Livvy, held out the gloves with a superior smile. 'How clever of you to visit this morning, Hattie…particularly as Sir Christopher thought you'd be here. I wonder how that came about?'

A distinct air of accusation rang in Stephanie's voice. She thought Hattie had arranged all this! Sir Christopher wore a smug expression as if it was precisely the outcome he'd hoped for. Hattie shifted uneasily. Why did he want anyone to think they had a flirtation? She could hardly be the type of woman with whom he generally flirted.

'I'll take possession of them. They have caused a great deal of trouble.' Hattie plucked them from Stephanie. A faint scent of sandalwood caressed her nostrils. She hurriedly stuffed them in her basket. When she arrived back at the Dower House, she would put them in her bottom drawer, never to be worn again.

'You really are too careless, Hattie. Those gloves were a *gift*. I spent hours getting those bows correct. First you mislaid them at the ball and then you place them in the basket all higgledy-piggledy.' Stephanie carefully poured a cup of tea. 'You were always the careless one of the family. When will you ever grow up and take responsibility for your actions?'

Sir Christopher cleared his throat. 'I was grateful for the excuse to call.'

'Will you and your godson be in the Tyne Valley long?' Stephanie asked in a speculative tone.

'It depends on a number of things.'

'It will depend on Aunt Harriet, that is what Sir Christopher means,' Portia said, bristling with self-importance.

'What on earth are you talking about, Portia?' Stephanie asked with an arched brow.

'Aunt Harriet is in the midst of a flirtation with Sir Christopher,' Portia burst out, her entire being quivering with excitement. 'Last night in the card room at Summerfield as well as today beside the cedar. Livvy told me. She swore me to secrecy, but that's why Sir Christopher kept the gloves. Why will no one tell the truth?'

'Out of the mouths of babes,' Sir Christopher said in a low tone.

'Next time I want to go, Mama. Things happen at balls. Please, Mama. Pretty please.'

'You are twelve, Portia,' Livvy replied with crushing firmness. 'You have years to wait.'

Portia stuck out her tongue.

'Portia, you know it is wrong to repeat tales, particularly highly embroidered ones,' Hattie said before either of her nieces uttered another damning phrase or their squabbling descended into all-out war. 'Sir Christopher has returned the gloves and seen the famous tree. His time will be required elsewhere. Do not seek romance where there is none, young Portia.'

Sir Christopher showed no inclination to take her hint and to depart. If anything, he seemed to be amused at her discomfort. He sat down and accepted the cup of tea that Stephanie held out. 'Fascinating place. Northumberland. My godson and I look forward to attending the Stagshaw Bank Fair.'

'Oh, the fair. Of course, I should have guessed the reason for you being here.' Her sister leant forwards. 'Mrs Wrigglesworth said it true when we first heard of your arrival—Stagshaw Fair attracts all sorts of people. Everyone had wondered. But hopefully having seen the delightful entertainment Northumberland has to offer, you can be persuaded to stay longer.'

Hattie bit her lip. Stephanie was up to something. She could feel the sense of impending doom creeping up her spine. She dismissed it. Stephanie knew of Sir Christopher's reputation. She'd never dare.

'I'm sure Sir Christopher is fully capable of finding entertainment to occupy his time,' Hattie said, seeking to end the discussion. 'We mustn't presume, Sister.'

'My godson and I would be delighted to take a full part in the village life while we are here. The estate I inherited has been neglected for far too long. And the company is utterly charming.' He inclined his head. The twinkle in his eyes deepened. 'We should go for a picnic out to Stagshaw to see what it is like before the fair. A local guide would prove of great assistance.' His voice became silken smooth. 'Would tomorrow suit, Mrs Wilkinson?'

Hattie's mouth went dry. There should be a thousand different reasons why she should refuse, but she heard herself say, 'Tomorrow would be wonderful.'

'Then it is all settled. Tomorrow at noon.'

'We will all go.' Hattie looked at Livvy, who suddenly straightened her back and blushed a violent pink at the hopeful glance Mr Hook gave her. Now that she knew Mr Hook was properly interested in making an honourable offer she was prepared to help. They did deserve a chance to get to know each other better, properly supervised. A picnic was hardly a debauched party. 'Livvy and Portia love picnics. It will make for a splendid expedition. You were saying just the other day, Stephanie, how we ought to picnic more often now that the fine weather had arrived.'

'Then it is settled. The day will be much brighter for the presence of all the ladies here.'

'Oh dear!' Stephanie banged her cup down. 'Tomorrow is no good at all. Far too much is on. Livvy and Portia have their dancing class. And I will be required at the Corbridge Reading Rooms. Colonel Cunningham will be thrilled to learn that we now have the world expert on newts in our midst. An illustrated lecture must be organised before Mr Hook departs.'

'Please, there is no need,' Mr Hook said, turning a violent red. 'It is nothing. My research is at an early stage.'

'I disagree, Mr Hook.' Stephanie raised an imperious hand. 'You mustn't be allowed to hide your light under a cloak of false modesty. You've informed me about your prowess and this must be shared with the neighbourhood. Immediately, before the schedule is cast into iron. There is a committee meeting tomorrow which I must attend.'

'Stephanie!' Hattie glared at her sister. Stephanie enjoyed the kudos of being on the village hall committee, but hated actually doing any work. She always produced the flimsy excuses to avoid the meetings where events like lectures were decided. 'We're talking about an invitation to a picnic, rather than this summer's lecture series schedule, which was decided weeks ago.'

'You must go of course, Hattie. You gave your word.' Stephanie waved a vague hand in the air. 'I feel certain that Sir Christopher and his godson understand why I must decline. Mr Parteger told the Colonel the other day that the lecture series was looking a bit thin. And the Colonel had the temerity to blame me. Schedules are made to be altered.'

Mr Hook turned a sickly greenish-yellow. 'I've not lectured before. I've no plans.'

'Then you must start. How else will you get on in this world? Mr Parteger has always said that we must have educated men as Livvy's suitors.'

'In that case, I…I would be honoured.' Mr Hook mirrored a tomato for colour.

Hattie curled her fists and attempted to ignore Stephanie's triumphant look.

'Of course, I will go on the picnic.' Hattie turned towards Sir Christopher. 'I would be delighted to accompany you and Mr Hook. Mr Hook can plan his lecture there.'

The flecks in Sir Christopher's eyes deepened. 'The picnic will be all the more memorable for it.'

Kit relaxed against the carriage seat, going over the morning events. It had unfolded differently than he'd planned, but not disastrously. After the picnic, he decided, he would send the flowers. He wanted to see Mrs Wilkinson fully blossom and realise the error of her censorious ways.

If he stopped prematurely, she would revert and cause her nieces problems. The lesson needed to be learnt thoroughly. Kit enjoyed the sense of goodness which radiated from his decision to take Mrs Wilkinson on the picnic.

'Do you care to explain precisely what happened while I was exploring the garden, Rupert?' Kit asked to keep from thinking about the precise shape of Mrs Wilkinson's mouth. 'How did you end up with a possible lecture engagement for a subject that you have never professed an interest in? Do you even know what a newt looks like?'

Rupert tugged at his neckcloth. 'Of course I know what a newt looks like. They are a type of amphibian, have four legs and a tail.'

'Is there some reason for Mrs Parteger to suspect that you are a world expert on newts?'

'I needed to say something to mark me out from the crush.' Rupert's ears turned pink. 'Miss Parteger is an angel. Two more bouquets arrived when you were touring the garden. I was desperate. Then I remembered how Miss James's father dismissed me as a know-nothing. It was not going to happen again. My tongue rather ran away with me. Newts were the first thing to pop in my brain.'

'You are now committed to giving a lecture about a subject you know nothing about. How is that going to impress anyone?'

'But I love her! I want to be with her. I know you will think me mad, but it is how I feel about her.' He thumped his chest. 'Sometimes, you know in here. The instant you see her. It was as if I had been waiting all my life and she walked into the room.'

Something inside Kit twisted. Rupert had no

idea about love. It was calf-love like he'd experienced with Constance, something that burned bright and fierce and vanished. And when it went, it hurt like the very devil. Every boy goes through it in order to become a man. And now he was a man, he protected that vulnerable bit of him so he would not get hurt again.

'You don't know what you are saying, Rupert. You hardly know her. How long will it last? Do you remember what you said about Miss James?'

'That was different.' Rupert flicked his fingers. 'I was merely a boy of nineteen.'

'You are only twenty!'

'What were you like when you were my age?'

'Young and foolish. Luckily your father stopped me before the folly went too far.' Kit shook his head. Never again would he allow a woman to share his secrets. All Constance had done was to mock him about his parents' scandalous past. 'I thanked him for it later.'

'Do you ever see her?'

'Who?'

'The woman who broke your heart? The one my father used to mention in his cups.'

'Your father was right. My broken heart lasted until the next dance when I found another lady who welcomed my attention.' Kit forced a laugh. His heart had been broken long before when his mother refused to look at him, despite his pleading, as she went out the door and his life. He'd settled for something less and kept his patched-up heart protected.

'Surely your heart was truer than that!'

'What heart? Didn't you know I'm heartless? How many women have despaired of taming me and thrown the accusation at me when I ended the affair?'

'My father didn't think that. He used to say—'

Kit held up his hand, stopping Rupert's words. 'Whatever he said, he said in confidence. Your father had a unique way of looking at life.'

'I wish he was here,' Rupert whispered.

'Your father asked me to look after you.' Kit glanced up at the carriage's ceiling, regaining control. 'I'm offering my advice. You keep your word. If you are determined to give this lecture, you study. My uncle did have an interest in amphibians and his papers and books are in the library. They should be enough to enable you to give an account of yourself. And you never make a false claim again. Lying never makes for a happy relationship.'

Rupert hung his head. 'Now you are committed to going on a picnic with The Widow.'

'Which I plan to enjoy.' Kit frowned. The lesson in flirtation was going better than he'd hoped. It would be one that Mrs Wilkinson would not soon forget. She might not thank him for it, but her two charming nieces might benefit. 'I could not have arranged matters better.'

'You and Mrs Wilkinson...but she is so old.'

'She is younger than I am.'

Rupert screwed up his face and stared out the window. 'I had always thought...they tell stories about you and the beauties. Mrs Wilkinson will never be a toast of London.'

Kit tapped his fingers together. He refused to indulge in speculation about Hattie Wilkinson's beauty. Rupert would not understand that it was precisely the point. Hattie Wilkinson possessed a refreshing charm that hadn't been powdered and primped to an inch of its life.

'One final lesson for today, Rupert. Never discuss a lady. Ever.'

'What precisely is going on, Stephanie?' Hattie asked once her nieces had been otherwise occupied with refurbishing their bonnets. For the first time in a long while, Livvy had expressed an interest in improving her mind, but the suggestion had been firmly quashed by her mother.

'Whatever can you mean, dear?' Stephanie looked up from where she was sorting out a variety of ribbons. 'I do hope you are not going to be tiresome, Hattie, and ruin your chances again. Simply because you had a wonderful marriage that was cut cruelly short does not mean you will not find happiness again.'

Hattie sighed. Her decision not to tell anyone about the full extent of Charles's betrayal did make for awkward moments. Stephanie refused to believe that her marriage was anything other than breathtakingly romantic. And this was the second lecture she had received today about making more of her life. Why didn't anyone understand that she was content as she was?

'This is Sir Christopher Foxton! Are you aware of his reputation? Marriage won't be on offer, if he has anything beyond mere politeness in mind.' Hattie clasped a hand to her chest and tried to regain control of her emotions. 'There, are you satisfied? I've said it. He is notorious in the extreme. He will be after more than an innocent conversation.'

'Why did he visit me and take pains to be correct?' Stephanie rolled her eyes. 'He brought the flirtation out in the open rather than hiding it behind closed doors. No man wants to remain a bachelor for ever.'

'You are mistaken, Sister. Some men are determined to remain bachelors. They are far from safe in carriages or conveyances of any kind. And Sir Christopher is first amongst them.'

'Sir Christopher seems very pleasant, rather sweet.' Stephanie crossed her hands in her lap and gave one of her Madonna-like smiles, which always grated on Hattie's nerves. 'On the other hand Mr Hook was painfully ill at ease. He droned on about his blessed newts. I doubt he even knows what women are.'

'You dislike Mr Hook's shyness?' Hattie stared at her sister in astonishment. She had anticipated Stephanie's objecting to Rupert Hook on the grounds of his association with Sir Christopher, but not because of his timidity. 'I believe you're wrong about the man. He has an abundance of confidence.'

'I dare say he will do for a chaperon for this picnic of yours or you can take Mrs Hampstead if you wish to have conversation on subjects other than amphibians. The man will not be moved. I did try.'

'Surely it is better for Livvy to realise what a bore Mr Hook is rather than to sigh for the love of his fine eyes. You can allow Livvy to accompany me,' Hattie said firmly, giving her final argument.

'Hattie, I do despair. Livvy is too young for such things.' Stephanie made a superior clucking noise. 'Sir Christopher Foxton pursues you. You should allow yourself to be caught and then force the marriage. It is how it is done.'

'You've muddled everything, Stephanie. The visit was about Mr Hook properly courting Livvy, rather than Livvy arranging clandestine meetings with her fan.'

'Pshaw!' Stephanie slammed her hand down on the table. 'My little Livvy would never do such a thing. Besides, Mr Hook was not acquainted with Livvy until today. Sir Christopher formally introduced him.'

With a heavy heart, Hattie rapidly explained the events of last evening, emphasising that Sir Christopher had only danced with her to prove a point about making assumptions. A forfeit, nothing more and then she'd left him standing on the dance floor.

'According to your tale, Sir Christopher was already chaperoning. Why was he there if not to ensure that nothing untoward happened to my dear girl? I do declare that people have done him a grave disservice in the past. He is the most perfect of gentlemen. I refuse to hear another disparaging word said against him.' Stephanie leant forwards and gestured with her fan. 'That is the end of the matter. Sometimes I worry that you became a walking ghost after your husband died. Why not enjoy the fun of a mild flirtation? After all, it is not as if you don't know where the boundaries lie.'

Hattie pinched the bridge of her nose. The conversation was starting to spin out of control. She refused to confess after all these years. At first it had been far too hard and Stephanie had never enquired. Her throat had swelled every time she thought about Charles and how he'd used her, how she'd stood mourning at his grave, bereft, and then had discovered about his other family, the woman he'd loved. And she had felt so stupid.

Her whole idyllic life had been a lie. Never again would she make the mistake of loving someone who could not love her back. Her blood ran cold every time she considered it.

'You would have to ask him why he was in that card room.'

'And you should ask yourself why he chose to dance with you and then to invite you specifically on a picnic. Now shall we speak about the colour of ribbon you will wear on your bonnet to this picnic?'

Hattie ignored Stephanie's peace offering. 'Why do you want me to go on this picnic alone? Do you truly want me to ruin my reputation?'

'You are a sensible widow of twenty-seven

who learnt your lesson years ago. If it had been anyone but Charles in that summer house, I shudder to think what would have happened. He worshipped the ground you walked on back then… It was utterly romantic. Your wedding when you fainted at the altar was so…so special. Then he had to leave to go to the front and wrote you such beautiful letters. They made me weep when you showed them to me.'

'Yes, I was lucky there.' Hattie fought to keep the irony out of her voice.

Stephanie smiled. 'I want you to have your last chance at a second marriage. Go on the picnic with Sir Christopher without distractions.'

'Livvy and Portia are not distractions.'

'I, too, remember last year when Portia put the lizard in Dr Hornby's tea. He had planned to propose to you that day. Portia and Livvy never gave you that chance.'

Hattie hid a smile. It had taken her the better part of three hours to capture that lizard. 'It happened for the best, Sister.'

'Hmmph.'

Stephanie in these moods was insensible to reason and ever likely to come up with more transparent schemes for entrapping Sir Christopher into marriage. Hattie gave an involuntary shudder.

There was no hope for it. She refused to sit

here and allow herself to become embroiled in one of Stephanie's projects.

She would have to go and explain to Sir Christopher the dangers. He had to understand why the picnic and any hint of intimacy was an impossibility. And she had to do it before she lost her nerve.

Hattie clicked her fingers. 'Moth, we are going.'

Her sister's face creased. 'Hattie, I am only doing this because I love you and want you to be happy. You need someone in your life. You looked happy when you arrived in the rose garden. Your cheeks were bright pink.'

'I like my life with Moth, with Mrs Hampstead and with you and your children.' She raised her chin. She refused to go back to that needy deluded girl who believed romance happened when two people's glances met across a crowded room. Going on a picnic with Sir Christopher was not going to happen.

'Hattie...'

'It satisfies me. Do not tell me otherwise.' Hattie hoped Stephanie believed her words because she was less than sure.

Hattie stood in the gloomy panelled hall of Southview Lodge. A variety of stuffed birds peered down at her. All the way here, she had planned her speech. Somehow it seemed right to explain the situation in person rather than writing a letter. Sir Christopher had to know what Stephanie was trying to do and why it would never work. The solution had come to her as she tramped home over the fields. Sir Christopher needed to know about her sister's machinations.

She had deposited Moth with Mrs Hampstead before driving the governess cart to Southview. She intended on handling this problem on her own without interference from Moth and her penchant for investigating.

'Mrs Wilkinson, what a pleasant surprise.' Sir Christopher came out of his study. His stock was undone and he was in his shirtsleeves. His black hair swooped down over one eye. Despite her intentions of being aloof, a curl of warmth twined its way around her insides.

Hattie inclined her head and was pleased her straw poke bonnet shadowed her face. 'Sir Christopher, I do hope you will forgive the intrusion.'

'I wasn't expecting any visitors. My uncle's affairs are in a bigger tangle than I had anticipated. He appears to have used a code...' He ran a hand through his hair, making it stand on end.

'But as you are here, you must stay and have a cup of tea. Come into the drawing room.'

'My sister was rude in proposing that Mr Hook lecture,' Hattie began before she lost her nerve. 'Take no notice of her. She became dreadfully confused and believes Mr Hook is a shy newt-fancier who needs bringing out.'

'Is this a problem?'

'Is he…a newt-fancier? A world authority? He appears awfully young for such a thing.'

The corners of his mouth twitched. Hattie risked a breath. She might not have to confess about Stephanie's other machinations after all.

'Rupert confessed. He misjudged the moment. Rupert shall be spending all his time studying the habits of newts until the lecture. He should know better than to lay false claim.'

'He doesn't know.' Hattie clapped her hand over her mouth. 'Oh dear. Just before I left the Dower House, Livvy arrived, looking for books on amphibians.'

Their shared laughter rang out.

His eyes turned sober. 'You didn't come all the way here simply to tell me about Rupert's folly. Out with it, Mrs Wilkinson. What else was your sister attempting to do? Why must I be wary?'

Chapter Four

He knows. Hattie's heart sank. Sir Christopher had known about Stephanie's intention all along. She twisted the handle of her reticule about her fingers and wished she was anywhere but here in Sir Christopher's hallway. She had made a mistake in thinking he was naïve or at best unaware. He was no fool, but a hardened and experienced rake. He must have foiled hundreds of marriage schemes in his lifetime.

Her first instinct was to slink away, but she had started so she had to continue—no matter how much she wanted the ground to rise up and swallow her.

'My sister wishes to play the matchmaker. You and I.' Hattie tried for a sophisticated laugh, but it came out strangled. 'How ridiculous! Anyone can see how ill-suited we are. I like to speak my mind too readily and you…you…well, you have a certain appetite for life.'

A flash of something—sorrow, disappointment?—crossed his face, but it was gone before she could really register it was there and his face became a bland mask.

'I would have used a different word,' he said.

'Stephanie refused the picnic invitation so that you would be forced to take me on my own. She knew I would never be rude and find a threadbare excuse to call it off.'

'Why did she think her being there would be an impediment?'

'My sister unfortunately recalled that I once used my nieces to sabotage her previous efforts.' Hattie knew her words were coming much too fast, tumbling over one another like a cart picking up speed as it careened down a perilous slope. 'A childish trick. I should have seen the possibility before it happened and saved everyone the embarrassment. What I was thinking… who knows?'

'Perhaps you were thinking that a picnic with me would be a pleasant way to pass an afternoon.' His grey eyes flashed. 'A picnic, Mrs Wilkinson, is not an invitation to a debauched party. Nor is it a prelude to sticking your neck through the parson's noose.'

'The expedition should be called off. Immediately.'

'Why?'

'Because it will encourage Stephanie and her folly,' Hattie said weakly, trying not to think about the way his mouth looked or how his eyes sparkled. A note giving a bland reason would have been simpler.

'I'm more than delighted to be spending time with you, Mrs Wilkinson. The arrangement suits me very well.'

'Does it?' Hattie gulped. She refused to consider that Sir Christopher might actually be attracted to her. The notion was completely absurd. She lacked the attributes that men like him prized. He had an ulterior motive. He had to. Her head pained her slightly.

'Had I thought you'd accept without your family for chaperons, I'd have proposed the current arrangement in the first place. For Rupert it was desolation but for me it is serendipity.' He lowered his voice. 'I take it you will bring your dog as a chaperon. It is always best to have a solitary chaperon…it provides cover.'

'My husband died at Talavera, Sir Christopher.' Hattie focused on a picture of an English castle which hung on the wall behind his right shoulder. It was easier to say the words when she wasn't looking at his face. She tightened her grip on her reticule. She refused to tell him the truth about the sham of a marriage and her humiliation, but he had to understand that whatever game he was attempting to play stopped here. 'I have no wish for another.'

'Marriage has never been one of my aspirations, Mrs Wilkinson. My parents were exceedingly unhappy. I trust you understand me.'

Hattie gave a little nod. She had thought as much, but the plain statement caused a tiny bubble of disappointment to flood through her. Just once she would have liked to have been wrong and for Sir Christopher to have had honourable intentions.

A tiny voice in the back of her mind whispered that he was the sort of man to make a woman believe in romance. She ignored it. That sort of thinking belonged to another woman. She knew what her responsibilities were. She liked her life as it currently was. She knew what was important to her. Free love was for women like Mrs Reynaud and her sheikh, not her.

'Thank you for being frank, Sir Christopher.' She met his gaze full on, never flinching or wavering. 'I must also inform you that I've no intention of our acquaintance becoming more intimate. I enjoy my current reputation and wish to maintain it. In the circumstances...'

'More intimate?' His grey eyes became flecked with a thousand lights. 'You do like putting the cart before the horse, Mrs Wilkinson. Most women wait to be asked. I shall allow you the opportunity to change your mind should the subject ever come up.'

'I find my sister's attempts at matchmaking intensely irritating.' Hattie quickly concentrated on the black-and-white tiles of the entranceway, rather than giving in to the temptation to drown in his eyes. 'Her schemes made my life a misery throughout the years until I found a way to halt them. Why should I have to seek another husband? There is no law against being a widow.'

He tilted his head to one side, his eyes coolly assessing her. 'Your husband must have been a lucky man. To have someone so devoted after his death.'

'He was a man in a million.' Hattie attempted to look pious and sorrowful. She had already had her folly with Charles. She had swallowed whole the lies of instant adoration, love and eternal devotion that dripped from his lips that night in the summer house.

She had continued to believe in the false illusionary world where she was the very heart of his universe until she had sorted his private papers, which arrived after his death. The stark black ink tore the illusion from her soul.

It was then she learnt what he truly thought of her, how another woman had had his regard and his joy at the birth of his son, a son he'd fathered after their marriage. That had been the hardest thing—reading about his joy at the birth and knowing how much she'd longed to have a child.

'I have no desire to change your mind. I only wish to go on a picnic with you.'

'And I should accept your word?' she asked. 'Without questioning it?'

His eyes flashed. 'I may be many things, Mrs Wilkinson, but I am no liar. Nor do I take advantage of unwilling women. Nothing will happen on this picnic that you do not desire.'

'Then I have no choice but to accept your assurance that the picnic will be between friends.' Hattie hated the way her heart jumped. The gloomy mood that had plagued Hattie on the way over vanished. Sir Christopher wanted to go on the picnic with her, despite knowing about Stephanie's machinations. She swallowed hard. Stephanie would not give up. The picnic would only embolden her. 'What am I to do about

Stephanie? I've no wish for you to become burdened or embarrassed.'

He took a step closer. 'A determined matchmaker needs to have a concrete reason to desist. You and I know of her intent and we can counter it…if we work together. If done properly, your sister might learn a valuable lesson. The world needs fewer meddlesome matchmakers. We will be doing a service to society.'

'Why are you willing to do this?' Hattie put her hand to her throat. She could see the sense in Sir Christopher's scheme but… She shook her head. 'You gain nothing.'

'Except the pleasure of your company for a few hours.' His eyes danced with a myriad of greys.

Hattie attempted to control the sudden fluttering of her insides. Mrs Reynaud had been completely wrong. Like most men of his ilk, he was probably attracted to sophisticated ladies of the *ton* or courtesans, rather than twenty-seven-year-old widows who were long on the shelf. 'I hope the company will suffice, then.'

'And now you have given me a further purpose. You need to be able to live your life free from your sister's interference. You should not have to worry about her matchmaking simply because you wish to enjoy the banter and repartee.'

'I welcome your assistance,' she whispered and held out her hand.

'You have it. To confounding the matchmakers, my intelligent friend.' His fingers curled around hers. Strong and firm. She swayed toward him, lips parting.

Somewhere in the bowels of the house, a clock chimed the quarter-hour. She let go abruptly, aware that she had held his fingers for a breath too long. She forced her mouth to turn up. He thought her intelligent, but unappealing. It reminded her of Charles's journal. *My new wife is a sensible choice, but far too intelligent for my taste.* Just once she wanted to be thought of as fascinating. A tiny piece of her had wanted Mrs Reynaud's scandalous suggestion to be true and that he'd pull her towards him and kiss her thoroughly.

She had entirely misread the situation earlier. A small shudder ran down her spine. She had nearly kissed him under the cedar. And now again here—just after she had proudly proclaimed no interest in marrying again! When had she become forward? And what if he thought she was an advocate for free love?

How embarrassing would that have been! *Poor silly deluded Hattie. Always gets it wrong.* Another of Charles's entries in his journal. She knew what she wanted from life and being one out of many women was not for her. 'I thank you for the compliment.'

'And you will come on the picnic with me? As a friend?'

He leant close and his breath laced with hers, doing strange things to her insides. He smelt of sandalwood and the faint tang of wood smoke. All she had to do was to lift her mouth a few inches. A slight tilting of her head was all it would take, except he wasn't interested in her, not in that way. Hattie concentrated on breathing, slowly and steadily, controlling her desire.

'I'd like that, Sir Christopher. True friendship is beyond price.'

'Kit. We are friends and intimates, Hattie.' His voice rolled her name.

'Very well, Kit.' Even saying his first name seemed intimate and wicked as if she was slowly but inexorably sliding towards the sort of woman who did indulge in serious flirtations. 'It took me three months before I dared think of my husband by his first name, let alone call him by it.'

'Then it is just as well that I'm not your husband.'

'Until tomorrow.' Hattie hated the way her blood leapt. She could stop any time she wanted. Going on a picnic did not mean she was going to become his mistress. It took more than a solitary picnic to ruin a reputation.

Kit made certain that he gave the appearance of relaxing back against an oak tree as he finished his share of the picnic, but his entire body was intensely focused on where Hattie Wilkinson sat, blithely eating strawberries. Her hair today was in a loose crown of braids with a few tendrils kissing the back of her neck.

The picnic had been far more pleasant than he'd anticipated. The conversation with Mrs Wilkinson had ranged from a mutual admiration of Handel and loathing of sopranos who added trills to arias to the games of chess and cricket. Mrs Wilkinson, he discovered, was a keen bowler and took pride in her ability to take wickets.

Having concluded the debate about the correct way to bowl off-side, Mrs Wilkinson reached for the few remaining strawberries in the dish.

'How did you guess I adored strawberries? Normally Livvy or Portia eat their fill before I get a chance to have more than one.'

'Another reason to be pleased you came without them.' Kit pushed the dish towards her. He'd nearly accomplished his mission. Mrs Wilkinson had blossomed. Perhaps it was as simple as her needing to understand that life went on without her husband. He hoped the man had deserved her devotion. He wondered how any woman could be so devoted? He doubted if any woman would shed real tears for him. Crocodile tears because he was no longer picking up the bills, but not real ones that came from deep within.

'One more, then.'

'You mustn't be shy. Take as many as you want. They are begging to be eaten.'

'When you put it that way, how can I refuse?' She gave a quick laugh and brought a berry to her mouth. Her teeth bit into it and the juice dribbled, turning her lips bright red. Kit silently handed her a handkerchief and indicated towards her chin.

She hastily scrubbed her face. 'Honestly, you would think after all these years I'd learn. How long has it been that way?'

'Long enough. You look delightful.' He leant back against the tree, put his hands behind his head and savoured the moment. 'This picnic is supposed to be about enjoyment.'

'And you think eating strawberries in the sunshine is a suitable pastime?'

'None better.' He shifted so his legs were stretched and struggled to remember the last time he had felt so content. There again, he found it difficult to remember the last time he had taken a woman on a picnic. The women in his life were far more inclined towards intimate late-night suppers, silken sheets and expensive presents. He had rarely wanted to talk to any of them about matters beyond the bedroom.

With Hattie Wilkinson, he wanted to hear her views. He enjoyed debating with her and disconcerting her in order to win.

A tiny frown appeared between her brows. 'I would have thought a man with your sort of reputation...'

'Simple pleasures are the best ones.' He reached across and popped the last strawberry into her mouth.

She half-closed her eyes and a look of supreme pleasure crossed her face. 'Those are exceptionally good strawberries. Don't you agree, Mr Hook?'

Full of more than his fair share of cold game pie, watercress sandwiches, fruit cake and elderflower cordial, Rupert sat with his head in a book about newts, mumbling about amphibians and their feeding habits and ignoring Hattie's attempts to bring him into the conversation. Mrs Hampstead, Hattie's housekeeper, likewise ignored the conversation and knitted.

It would be easy to do this every day.

Kit inwardly smiled at the thought—the great *bon vivant* Sir Christopher Foxton indulging in rustic pleasures. He could imagine the caustic remarks. He should end the flirtation now, before he was tempted to enjoy it or, worse still, repeat it and start to count on it. Counting on women for anything beyond the basics was a bad idea. He'd learnt that bitter lesson long ago. His mother had turned her elegant back on him and never attempted to make contact with him after she left.

Kit struggled to his feet. His mother, her lack of care and her penchant for scandalous behaviour were far from suitable topics for conversation or thought on this glorious day.

'Is there something wrong?' Hattie asked at his sudden movement. The light in her eyes flickered and died.

'Shall we explore the area to work off some of the lunch? You may have eaten the strawberries, but I had game pie,' Kit said, gesturing towards where the busy coaching inn stood.

Physical activity was what was required. It would keep his mind from wandering down unwanted paths. After today, there would be no more picnics with Hattie Wilkinson. This was about a lesson in short flirtation rather than a prolonged friendship.

'There is nothing much here,' Rupert said unhelpfully, looking up from his book. 'Just some empty fields.'

'When you see the two crossroads, there is little mystery as to why the fair is held here,' Kit continued, giving Rupert a meaningful glare. 'Do you know how long the fair has been going on, Hattie?'

'Since time immemorial,' Mrs Wilkinson replied, dusting her fingers with a white handkerchief.

She leant back and the bodice of her gown tightened across her breasts. In other women, he'd suspect that it was done deliberately, but with Hattie, he was sure it was unconscious. All too often recently, his life had been filled with women who knew what they were on about and sought to accentuate their sexuality, leaving him cold.

'There are some Roman remains just to the north of the inn. We could walk there.' Her long lashes fluttered down, hiding her expressive eyes. 'It is possible they had a fair. I've never really considered it.'

The tension went out of Kit's shoulders. Virtue radiated from every pore. He could end the flirtation there. Something simple and it would be over. It was better to be done now, than to risk liking Mrs Wilkinson. They had no future. She'd never agree to an affair and he had no wish to become respectable.

The thought sent a pang of unaccustomed melancholy through him.

'The perfect destination for an afternoon stroll.' He made a bow. 'If you are up for exploration and exercise...'

Mrs Wilkinson stood up and shook her skirts. Her carefully arranged crown of braids slipped to one side. With a laugh she brushed the grass stains from her skirt.

He considered his last three mistresses, all high-stepping courtesans, and if they would have reacted so favourably to a picnic or to eating strawberries or, worse, having any of their immaculate clothes soiled. The thought of the hysteria, shrieks and sulks which would have ensued made him shudder.

'Shall we all go and explore? Mrs Hampstead and I will take the rearguard while you and Rupert...'

'I do believe Mr Hook can stay with me,' Mrs Hampstead said, looking up from her knitting.

'But why?' Hattie tapped her fingers together. 'I can remember you always proclaiming about the virtues of a walk.'

'I wish to find out about newts and I have

seen enough stone to last me a lifetime. Why a bunch of old stones provides such amusement I'll never know. But I know all about you and your walking, Miss Hattie. You were never able to sit still as a girl and you've never changed,' Mrs Hampstead said with a placid smile. 'Walk off your energy with Sir Christopher. You are a grown woman, not an impetuous girl of sixteen. I trust your judgement, even if you don't.'

Rupert turned a dull purple and swallowed rapidly. 'I'm sure you will find the subject quite dull, Mrs Hampstead. That is to say—a walk will do everyone some good.'

'Not at all. It will do my bones no good to go clambering over rocks and stones.' Mrs Hampstead patted a place beside her. It amused Kit that so many people in Mrs Wilkinson's life seemed to think a bit of romance would do her good. 'I have an enquiring mind and Miss Parteger came over yesterday to specifically ask about the subject. She assures me that you are a great authority. You are going to give a lecture in Corbridge and she plans to sit in the front row listening.'

'Miss Parteger said that? She plans to?' Rupert dropped the book and the page flopped open to lesser spotted newts and their habits. He hurriedly shut it and his face grew even redder. 'Of course the lecture was pure speculation on her mother's part… I mean, if called upon, I will be delighted to lecture. I believe I can give a convincing lecture…on newts.'

'It is good to see that you are willing to rise to the challenge, Rupert,' Kit said, looking at his protégé. Rupert was learning to honour his commitments and hopefully to think carefully before laying claim to any prowess again. He would repay his debt to Rupert's father.

Rupert ducked his head. 'I would endeavour to do my best.'

'Practice always makes perfect.' Mrs Hampstead fluffed out her skirts. 'Mr Hook, I've waited a long time to hear about such things and I trust you will oblige me.'

'You will have to imagine the illustrations.'

'I have an adequate imagination.' Mrs Hampstead reached for another ball of wool. 'I told Dr Hornby that last year when he did his lecture on battles in the Bible. My imagination is more than adequate for the task required. What are you two waiting for? Go and enjoy yourselves.'

Kit exchanged an amused glance with Mrs Wilkinson. She gave a little shrug as if to say she knew about the stratagem.

'Shall we leave Mrs Hampstead and Rupert to their discussion? I fear I don't find newts as fascinating as Rupert currently does.'

'I'm sure Moth would enjoy the exercise,' Mrs Wilkinson said, snapping her fingers towards where Moth lounged in the sun.

'I believe Moth would like to stay as well. The summer sun is a bit hot for her.' Mrs Hampstead gave Hattie a significant glance. 'You can tell us all about the ruins when you return. Take your time, my dear. We will be here when you return.'

Hattie concentrated on smiling sweetly rather than screaming. The disease of matchmaking appeared to be highly contagious. First her sister, and now Mrs Hampstead felt she should be encouraging Kit with a view towards matrimony. She shook her head. The man had dodged more marriage traps than most. Besides, he was a person to be enjoyed, rather than to lose one's heart to.

A walk alone with Kit—the very prospect was enough to set her nerves jangling like some young débutante's.

There again, sitting in the blanket, gazing at his regular features and listening to his voice rumble over her had done nothing towards eliminating the attraction she felt for him. Familiarity was supposed to breed contempt...when in this case all it bred was the desire to be kissed. She clenched her fists.

She refused to start believing in romance again. It led straight to heartache.

Hattie picked up her parasol and hoped that Kit would not see her heightened colour and attribute it to the wrong reason. 'A walk will be just the thing.'

'You obviously haven't informed your housekeeper about our arrangement,' Kit observed when they reached the small pile of stones which marked the remains of Portgate.

Hattie stumbled over a stone. They had covered the ground between the picnic and the ruins in silence. She'd kept thinking up topics for conversation and rejecting them as unsuitable. She'd finally settled on the weather when, without warning, he mentioned the very topic she wished to avoid—the blatant attempts at matchmaking.

'What sort of arrangement do you mean?' she asked, attempting to stay upright.

'Our friendship. Or is everyone chronically addicted to matchmaking in Northumberland?'

'In my defence, I tried to warn you.'

'Surely you confided in someone about this? Women always confide in their female friends.'

She glanced upwards to see how he felt about it, but the planes of his face gave no clue. Her heart sank. Of course, he could scent matchmaking wiles. Such men always could.

Her grip on the parasol tightened.

'Mrs Hampstead used to be Stephanie's nurse as well as mine. They remain close. If I want to fool my sister, I can hardly confess to Mrs Hampstead. You do understand my reasoning, don't you?'

'Perfectly.'

Hattie shook her head. Even the thought made her blood run cold—confiding in Mrs Hampstead. The fewer people who knew about her arrangement with Kit, the better.

'All I can do is to apologise.'

His eyes widened. 'Why apologise? None of it was your doing. And I do think I am old enough to see through a simple matchmaking stratagem. I'd have hardly remained single for this long if I didn't. It amused me to see it happen. Do you think she will tell your sister?'

'Yes, of course.' The words tasted like ash in her mouth. Hattie pulled her bonnet forwards. She hadn't asked for Livvy to list her shortcomings this morning—passable figure, too long of a nose and far too inclined towards sarcasm. And she failed to smile enough.

'All we are doing is going for a walk, Hattie.

Relax and enjoy the moment. Nothing untoward will happen. Nothing to cause adverse comment.'

Hattie hated the butterflies which had started beating in her stomach and the way her jaw hurt from trying to keep a smile. This going for a walk alone was a poor idea.

If anything it emphasised that she wanted to be with him as more than a friend. She liked thinking of herself as independent and not needing a man, but right now all she could think about was how alone she was and how his arms felt when they waltzed.

'It was sweet of Livvy to ask Mrs Hampstead about newts,' she said, attempting to keep the subject away from the matchmaking scheme.

'Rupert is learning a valuable lesson in the folly of trying to please people.'

'Please people?' Hattie stopped beside a large pile of stones. 'It certainly backfired on him. Livvy still likes his well-turned calf muscles, but if his object was to impress her mother, he singularly failed. He is about to endure a baptism of fire. They still speak about the great Hollingbrooke disaster from '98 when Mr Hollingbrooke tried to give a lecture on the history of lime kilns and people began to throw rotten fruit.'

He reached out and caught her elbow. 'Hattie.'

'We have exhausted the subject, yes, I know.'

Hattie gulped air. She babbled when she was nervous and today was no exception. 'You have no interest in the great Hollingbrooke disaster and it was wrong of me to bring it up.'

'Hattie,' he said again. He stood looking at her with his top hat pushed back, giving him a rakish look. 'I didn't go on this picnic to discuss my godson or his prospects. I came because—'

'We don't need to discuss why,' Hattie broke in before he could finish. The last thing she wanted to hear was his proposal for confounding the matchmakers. She needed to end this now, before she started to enjoy his company. She refused to go back to that naïve girl whom Charles had taken advantage of. 'When we return to the picnic, it will appear that we had a quarrel. The nature of said quarrel will be highly trivial, but on an important point of principle. I will inform my sister that we will have fallen out of civility with each other. After that we become civil but distant acquaintances. The only thing I need from you is to decide how long we stay out here. I'm sorry if my words are blunt, but there you have it.'

She waited for him to agree. Or to at least comment on her rudeness. The solution had come to her in the middle of the night, when she had awoken from a dream about his mouth against hers.

'Hattie.' He took a step closer. She became aware of his elusive scent and the way his stock was intricately tied. It was one thing to make plans to counter a dream Kit and another to be confronted with the living and breathing man.

Her mouth went dry. His eyes were a luminous grey and his face seemed suddenly intense and serious. She knew she ought to pick up her skirts and run like the very devil was after her. She stood still. Behind her, some bird burst out into a trill of song.

'Kit,' she breathed.

He lowered his mouth and his lips lightly brushed hers. The kiss, if you could call it that, was over in a breath.

Hattie fingered her lips. They ached slightly. Two bits of knowledge hammered through her. First she wanted to be kissed again, more thoroughly and second, perhaps more importantly, he was attracted to her. The realisation made her wary, in case she had mistaken it. 'What…what was that for?'

'You wanted a reason for us to fall out of civility. I gave you one.' He snapped his fingers. 'I refuse to apologise. It was the most agreeable part of my day so far. What happens next is up to you.'

Hattie nodded, and attempted to ignore the way her heart thudded. 'You expect me to pick up my skirts and run as if the devil is after me?'

He tilted his head to one side. The grey in his eyes deepened. 'Did I mistake the moment?'

'You have a funny idea of women.'

A dimple showed in the corner of his mouth. 'You don't think it was enough. You want more.'

'I am made of sterner stuff and fail to wilt when someone seeks to mock me. In any case, a simple quarrel over the Romans would have sufficed.' Hattie concentrated on a particularly nondescript piece of rock. Her mouth ached and she knew she wanted more, but that went beyond the bounds of propriety. She refused to get herself into a situation where she jeopardised her reputation. 'Your choice of topic leaves a lot to be desired.'

'You want to be kissed again. Immediately and more thoroughly.'

'You are being ridiculous.' Hattie pressed her lips together and attempted to banish the strange quivering in her stomach. 'I never said anything of the sort.'

'You told me to pick the topic and I have. It is

far better to fall out of civility over something like a kiss than over anything else.'

'The question of whether or not I want to be kissed by you is inappropriate.' She crossed her arms over her breasts and tried to ignore the way they felt. 'Completely and utterly inappropriate. I could hardly confess to Stephanie that I fell out of civility because of a kiss! Imagine the commotion.'

'But you do want to be kissed.' He cupped her cheek with firm fingers. She fought against the impulse to turn her face into his palm. 'It is in your eyes.'

'In my eyes?'

His thumb traced the outline of her mouth.

'And your lips.'

He lowered his head. This time his kiss was slow and coaxing. Instead of merely brushing her lips, he tasted and explored. Slowly and steadily. Tiny nibbles at her lips made her stomach contract and warm pulses shoot through her.

Hattie brought her hands up and rested them on the solid broad cloth of his coat. His hand moulded her body to his. At the insistent pressure, her lips parted slightly and she tasted the cool interior of his mouth. Nothing in her life had prepared her for the sensation rippling through her. It made the memory of Charles's kisses seem like poor milk-water.

He groaned and deepened the kiss, drank from her. His hand tangled in her hair, pushing her bonnet off her face. He rained kisses down her cheeks, her eyes and her nose before returning to plunder her mouth.

Hattie allowed herself one more heartbeat of pleasure. She felt ridiculously feminine and pretty, someone to be cherished. Cherished?

The thought poured ice water into her veins. She refused to become like one of those women who fell at his feet. She was never going to become another notch, to be enjoyed and then tossed away. She had been there with Charles and never again. No romance required.

She beat her hands against his chest. Instantly he loosened his arms. He looked down at her with a quizzical expression in his eyes.

She stumbled backwards and attempted to breathe normally. Her body protested at the sudden rush of air between them. She knew her eyes were too large and her lips too red. She grabbed at her bonnet and tore a ribbon. It lay glistening in her hand, mute rebuke of what she'd done.

Anger at herself, at him and at life in general washed over her. After all her promises, all she had been through, the first man with a reputation crooked a finger and she behaved like a babbling schoolgirl. This stopped before it ever started.

'That should never happen again. Ever!' she said when she had regained her balance. 'I forbid it!'

Chapter Five

'Forbid?' Kit watched Hattie through narrowed eyes.

Hattie's breath was far too quick and her eyes were huge blue-green pools. It took all of his self-control not to pull her back into his arms. His response to her was entirely unexpected. Ever since Waterloo, nothing—not even with the most experienced courtesans London could offer was there any excitement or response, but one gentle brush of his lips against hers and his body started to rage out of control. He'd kissed her again to make sure and had nearly fallen off the edge.

He wanted to drink from her mouth and leisurely explore the contours of her body. Silently he willed her to come back into his arms and to allow the kiss to develop further. With a great effort, he concentrated and brought his breathing under control.

'You only needed to tell me to stop,' he said when she continued to stand away from him, looking at him with those huge eyes. 'And I will, if that is what you truly desire.'

'I should never have done something like that. I'm not like that. I'm not given to…'

'I'm very honoured.' Kit clung on to his sanity. She was frightened of her response. Intellectually he should have expected it, but it still hit him in his gut. She had enjoyed the kiss until she had started thinking and remembering that she was a respectable person.

'All I know is that it must not happen again. I'm not that sort of a woman. I'm a widow who has responsibilities. I'm not looking for a quick tumble in the hay.'

'Do you see any hay around here?'

Hattie gave an impatient stamp of her foot. 'You know what I mean!'

Hattie took a step backwards, half-stumbled on a rock and tumbled down on her bottom. She gave an exasperated cry.

'Do you need help?' Kit held out a hand to help her up, but she ignored it and scrambled to stand up.

'I can manage on my own. I always do.'

'Your bonnet is crooked.'

'Is it? I...I hadn't noticed.'

Kit reached out and straightened her straw bonnet, placing it firmly on her head, pulling it forwards so she was once again the perfectly proper woman he'd first met. He should say the words he'd planned to end it, but they stuck in his throat. He wanted more of her. He wanted to see if the promise in the kiss held true, but he knew he'd have to go slowly, coax her and discover why the physical frightened her. He wanted to see what would happen when she fully gave in to the passion that simmered under the surface.

'There, no one will guess. Your armour is back on.'

'Armour?'

'To keep you safe from the world's scrutiny. No one will remark if that is what you are afraid of.'

'Nothing. I am not afraid of anything.' Her words were barely audible as she half-turned from him. 'It has to be this way for both our sakes.'

Kit allowed his hand to drop to his side. Not only did her body have to crave his touch, but her mind as well. He wanted her to want him as he wanted her. He'd felt the passion in her kiss. He wasn't ready for the flirtation to end. He wanted it to continue and for them to explore this white-hot spark that flickered between them. He'd be a poor person if he gave up at the first hurdle. 'I'll respect your wishes, but will allow you the luxury of changing your mind.'

A long sigh escaped her mouth before she straightened her back. 'I can't. I won't. It ends here. It has to. Things like this don't happen to me.'

'Denying your passion won't bring your husband back.'

'You seek to discomfort me. Never mention Charles Wilkinson again. He has nothing to do with this. He died seven years ago.' She wrapped her arms about her waist. 'That…that demonstration of your prowess was totally unnecessary.'

Kit clung on to her response as a dying man might cling to a wooden spar. She didn't say unwelcome. He hated that it mattered and that he wanted her to want him. Silently he cursed her husband and what they must have shared. He'd never had to compete with a ghost before.

He could just imagine the upright Army hero who had won her. Someone who had more to offer than he ever could. A sudden irrational hatred of the man filled him.

'Why did you do it, Kit?'

'If we intend on falling out of civility, I wanted it to be for something real,' he said lightly, pushing the unaccustomed jealousy to one side. He never examined the past. 'The truth is far easier than a lie. The mealy-mouthed kiss earlier was nothing, but this, this will make the falling out worthwhile.'

The colour rose in her cheeks, rivalling the dusky pink of her lips. 'Just so you understand, there can be no future.'

'I try never to look to the future,' Kit said stiffly. 'And I never regret the past where women are concerned. It helps.'

She clasped her hands together so tightly he could see the knuckles through her gloves. 'Just know that I have no intention of becoming somebody's mistress. Anyone's mistress. I wouldn't want to soil...to soil my spotless reputation.'

'We are friends.' Kit bit back the words that he didn't want her to become just anyone's mistress—he wanted her to be *his*.

It would be laying claim to her. He'd never laid claim to anyone. To claim someone meant that you cared. And if you cared, you got hurt.

'We should go back to the picnic.' She turned away from the ruins. 'Mrs Hampstead may need rescuing from Mr Hook's lecture.'

'We should indeed.' Kit put his hand in the

small of her back. 'Careful. The path is unsteady.'

'I can walk on my own.' She made no attempt to move away.

'Sometimes everyone needs help.'

'I'll remember that.'

'You appear far more serious than I intended,' Kit remarked when they neared the picnic area. Rupert's voice declaiming loudly about the sleeping habits of the great crested newts punctuated the air. 'What have I done to cause the frown besides kissing you?'

'I was considering how to break the news to my sister of our incompatibility so I can prevent further meddling.'

'Surely the kiss is excuse enough?'

Her hand flew to her mouth. 'There is no need for anyone to know about the kiss. I have no plans to tell.'

'Honesty is always best.' Kit stifled a smile. The kiss had caused her to go off balance by a bit, but she hadn't fully capitulated. A wise man knew when to retreat and when to advance. He'd pursue her slowly and see what happened, but first he'd give her the protection she craved. 'We quarrelled and you see no way to mend the quarrel. You are far too distraught to talk about the quarrel because it was over a trifling matter.'

'That excuse might do.' She gave a heart-stopping smile. 'It will do very well indeed.'

Kit raised two fingers to his hat. They said that there was a first time for everything, but he had never considered that he'd be involved in this—pursuing a woman by giving her advice on how to break up with him. Quarrels were made to be mended. He would see this one was. 'Until the next time.'

'Will there be a next time?'

He leant forwards and brushed her cheek with his forefinger. 'You can count on it.'

Reasons why she was not interested in Kit Foxton...
Hattie read down the list of reasons, starting with his notoriety and his lack of reliability and ending with the taste of his kisses making her unsettled. She frowned. The taste of his kisses was not something she wanted to consider. With a furious stroke of her pen, she crossed it out.

'There you are, my dear,' Mrs Reynaud said, bustling into the drawing room of the Dower House. Unlike the day before, which had been bathed in brilliant sunshine, a steady rain fell, adding to the general air of gloom.

Hattie nearly dropped her pen in surprise. She was hard pressed to remember when Mrs Reynaud had last come calling. Hattie slid a piece of paper over the list.

'Is something the matter, Mrs Reynaud?'

'I feared something had happened to you,' Mrs Reynaud explained in a rush as she removed her veil, depositing it on an armchair. 'You failed to stop by this morning. There were things I wished to discuss with you. The picnic you had yesterday with Sir Christopher…did everything go as you would wish?'

'I went on a picnic. For the most part, it was highly pleasant. Mr Hook practised his proposed lecture and sent Mrs Hampstead to sleep. I ate my fill of strawberries for once as neither Livvy nor Portia were there.' Hattie folded her hands in her lap and tried to keep from looking at the list. 'There is little to discuss. A typical picnic. Nothing exciting. No handsome highwaymen or rescuing distressed maidens like you always seem to be encountering.'

'No picnic is typical if it involves Sir Christopher.' Mrs Reynaud lifted her chin. 'Your sister quite bristled with importance when she called yesterday. You dined with Sir Christopher Foxton. Your sister has expectations, great expectations. Left to her own devices, I believe she would be calling for banns. Do you have expectations, my dear?'

'My sister came to see you,' Hattie said slowly. How many other people had Stephanie happened to tell? Expectations indeed! Silently she offered up thanks that she had already dispatched her note to Kit, severing any connection. It had come to her last night. After the kiss they enjoyed, sending a letter was her only course forwards, but it had to be carefully worded, coded without appearing to mention That Incident. She had retained a copy to show Stephanie when she appeared, but she didn't want to appear too eager to share the news.

'Mrs Parteger required urgent advice about Mr Hook and her eldest.' Mrs Reynaud narrowed her eyes. 'I believe you mentioned something about me knowing Sir Christopher...'

'Only in passing.'

'It was many years ago.' The elderly woman fluttered her hands as two bright spots appeared on her pockmarked cheeks. 'I wouldn't want Sir Christopher to feel that I claimed an acquaintance. And I have no knowledge of Mr Hook's antecedents in any case.'

'Stephanie should never have bothered you with such a trivial matter. I fear she wanted to gossip about the picnic.' Hattie leant forwards and lowered her voice. 'No doubt she neglected to mention that Sir Christopher invited the entire family, but she declined, preferring to concentrate on arranging a series of lectures.'

'No, your sister never mentioned that.' Mrs Reynaud gave a merry trill of laughter. 'I thought Colonel Cunningham had charge of the lectures this year because it was something your sister loathed. Indeed, we very nearly did not have any lectures last year because your sister forgot.'

'Stephanie changed her mind. She thinks Colonel Cunningham needs some assistance now.'

Mrs Reynaud's eyes danced. 'Fancy forgetting that piece of information about who was originally invited. It puts the invitation in a different light.'

'My sister is rather inclined to make overmuch of the matter.' Hattie stood up and faced Mrs Reynaud. The sooner she stopped the gossip, the better for all concerned. 'The matter is now closed.'

'The matter with Sir Christopher or Mr Hook?'

'Both.' Hattie remembered the uncomfortable way Mr Hook had shifted in the carriage and how Mrs Hampstead had confided that she doubted anyone, even Livvy, could sit through something that dull and tedious. It was better for all concerned if they drew a line under the entire episode. 'Livvy might suffer for a few weeks, but London gentlemen never stay. It is no good hoping they will. They never do. I will inform Stephanie and the lecture can be postponed before real harm is done. I would hate for anyone to be disappointed.'

Mrs Reynaud tilted her head. Her sharp eyes assessed her. It seemed as if her gaze bore into her soul. Hattie toyed with her pen as her cheeks flamed.

'He kissed you. More than once, I reckon,' Mrs Reynaud said in solemn tones. 'It is far from a crime and occasionally most enjoyable. You were discreet. Yes. Yes, that goes without saying. You are the sort of woman who would be discreet. It was always part of my trouble when I was young and foolish. I forgot to be discreet.'

Hattie put her hand to her throat. How had Mrs Reynaud guessed? Nearly twenty-four hours later, and there should be no mark on her. Hattie glanced down and saw the word kiss, underlined, rather than scratched out. She moved the piece of paper more firmly over the list.

'We quarrelled. I doubt he will kiss me again. Nor would I wish him to.' She tilted her chin upwards. 'I sent him a note explaining the situation. It is impossible. He is impossible.'

'Why did you do that if you wanted to end it?'

Hattie put her hand on her stomach and concentrated on keeping her shoulders straight. She could hardly explain that she saw herself becoming like the woman whom Charles had loved, living on the margins of society, and for the first time it had tempted her.

'Because I have Livvy and Portia's reputation to think about,' she said firmly. 'How could they make the matches they need if their aunt is pilloried for being wicked? Sir Christopher does not believe in marriage. His parents had a dreadful one, I believe.'

The colour drained from Mrs Reynaud's face. 'He spoke to you about his parents and their marriage?'

'Only briefly to explain why he intends to remain unwed.' Hattie resolutely did not look at her list.

'People should not visit the sins of one generation on the next.'

'It was a brief interlude and now it is over.' Hattie walked over to the window and looked out over the garden with its gravel paths and roses. Off to her left, she could just make out Highfield's chimneys and the great cedar of Lebanon. This was home and safe. She was not prepared to risk her heart again. Charles had seen to that. Life would have been much easier in ways if Kit had been the marrying kind, but he wasn't. His honesty made her decision easy. 'I love the girls like my own and I would hate anything I did to ruin their chances of a good marriage.'

Mrs Reynaud made an impatient noise. 'Stop using them as shields to stop you from living. You are as bad as a foolish débutante who believes that a man's promise in a summer house offers a life of undying romance.'

'The heat of the moment overcame me, but I recovered before any real harm was done. He accepted my verdict.' Hattie pressed her hand into her stomach. Even a day later, the intensity of the final kiss made her senses reel. She had been so close to giving in completely. And she knew the next time she kissed Kit, she'd lack the will-power to stop. A very large part of her had wanted to drown in that kiss and blot out any memory of Charles's rough love-making. And she worried that it made her very wicked indeed, whatever Mrs Reynaud might say.

'As you say, it is all over. Then no harm is done.' Mrs Reynaud came over to her and put her hand on Hattie's shoulder. 'In my experience with men like Sir Christopher, they wish to be the one to end things. Formally. Informally is quite another matter.'

'This time it will be different,' Hattie said decisively as she gave Mrs Reynaud a copy of the letter. 'I was very firm and unyielding.'

'And you are prepared for the consequences, my dear?' Mrs Reynaud handed the letter back to Hattie. 'If Sir Christopher is half the man I have heard him to be, he will not give up at the first hurdle. He will see your letter as a challenge, an invitation to raise the stakes.'

'A challenge?' A pulse of warmth went through Hattie. 'You're wrong. He will see the logic of my argument. After all, it is not as if it were a serious flirtation.'

Kit tapped the note with his forefinger. The various scrawled words leapt out at him. Faint aromas of Hattie's jasmine scent permeated the paper and forcibly reminded him of how her lips had yielded. How she had forgot herself and given in to the passion for a moment.

Hattie had put her case for breaking with him in flowery language which did not detail the situation. She regretted that they were incompatible and that the picnic had proved a great trial. From now, they would have to be distant friends.

'Liar,' he whispered. 'All a quarrel means is a chance to become closer. You want this friendship. And I'm going to prove it to you. I do not quit over a simple misunderstanding. Or a base-less fear.'

Kit held Hattie's note over a candle and watched it smoulder and burn to ash. Over? It wasn't over until he ended it. He made a point of it. No woman had left him since Constance and she had begged in the end to return.

He paused. Hattie wasn't like any woman he'd been involved with before.

It didn't matter. He refused to allow Hattie to end it on such a slim pretext. No woman had ever written to him like that. And Hattie certainly had not kissed him like they would not suit. He had allowed her a chance to raise her drawbridges and retreat. But retreat was not for ever. The next stage needed to begin. Today, before she had a chance to think.

'You wanted to see me, sir?' Johnson, his valet, appeared in the doorway.

'I find I require my evening clothes after all today.'

'You are going out?'

'The musicale in celebration of Waterloo awaits.'

'Sir?' Johnson struggled to keep his face blank. 'You loathe such things. Tuneless playing.'

'I shall go and enjoy myself. Where was that

note from Mrs Parteger? After all, I do have an invitation. A seat has been saved.'

'You were wrong to send that letter discarding Sir Christopher.' Stephanie sank down next to Hattie in a flurry of feathers and ruffles.

'This is not the time to discuss it, Stephanie,' Hattie said through clenched teeth. She had to wonder how much Stephanie knew of the contents. 'The concert to celebrate the deliverance from Napoleon is about to begin.'

'You always do such things to me. At least this time, hopefully I learnt about it early enough.' She glanced over her shoulder. 'Oh dear!'

'I have no idea what you are talking about, Stephanie.' Hattie slid towards the vacant chair on her right. Stephanie's feathered turban kept tickling her nose. The last thing she needed now was a frank-and-public discussion about her severing relations with Kit. 'What is the problem?'

'Maria Richley has waylaid Sir Christopher.'

Hattie fought against the inclination to turn her head. She had counted on Kit not appearing at this concert. 'Really? I wish her the joy of it.'

'I feel certain that the Widow Richley will not squander any opportunity. No...hush.' Stephanie laid a proprietary hand on Hattie's arm. 'All might not be lost, Hattie. Be civil if he approaches.'

'You are making it seem like I am younger than Portia.'

A trill of laughter cut through the musician's tuning. Hattie turned her head. Maria Richley clung to Kit's arm as if she were drowning. Over the heads of the other concertgoers, Kit nodded directly at her. A sardonic smile curled on his lips. He leant down and said something to Maria Richley, which sent the woman into further peals of laughter.

Hattie forced her eyes forwards. She crumpled the music programme in her hand. It was none of her business if he chose to enjoy Maria Richley's favours. All it did was to confirm that she'd been correct in the first place. That man was trouble.

Only she wished that he had not stood quite so close to Maria Richley.

Her view was suddenly obscured by a large expanse of black broad cloth.

'Mrs Parteger, Mrs Wilkinson…if I may squeeze in? You have a free seat, I believe.'

Hattie shrank in her seat. She was now going to have to spend several hours trapped between Stephanie's headdress and the vicar, Dr Hornby's, bulk. The perfect way to spend an evening. No doubt Kit would have secured a place with plenty of space for Maria Richley.

'Doctor Hornby.'

'Your sister said that you would be here, Mrs Wilkinson. How delightful to see you again.' Doctor Hornby gave a jowly smile. 'I'm looking forward to the planned lecture series now that it is finally settled. You will come to my lecture on the problems of mapping the Holy Places in two weeks' time?'

Murder, Hattie decided, was too humane a punishment for Stephanie. She needed to be tortured slowly. 'I look forward to it.'

'My dear Mrs Wilkinson, you do me such honour.' Doctor Hornby made a grab for her hand and froze. His face became a mottled purple.

'Are you well, Dr Hornby?'

'Perfectly fine. I must leave you ladies.'

Hattie had half-turned and saw Kit glowering. He gave her a cold nod. 'As long as you are certain.'

'On second thoughts, I do believe Miss Gormley has saved me a seat. I would hate to disappoint her.'

'I understand completely.'

Hattie drew in a breath of air and concentrated on steadying her pulse. She resisted the urge to turn around and see Kit's reaction. They were finished, and she was not going to be kissed again. Ever. The thought made her unbearably sad.

'If you will excuse me...I believe this is my seat.' Kit pushed passed her and sat down in the chair Dr Hornby had just vacated.

'I hadn't realised it was spoken for.'

'It was.' He turned his back on her. 'Mrs Parteger saved it for me.'

Stephanie developed a sudden interest in her programme and ignored Hattie's sudden jab to her side.

Hattie spent the entire concert busily trying to ignore his very existence. And failing. She rejected a number of possible conversation topics but finally settled on a polite discussion of music. She'd demonstrate to Stephanie and Kit that she bore no ill feeling. The remainder of the concert was spent in happy contemplation of what she would say.

When the concert was over, he stood up.

'It has been a pleasure, Mrs Wilkinson, Mrs Parteger.'

Before Hattie could utter another word, he was gone.

'You could have done more, Hattie. I am highly disappointed in you.'

'He nearly cut me dead.'

'You were the one to send the letter. Ill timed and ill advised. I was attempting to mend bridges. Sir Christopher is a neighbour.'

He'd only sat with her to prove a point. Stephanie in her misguided way had given him an opportunity. Hattie narrowed her eyes. 'If you ever do that again, Stephanie, I will create a scene and, more than that, a scandal. How would you like me to be embroiled in a scandal?'

'Some people are entirely too touchy.' Stephanie gave a loud sniff. 'Very well, you will hear no more from me on the subject. I entirely wash my hands of you, Harriet Wilkinson. I hope you enjoy your widow's bed.'

'I find it utterly comfortable. Far better than my marriage bed,' she muttered under her breath.

'Aunt Hattie, it is his carriage. I know it is,' Livvy breathed when Hattie turned the governess cart into the Corbridge High Street the morning after the concert.

'Whose carriage?' Hattie asked absently as she brought the cart to a halt outside the ironmonger's. Her dreams had been confused last night after the concert. Twice she had woken with her mind full of thoughts of Kit and the way his lips had moved over hers. She should have said something before he left. It was quite possible he considered that she had a part in that saving of a seat débâcle. She couldn't decide which was worse—Stephanie's behaviour or the fact she had been supremely aware of him.

Today was a day for concentrating on the jobs that needed to be done before the Stagshaw Bank Fair, rather than considering what might have been. Once the fair was over, he'd depart the neighbourhood and she would not have a constant reminder. She could get over this attraction.

'Whose carriage, Livvy?'

'Sir Christopher's, of course!'

Hattie ignored the sudden fluttering in her stomach. She had made the correct decision. She'd no other choice. Any lady would have done the same thing. 'I wasn't aware that you ever paid much attention to carriages.'

'It has butter-yellow wheels and is quite new. Mr Hook told me all about it. Sir Christopher purchased it once they arrived in Newcastle by packet boat.'

'Other carriages have butter-yellow wheels,' Hattie said, more to control her own sudden onset of nerves than Livvy's. After the concert where he'd barely spoken to her, she wasn't entirely sure what to expect.

Livvy kicked the board under her seat. 'Can I go to the circulating library?'

'May I. Where are your manners today, Livvy?'

'May I go? Portia, you will come with me.' Livvy grabbed her sister's arm. 'Aunt Hattie, surely you can't object if I have a companion. I wish to improve my mind.'

Portia gave an indignant squeak.

Hattie pinched the bridge of her nose. 'I thought you wanted to go to the haberdasher's for more ribbon.'

'I can do that after. Please. I want to see if the latest by the author of *Waverley* is there. And Papa wants a book on animal husbandry. He wants to settle an argument with Colonel Cunningham. I will catch you up in the haber-dasher's.'

Hattie gave a weary wave. It would make life easier if neither Livvy nor Portia accompanied her on her errands, particularly when she needed to find out if indeed the firebox for Mrs Belter's cook stove could be repaired as Mr Ogle had promised weeks ago or if she'd be better inves-tigating the range of stoves at the Stagshaw fair for Mrs Belter. The fair did represent an oppor-tunity to buy a wider range of goods than were generally available in the Tyne Valley.

She watched the pair for a few steps and decided that they would be all right. Livvy could not get up to any mischief at the circulating library and the probability that Mr Hook was actually there was slim. The back of her neck crept. The last person she wanted to encounter was Kit and if Mr Hook was in the library, Kit would not be far behind. And she certainly did not want to explain about the concert.

She stepped into the ironmonger's and collided with a solid expanse of chest. Hattie inhaled the sandalwood scent. Strong fingers caught her elbow and steadied her.

She hurriedly took a step backwards out of the shop. She ducked her head, hoping that he wouldn't see her flaming cheeks. 'Sir Christopher. This is most unexpected.'

'Mrs Wilkinson.'

Hattie shifted in her boots. Of all the people! This time she refused to be cut. 'I wanted to make sure Mr Ogle had finished a job for me.'

'It is your habit to enter establishments without checking to see if anyone is coming out?' His grey eyes danced.

Her heart did a little flip. He wasn't angry with her. He was flirting with her as if the breach never happened.

'Yes, I mean, no. I was thinking of other things.'

'Obviously of great import.'

'Domestic triviality.' She squared her shoulders. This encounter would not throw her off balance. She had made her decision, but it did not prevent her from being civil. 'You understand how it is.'

'Wool-gathering,' he said decisively. A smile tugged at his lips. 'It is a bad habit. You neglected me dreadfully during the concert.'

'You left straight after the concert.' She pulled at her gloves, straightening the fingers. 'I wanted to thank you for rescuing me.'

'Rescuing you?'

'From Dr Hornby. He can be difficult to sit next to.'

He tilted his head to one side. 'It was my seat. Your sister signalled to me when I came in, I thought you knew.'

'Obviously I was mistaken.' Hattie picked at the seam of her glove. She wished she had thought of that scenario. She should have guessed something like that had happened. Stephanie could be singularly stubborn. 'Despite my best efforts, my sister harbours hopes.'

'If he bothers you again, let me know. Simply being the vicar does not give him the right to touch people.'

Hattie glanced up quickly. 'You saw that.'

'I happened to look over. Even if it had not been my seat, I would have done something.'

'You would have?'

'You are the only true friend I have in the neighbourhood.'

'You plan on staying in the neighbourhood?' Hattie gripped her reticule tighter. He was going to stay for longer. A mixture of fear and excitement vibrated through her. She would have to see him again and again, but on what terms? Friendship was the only sensible course. She had to think about safeguarding her reputation.

'I am undecided about what to do with the Lodge.' The tone in his voice seemed to indicate something troubled him more than the Lodge.

'And will you be doing up your tenants' houses?' Hattie asked, trying to steer the conversation away from their friendship.

'They appear to be in good order. My uncle may not have cared for his own comforts, but he did make sure that his tenants all had a roof over their heads.' Kit drew himself up to his full height. 'I do employ the same estate manager. No one has been to me with complaints about him.'

She thought about Mrs Reynaud and how she

had mentioned him. It would be the perfect opportunity for them to renew their acquaintance. 'Perhaps your tenants might like to meet you. People like the personal touch rather than being treated like a component in one of those newfangled machines. You hardly want to be considered aloof.'

He quirked his eyebrow. 'Are you seeking to teach me my duty now, Mrs Wilkinson?'

'No. It was merely a suggestion. I believe they feared you would never arrive.'

'Sir Christopher, there you are.' A trilling voice called behind Hattie. 'Mama and I thought we had lost you. I should be most distressed if that happened.'

Miss Dent and Maria Richley. How many other women after that? Hattie ground her teeth. Had he lied when he said that he only pursued one woman at a time? Kit knew what he was on about. She shouldn't have to spell out how tenacious the Dents could be. He had the perfect right to see anyone he wanted.

'Miss Dent, I was endeavouring to follow, but circumstances dictated otherwise. Please go on to our arrangement. I will follow you shortly.' He inclined his head. 'You must excuse me, Mrs Wilkinson. We must continue this highly interesting conversation some other time. I did promise Miss Dent that I would join her father for a cup of coffee in the Reading Room. He apparently knows a good joiner and the staircase at the Lodge will have to be replaced.'

Hattie kept her head up. It was not as if she had any claim on him. She had made her choice the other day. And if anything, her encounter showed that she was wrong to suspect his hand in Dr Hornby's odd behaviour.

'You are busy, you should have said. The social whirl surrounding this year's fair has been phenomenal. I've no wish to keep you...from your duties.'

'I'm never too busy to speak with a friend.'

'I thought...' She attempted to focus on the coal scuttles, grates and variety that adorned the walls of the ironmonger's rather than on Kit's face.

'We remain friends.' There was no mistaking the finality in Kit's voice. 'We may have quarrelled, but it is settled now. What is friendship without quarrels? Life would be very dull indeed.'

The air rushed out of her lungs. He was determined to ignore her letter. It shouldn't make her heart feel so light, but it did. 'Yes...yes, of course.'

His smile brought sunshine into the gloom

of the ironmonger's. She wasn't going to ask for more than he could give. She knew what he was. He was precisely the same as Charles and if she ever forgot that for a moment, she'd lose her way. She was not going to be betrayed like that again.

'I knew you'd see it my way.' His smile increased as he rocked back on his heels. 'I burnt your letter. It held little of value.'

'You burnt it? Did you even read it?'

'I know why it was written, Hattie. And you are wrong to be afraid. I wanted to let you know that.'

She was conscious of staring at him for a heartbeat too long, of drinking in his features. She was very glad now that he hadn't read the pretentious twaddle. It didn't change things. Serious flirtations were out. The risks were too great. 'I'm not afraid.'

'That is good to know.'

'There are things I must do.' Hattie forced her chin upwards so she looked Kit directly in the eye. Here she retook control of the conversation. 'Mr Ogle was going to fix Mrs Belter's firebox. It needs to be done or I shall have to order another stove at the Stagshaw fair.'

'Who is Mrs Belter?'

'One of my brother-in-law's tenants. Stephanie can't be counted on to ensure my brother-in-law knows how they are doing. Over the years, I took the responsibility on. It keeps me out of mischief and makes everyone's lives happier.'

'Far be it from me to keep you from doing anything.' He put two fingers to his hat. 'Until the fair, Mrs Wilkinson.'

Hattie put a hand to her head as she stepped back into the shop. He probably thought her sighing from love just like Miss Dent and Maria Richley. She gave a little smile. The next time she encountered him, she would not feed his self-importance. *Until the fair.* Had she agreed to meet him? Did he think they were going to meet? Impossible! She had to find him and tell him that it was not going to happen.

Hattie hurried back out of the ironmonger's. Her feet skittered to a stop.

Kit stood facing the door, arms crossed. He raised an eyebrow and inclined his head. She curled her fists. He knew she'd appear. He had waited for her to appear. Silently she cursed for behaving precisely as he thought she would. Seven years after Charles's betrayal and she acted worse than Livvy.

'Is there a problem, Mrs Wilkinson?'

'I…that is…' The words stuck in her throat. She swallowed hard and tried again. This time she stuck her chin in the air and took refuge in her dignity. 'I had no plans to see you during the fair.'

'But you have no objections, should it happen?'

Hattie waved her reticule in the air in a gesture of magnanimity. 'If it happens, I will not cut you.'

'You have relieved my mind.' His eyes danced. 'The thought has kept me awake in recent nights. What could be worse than being cut by Mrs Wilkinson at the Stagshaw fair? How can I prevent it?'

Hattie allowed her hand to drop to her side. All the pretence flowed out of her. 'You are laughing at me. You think me a censorious widow who has forgotten what it is like to be alive.'

'Not at all. I'm not given to flights of fancy. I do have the honour of having been on a picnic with you. I have heard you laugh.'

'Then what?' She found the answer mattered suddenly.

The dimple in the corner of his mouth deepened. His gaze seemed to pierce her very soul. 'I'm merely welcoming our return to friendship. Nothing more. Your servant, Mrs Wilkinson. Stop being so hard on yourself.'

Chapter Six

'Hurry up, Livvy,' Hattie called from the governess cart just after ten on the fourth of July.
'You don't want to be late for the fair. Your
mother and father left over an hour ago.'

Portia had run over and clambered immediately in, but Livvy slowly picked her way across
the puddles, holding a white parasol over her
head. Hattie wanted to get out of the governess
cart and bodily pick her up. All night she had
thought about Kit and how she'd behave during
the fair. They were friends. The fact that she
kept remembering the kiss they had shared was
her problem.

'Isn't the sun fierce this year?' Livvy said, finally getting into the cart. 'You will freckle, Portia, if you don't pull your hat forwards.'

Portia stuck out her tongue and pushed the straw bonnet back.

'If there is any bickering, you can stay at home.' Hattie gave the reins a shake and the horse started off smartly. All she could hope was that the day improved. This was the sort of thing she loved—being with her nieces. Except today, it felt a bit like everyone took her for granted. There was a question of how she greeted Kit as she had not bothered to inform Stephanie about the precise ending of hostilities. 'I mean it, Portia and Livvy. I want no repeats of last year.'

'You can't do that!' Portia's eyes went wide. 'I have been waiting for oranges and gingerbread for ever so long. Whenever I'm feeling sad, I tell myself—oranges and gingerbread lumps as big as hats at the Stagshaw fair. Somehow it makes everything seem more bearable.'

'I am sure there will be time for both oranges and gingerbread...provided you both behave yourselves.' Hattie concentrated on navigating the rutted road. The short journey to Stagshaw was fraught with difficulty after so many carriages and carts had churned up the road. The last thing she needed was a broken wheel or to get stuck in the mud. She had taken pains with her dress and had tried out a new hairstyle. 'I've saved some pennies for you. Shall we see how many squares of gingerbread we can eat?'

'Can I use the money towards a pair of Hexham Tans?' Livvy smoothed her skirt and tilted her chin. From where Hattie sat, it appeared that she was striking a variety of poses, trying them out to see which suited her best by looking at her shadow. Hattie remembered the phase all too clearly. 'I would like a pair of gloves more than anything and I have almost enough. I've saved my Christmas and birthday money especially.'

Portia snorted. 'You mean you are hoping to run into Mr Hook and don't want your face grubby. Personally I fail to see what the fuss is about. He doesn't appear to know much about newts. I asked him about the toads in our garden when we ran into him at the Halls' At Home. And he kept primping his curls when he thought no one was looking. The tousled look.'

Livvy rolled her eyes. 'There is a difference between toads and newts, Portia. Any fool knows that.'

'Will he be giving the proposed lecture before he departs? I understood they were only staying for the Stagshaw fair,' Hattie asked, attempting to keep her voice casual. Her mind raced to think about whether Kit had actually said they were staying or if today was truly going to be goodbye. Her heart sank. She wasn't ready to say goodbye.

'It depends on what Colonel Cunningham decides, but I plan to sit in the front row when it happens.'

'Livvy, we weren't going to speak about meeting Mr Hook in the High Street. Mama said. Sir Christopher would barely speak to Aunt Hattie at the concert. They have fallen out of civility and it is all Aunt Hattie's fault. Her best chance for marriage in years is gone.'

Livvy clapped her hands over her mouth. 'I'm so sorry, Aunt Harriet. I understand now about the sorrows of the heart.'

'Is there a particular pair of gloves you want or are you going to look over the stalls?' Hattie asked, silently damning Stephanie. Sorrows of the heart and Kit being a good marriage prospect indeed. She was not wasting away for love or looking for a loveless marriage with a charming but unreliable man. The only person who would see the irony was Kit.

'Oh, I thought I would wander up and down the stalls until I found the one I wanted.' Livvy gave an elaborate shrug.

'Does your mother approve of your plan? You are hoping to meet Mr Hook.'

'Mama fails to understand.' Livvy bent her

head and fussed with her lace gloves. 'I'm sixteen, but I also have a brain. I want to go to
London and have a Season. I'm not about to do
anything foolish.'

'You did go into the card room.'

'Mr Hook explained that it was not my best
idea, but how else could I meet him?' Livvy
screwed up her nose. 'Sir Christopher gave him
a talking to. Being young is no reason to be ignorant of society's pitfalls.'

Despite her earlier misgivings, Hattie was
impressed. Mr Hook had obviously considered
his position and decided that he wanted to court
Livvy. She might not agree with everything, but
the light romance would not put anyone in danger. 'I agree with Sir Christopher.'

Livvy clapped her hands together. 'Why did
you have to fall out of civility with Sir Christopher? It makes everything much more difficult.
Mama has taken against Mr Hook for some unknown reason. And now they say Sir Christopher has taken up with one of the Dent sisters.
The elder one who has the annoying laugh. And
the younger one probably will get her claws into
Mr Hook.'

'I heard that it was Maria Richley.' Portia put
her hand over Hattie's. 'We weren't meant to tell.
Mama made us promise.'

Hattie pasted a smile on her face. Stephanie obviously knew that Portia would be unable to keep a secret and had primed her. After the incident at the musicale with the seating arrangements, she should have guessed that Stephanie was not going to give up her matchmaking scheme easily. Still the gossip caused a slight jealous twinge and that surprised her.

All in all it was safer if no one knew about her renewed friendship with Kit. Hattie forcibly turned the subject away from Sir Christopher and back towards safer subjects like gloves, gingerbread and the possibility of exotic animals.

The odour of spice and citrus fruit mixed with animal and overlaid with sawdust took Kit back to his childhood. He could remember every step of the fair even though he had not been in twenty-five years. The stalls looked tantalisingly familiar—here one for London Spice and there another selling oranges. Still further on were the stalls devoted to all manner of pots and pans. It appeared as if a large tented city had sprung up overnight. Kit struggled to see the windswept field where he and Hattie had picnicked only a few days before.

The memory of waiting outside the ale tent and hoping that his uncle would not turn out like his father sliced through him. *Your father has it all wrong, Kit. Bad blood doesn't mean you have to be bad. Damn your mother to hell. Never wait on a woman.*

Kit frowned and pushed the memory away. Over the years he'd perfected the art of not thinking about the past and only living in the present. And the present meant deciding what to do about Hattie. He wasn't ready to face that…yet, and it was unlike him to be mealy-mouthed. He would end it after the fair. The gift he gave her would be special, but in keeping with their relationship. The weight on his shoulders eased. He was going to do the right thing.

'Do keep up, Rupert,' Kit said as Rupert endeavoured to linger at the gun stall and then at Moles Swords where the latest models were hung with precision and a crowd of ten deep stood. 'You purchased a sword before we left London. Maybe now you will understand why I urged you to wait. Moles always brings out its new range for the Stagshaw fair.'

Rupert put down the rapier with a loud sigh. 'You are right. Nothing, not even a sword, can give me pleasure when the sight of my beloved is denied.'

'Petulance does you few favours,' Kit murmured. 'You were the one to get into this muddle. Women should be enjoyed, not mooned over.'

Rupert gave a glance behind him and his entire countenance lit up. 'Miss Parteger is at the glove stall, right when she said she would be. You are wrong, Kit, some women you can count on.'

Kit tensed. Hattie stood next to Miss Parteger, seemingly absorbed in choosing a pair of butter-yellow gloves. Her straw bonnet trimmed with green ribbons made a pleasant contrast with her round gown. Not a London sophisticate, but refreshing, someone who was comfortable in their skin. Was it just the novelty of freshness that intrigued? Kit frowned. It didn't matter. He would return to London soon and the flirtation would be over.

'Shall we go and investigate the famous Hexham Tans?' he said.

As he approached, Hattie looked up. Her straw bonnet framed her face, shadowing her features and making her look far more desirable than the majority of women of his acquaintance.

'Are you buying gloves?' he asked after they had exchanged pleasantries.

'Livvy is. She desires a new pair and they always do specials on fair days. She is looking at the other stalls, but I always come back to Hedley's. There is a certain something about the way they soften the leather.' She stretched out her hand. 'I can't make up my mind about whether the butter yellow or light tan is best.'

'For riding?'

'General purpose.'

He looked down at her hands. Her fingers were small and slender, but there was a certain indomitable strength in them. She was the sort of woman who would bend, but not break. 'Can a lady accept gloves from a gentleman or would it be too intimate a gift?'

Her eyes twinkled, warming him. He found he'd missed the barely suppressed humour. 'I suspect you already know the answer.'

'A pity as those butter-yellow gloves suit your hands perfectly.' He waited for her to agree. 'It is a fair day after all and the normal rules don't apply.'

'I would hate to cause talk. And you make your rules as you go along in any case.'

'Not all my rules. Some are immovable.'

'But most of them. It lulls people into a false sense of security.'

'Is it my fault if they wish to be lulled?'

Hattie stripped off the glove and handed it back to the stall owner with a decided shake of her head. As she began to make a pile of the various other gloves, Kit signalled first to the stall owner and then to Rupert, handing the stall owner some money. He'd give Hattie the gloves when the time was right.

'Is the fair everything you hoped at Waterloo?' she asked, glancing up just after he had completed the transaction.

'It is everything I remember, but it is as if I am looking through a Claude glass rather than actually being here.' He gave a laugh. 'Perhaps I need a guide.'

Her hand brushed his as she reached for the next set of gloves. 'Is there anything missing? Something that would help make the day perfect?'

Kit contemplated saying her exploring the fair with him, but decided that it would be revealing too much. He opted for something safer, less declaratory. 'I need to find a toy manufacturer.'

Her hands stilled. 'What sort of toys? Dolls? Wooden tops? You hardly seem like the child-loving sort.'

'Jumping-jacks—little men or women with a string you pull. I had one from the fair when I was a young boy. My uncle bought it for me.' Kit gazed over her shoulder and knew it would help ease the unsettled feeling if he could find the stall. It would reassure him that there was nothing magical about the stall. The jumping-jack was just that, a wooden toy. 'I wanted to see if such a creature still existed. The stall holder had a humpback and a hook nose, but he made the most wonderful wooden toys.'

Her mouth became a perfect O. 'You had one as a boy. From this fair. It is why you wanted to come back here?'

'That's right,' he agreed, surprised that she had guessed. 'My uncle gave me one as consolation.'

'Consolation? That is a strange word to use. Why did you need consolation? Had someone died?'

'I had waited outside the ale tent for hours.' Kit clamped his mouth shut. He had explained too much already. He remembered thinking that he'd meet his mother. Of course she had never appeared. He'd blocked the memory until now. The last thing he wanted was to discuss his mother, particularly not with Hattie Wilkinson. He'd already revealed more about his past than he'd intended. He never spoke about her. It saved having people look at him with pity.

'You won't find one on this row.' Hattie's brow knitted. 'The toy manufacturers are two rows down, near the London Spice merchant. I think I know the one you mean. I used to buy my nieces and nephews toys from him when they were little.'

'It sounds straightforward enough.' Kit touched his hat. He silently thanked her for not pursuing the topic. 'Rupert…'

Rupert had wandered down the stall and appeared to be in earnest discussion with Miss Parteger over a pair of gloves. Instantly he broke off the conversation and stood up straighter. Rupert appeared to have taken their conversations to heart. Kit gave a wry smile. Then he *was* Brendan's boy and Brendan could always be counted on to do what was right.

'I'm about to go that way after Livvy finishes and I return her to her mother.'

He caught her hand. 'And you won't lead me astray?'

She tilted her head to one side. Her eyes danced with mischief. 'I can show you if you like. As for leading you astray, I fear you went from that path long ago.'

Kit laughed. A heartbeat later, Hattie joined in.

The sound of her laughter made the whole day seem brighter. Kit knew he would get his way. He'd enjoy today and finish the flirtation before it started to mean anything. It was better that way. He'd retrieve the gloves from Rupert later and send them with a note before he left for London. And he would leave for London, once his business here was finished.

'That would be perfect. With you by my side, Mrs Wilkinson, I know I shan't lose my way.'

'I'll tell Livvy to hurry up. She has lingered far longer than I thought she would. Portia and Stephanie went off to buy oranges over an hour ago.'

'Rupert can look after your niece. He is quite safe.'

'Are you sure? The memory of the card room lingers.'

'He has grown on this trip. You must take my word for it.'

'I shall.'

Kit called to Rupert and told him to take Miss Parteger back to her mother without stopping for refreshment on the way. His godson blushed a deep scarlet.

'Very neatly done.'

'I like to think so.' Kit tucked her hand in the crook of his arm before she had a chance to pull away. 'What is the wagering that they do stop? Maybe not for refreshment, but to watch a Punch and Judy show or one of the other entertainments?'

'Just so you know, I never bet on a sure thing.

It takes the fun out of it. Everyone should have a little romance in their life. It will be harmless.'

'You surprise me, Mrs Wilkinson. I was willing to wager on you not understanding about young romance except I make it a policy never to wager on a lady, only with her.'

Her eyes turned cloudy and something close to sorrow tugged at her mouth. In that instant, Kit hated her late husband. Seven years and he retained a hold over her. 'You are wrong about that. I understand about romance and its perils all too well.'

'Is this the one you want? Now that we are finally here.' Hattie held up a red-coated jumping-jack.

'And whose fault is that?'

'Yours, I believe.' She gave a light laugh, basking in the warmth of his smile. 'You kept seeing another stall you wanted to investigate.'

'It has been an age since I've been to a fair. I wanted to make certain things were here.'

'Including having a go at the ha'penny man?'

'I did win.'

The toy stall had proved more difficult to find than she thought it would be, not the least of which Kit seemed intent on taking the most circuitous route. Not that she had strenuously objected. She had enjoyed talking with him and laughing. They seemed to share the same sense of humour. They were friends, nothing more. It could never be anything more.

She refused to go back to the girl she had once been, and in any case, Kit had been clear about his views on marriage. She wished that she could be like someone in Mrs Reynaud's stories, but there were considerations. She shivered slightly, remembering how Charles's mistress had said that they were more alike than she thought.

To banish the unwelcome memory she blindly reached for another toy.

'Do you like this jumping-jack? Personally I think he has a roguish smile, just the sort of thing for a man like you.'

'It will do.' His hand closed over it. A sudden fierce longing crossed over his face. 'The one I had as a boy had a dark-green coat with white trim.'

'You must have loved it.'

'It meant a lot to me once. It was about my only toy.'

Hattie's heart bled for the lonely boy that he must have been. 'Your only toy?'

'My father didn't hold with such things, but as it was a present from my uncle, he allowed me to keep it.'

'Then it was good that you loved it so much.'

He tilted his head to one side. 'I suspect you find it strange. But my father had his own views on life.'

'Not at all. Just tell me that he died a lonely and bitter old man.'

He lifted an eyebrow. 'Why?'

'It saves me from having to kill him. Children should have toys. There is time enough to be grown up.'

'My father would not have agreed. Boys need to learn to be men. My father was a hard man.'

'But you are not your father.'

'I'm grateful you realise that. I try not to take after either of my parents.'

Hattie relaxed in the sunshine of his smile. A sharp longing sliced through her. If only… Hattie pushed it away. It was far too late for regrets. She was not the type to indulge in casual affairs of the heart. She had her responsibilities and duties to think about. This had to be the last time she indulged in a flirtation with Kit.

'The jumping-jack will be a present from me,' she said, taking control of the conversation.

His eyes narrowed. 'Are jumping-jacks different than gloves?'

'Jumping-jacks are better given as gifts. Every

child since time began knows that. It adds to the magic.'

'I agree.' There was a catch in his voice and he turned his face from hers.

'Is something wrong?' She laid her hand on his arm. 'Kit, explain. We are friends. I want to know.'

He turned back towards her. His eyes held a distinctly sultry look which caused a warm curl to wind its way around her insides. 'I normally never let my lady buy me anything.'

A warm shiver went down her back. She envied the unknown lady who would be his. A longing to feel his lips against hers and the touch of his hand against her skin filled her.

'But I'm not yours, am I?' she returned more tartly than she had intended. 'It is a gift from a friend, nothing more.'

His eyes bore into her, searching down to her soul. Hattie returned his gaze as steadily as she could, hoping he didn't see the white lie.

'I stand corrected,' he said finally. 'In that case I shall be delighted to accept the gift. Child that I am.'

'Play with it wisely. It is what I always tell my nieces and nephews when I give them a toy,' she joked after she had paid the wizened toymaker.

Keep it light. She needed to keep it light. She

gripped her reticule tighter. Their time was coming to an end and she didn't want it to.

She could easily imagine what one of his London mistresses would be like—the highly sophisticated way she'd laugh and how her gestures would be perfectly poised. Everything she wasn't and could never be.

'I intend to treasure it.' Kit tucked it into his breast pocket. 'It should be safe there. Thank you, Hattie. It is a first being given something like this from a woman, but then you are unique.'

Hattie dipped her head. There was a wealth of meaning in those words. If she wasn't careful, she would start wanting to be kissed again. And that would be a very bad idea. 'I should get back to the family. Livvy and Portia will be wondering what has happened to me.'

'Surely they can spare you for a while longer yet? There must be some part of the fair you haven't explored. Perhaps you'd like your fortune told. There are always gypsies at fairs like these.'

'I'm not overfond of fortune tellers. My husband used to enjoy such pastimes.'

'And you gave them up as frivolous on his death.' He held up his hand. 'Say no more, Hattie. Your past defines you.'

'That is not it at all.'

'Why can't you linger with me a while? We

won't have our fortune told. We can enjoy the fair in other ways.'

'They count on me. I don't know where I'd be without them.' A sudden chill passed through Hattie. She'd been so close to agreeing. She needed to keep this friendship light and easy, but not lose sense of what was truly important in her life, permanent and lasting—her family. 'It helped so much to have them near after Charles's death. They restored my faith in humanity.'

'You should try living for yourself more.'

'It's funny...that is precisely what Mrs Reynaud said.' She straightened her back. 'You mustn't worry. Once they are grown, I intend to travel the world, really travel. There are so many places I long to see. I make a list every year. I only stay in Northumberland because Stephanie and her girls can't cope without me.'

'Mrs Reynaud?' A puzzled look came on his face and he seemed to go rigid. 'Do you know someone called Reynaud?'

'An elderly lady. One of your tenants. At Pearl Cottage.'

'None of my tenants is called Reynaud. I would know.'

'Perhaps she used a different name.' Hattie gave a little shrug. 'Her agreement was with your uncle. I think she knew your family when she was younger.' Hattie lowered her voice. 'She has led an exciting life and doles out tales of her wickedness. Stephanie doesn't entirely approve of her, but I enjoy her company.'

Kit's face became carved out of stone. All humour and goodwill had vanished. 'I can't remember ever meeting a Mrs Reynaud. What does she look like?'

'She says she is much altered. A few years ago before she came to the Tyne Valley, she suffered from smallpox and totally lost her looks. Recently she has become more of a recluse than ever. Mrs Belter told me that she had refused to come to the fair because the children might point their fingers and call her a witch.'

Kit tapped his fingers together. He looked her up and down in an assessing sort of way. Hattie was aware of the simplicity of her dress and the fact that it was several seasons old. He must consider it hopelessly naïve and unattractive. He took a step closer to her and his eyes became almost feline.

'I agree with her assessment, whoever this Mrs Reynaud is. You should have a life, Hattie, and let your nieces lead their own.' His hand slid down her back and his breath tickled her ear. 'It is your life to live. You only have one. Seize it.'

'I don't understand what you are saying.' She

hated the way her voice caught. Her lips ached as if he had kissed them again.

'I think you do.' His voice rolled over her, silently urging her to move closer. Seductive in the extreme. 'I think you understand me very well. We could be good together.'

Hattie pulled her hand away. She pressed her fingers to her temples and willed the siren call to be gone. She knew what he was asking and she also knew she wasn't ready. Not today and probably not ever. She had to leave now and not look back.

'Hattie?'

'When I require your advice, I'll ask,' she said stiffly. She had nearly done it and she couldn't. She'd hate herself later if she embarked on an affair. She wasn't going to be like...like her late husband's mistress. She shuddered, remembering the time she'd visited and how awkward it had all been. She had to stay with where she was safe. She started to walk away from Kit.

'Where are you going now?' He reached her in two strides and put his hand on her elbow, bringing her against his body. 'I didn't think you were given to false modesty, Hattie.'

'Stephanie will have created a small camp for us near the black-faced sheep. She worries about my brother-in-law becoming lost and so they go back to the same place every year.' Hattie jerked her arm away. To think how close she had come! Poor deluded Hattie had nearly done it again. Been swept away on the romance and forgetting the cost. 'They will be wondering where I am. It was bad of me to go off like this.'

The dimple shone in his cheek, highlighting his lips. 'Your brother-in-law gets confused?'

'It is the one day of the year that he spends time in the ale tent. Stephanie refuses to go in, but always waits to take him home.' Hattie gave a careful shrug, but she was aware of how near he stood and where his hands were. Her sister and brother-in-law were very different but they did seem to have a happy marriage, something that was for ever going to elude her. All she wanted to do was to find a quiet place and regain control of herself. She'd been so close to giving in to temptation. It had been seeing the longing in his face when he held the jumping-jack in his hand which had nearly undone her and made her think that he might want something else. 'It is an arrangement which has served them well.'

'Shall I walk you there? Fairs can be notorious for drunks and others making a nuisance. Allow me to keep you safe.'

'I can find my own way.' Hattie used her reticule as a shield. 'The fair has so much to offer.

You must try the ale tent yourself. If you find my brother-in-law, remind him that we are expecting to go home at a reasonable hour rather than at eight when the fair finishes. Please let me go, Kit.'

'Independent to a fault.' He held up his hand and his eyes became steely grey. 'I understand.'

Hattie didn't flinch even though she was dying inside. 'It is the way I like it. Independent but respectable. I can't have it any other way.'

'Because of your husband's memory?'

'Do not bring my late husband into this.' A cold chill went down her spine. She couldn't lie about Charles. Not to Kit. The thought stunned her.

'Let me know if you ever feel lonely.'

'I bid you adieu, Kit. I'll understand if you have to go back to London suddenly.' She made an expansive gesture as her insides wept. 'I hope this is everything you wanted.'

His hand curled about hers and then let go. 'Thank you, Hattie…for my jumping-jack.'

Hattie forced herself to walk away without looking back. It was one of the hardest things she had ever done, but she knew it was the right thing. Kit suddenly appeared to be taking liberties, to misunderstand why she'd purchased that stupid jumping-jack. She was safer on her own.

Chapter Seven

Walking away from Kit was the right thing to do, Hattie thought as she strode away from where he stood. To stay would mean giving in to temptation and starting to believe that there was something between them. She had nearly cried when he told her the story about the jumping-jack and then he became so cold, practically accusing her of trying to interfere. And then he'd made the suggestion and it changed everything. She was not going to tumble into bed with him. Ever.

Hattie pushed past the gawkers around the find-a-penny man and the farmers and their wives outside the exotic curiosity stall. She resisted the temptation to turn around and see where Kit was.

A gypsy cart had become stuck in the middle of a boggy bit. Hattie attempted to squeeze around the back, ignoring the gypsy woman who offered to read the pretty lady's fortune. When she was a little girl, Mrs Hampstead used to tell stories about how gypsies spirited people away, over and over again because Stephanie loved being scared. Even now, Hattie was not entirely comfortable around them. They were harmless for the most part and a simple 'no' generally sufficed.

A gypsy man with a scarlet bandana and a gold earring loomed up in front of her, asking if she wanted a bit of lucky heather.

Hattie shook her head 'no', picked up and hurried off in the opposite direction.

By the time she'd recovered her composure, she realised that she was in completely the wrong place, close to the rough end of the fair where the cockfighting and bear-baiting happened, with no easy or straightforward way to get to where Stephanie had set up camp.

She wished she had taken Kit's offer to escort her back but that would have only prolonged the agony. It was over and done. She could go back to her dull, unexciting life.

'Hey, watch where you are going.' a man

shouted at her and she managed to duck before she was hit by a large metal trap.

'That was far from my fault,' Hattie muttered and turned down another row of stalls. These were devoted to all manner of farm equipment. She turned another way and heard the cries of a cockfight. She could never understand why anyone would think such a thing was entertainment.

She rubbed her hand over her face. Several painted women sauntered passed, with swinging hips and fixed expressions. The distinct odour of stale alcohol choked the air.

Hattie picked up her skirts and began to hurry towards the ale tent. It was early enough so there should not be too great of a problem. But once there, she'd get her bearings. Stephanie was going to be annoyed. She could handle Stephanie, but she knew if anything had happened to Livvy or Portia, she'd never forgive herself.

What could she have been thinking about, going off with Kit like that? She'd abandoned Livvy for nothing but her own pleasure. Hattie quickened her steps. *Idiot. Idiot. Idiot.* Her boots seemed to pound out the words. Hattie reached for a handkerchief and covered her nostrils.

'What's your hurry, my dear?' A rough hand grabbed her elbow. Her captor sported a purple scar stretching from the corner of his right eye to his nose. Two more men stood behind him, egging him on. 'We can have some sport with this one.'

'I am not your dear.' Hattie drew herself up to her full height and gave her most imperious stare. The last thing she wanted to show was fear, particularly not to a man who looked the worst for drink. It was all a misunderstanding. 'Unhand me and allow me to go about my business unhampered.'

'Pardon me for breathing.' His hand loosened. He said something in an undertone to his loathsome companions.

A nervous trembling filled Hattie's limbs. It was that easy. Mrs Reynaud was right. A positive attitude could work miracles. Her virtue was her shield.

She started to move on, slowly and sedately, but purposefully. The men were drunk. They'd leave her alone. Once she'd returned to Stephanie, she was never going to hanker after travelling or adventures again.

'Give us a kiss. Proud lady.' Another hand caught her upper arm. The stench of sour ale and tobacco filled her nostrils. This time she was pulled back against his fat chest.

'Let me go.'

Kit let Hattie walk away into the crowd. It had all gone wrong when she'd mentioned the name

Reynaud. Stupid, really. There were hundreds of people with that name. It wasn't Hattie's fault that his mother had abandoned him for a Frenchman named Jacques Reynaud. The woman in question was probably another innocent caught up in the mess his mother had left behind.

He'd taken the crude and insulting way out, using his seductive voice to make suggestions, making her unsure. He'd known that she'd leave. Coward that he was. And all because of a name from the past that should no longer have any power. He was a man, not a youth who had been teased endlessly about his mother and her morals. Disgust filled him. He knew the proper way to act in society. But it was better this way. Their friendship had to end before…before he started to care.

He curled his hand about the jumping-jack and regarded the various faces of the farm labourers and other men. The noise from the ale tent had increased. Hattie might think that she didn't need his help, but he was not about to abandon her. Not when it was his fault to begin with.

He watched her take a wrong turning and then followed a few paces behind. Once she was back with her family, he'd relax and she'd cease to be his problem.

He lost sight of her when she rounded the

gypsy caravan. Kit went down one aisle and then another, but nowhere did he see Hattie's back. He started to circle around towards the ale tent, ignoring the shorter route by the cock and bear pits. Hattie with her strict sensibilities would never go there.

Let me go.

Her voice floated on the air.

Kit broke into a run. Near the cockpit, he saw her, surrounded by a group of farmhands who were the worse for wear with drink. Several of them gave coarse laughs and called out obscene suggestions.

Hattie's hand beat against the largest one's chest. Her straw bonnet had slipped off her head and lay abandoned in the mud. Kit cursed. Her predicament was all his fault.

He knew the dangers that a fair could bring and he'd been the one to allow her to wander about on her own. His mistake and he always owned up.

He glanced around. Four against one. The odds were not good, but he refused to stand by. Going and fetching the parish constable was not an option. But if he started something, others would join in and lend a hand.

'Unhand that lady!'

'Mind your business. We are having a bit of sport.'

Kit clenched his fists. His eyes flickered from face to face, memorising their features. He'd lost count of how many fights he'd experienced, but he knew how to fight and he was sober. 'I doubt that is possible. She is with me. I look after my own. Unless you want to be seriously injured or worse, let her go now.'

The mountain of a man loosened his grip on Hattie. The primitive urge to tear him limb from limb filled Kit. He struggled to keep his temper. Cool and collected won fights—giving in to anger resulted in errors. He'd learnt that back at Eton when he'd tried to defend his mother's name.

'Who will stop me? You? On your own? I have won my last six bouts in the ring.'

A would-be pugilist who had had far too much to drink. Kit stifled a laugh. It was going to be easier than he thought.

'It is a serious mistake to doubt my ability. My pugilist ability is renowned in London. Ask at any pub about Kit Foxton and see what they say.'

The mountain scratched his nose. 'It ain't known up here.'

'We could have a bare-knuckle fight if you

wish, but allow the lady to go about her business,' Kit said in a deadly voice.

'And you think to come from London and tell us our ways.'

'You should respect your betters.' The blood pumped through Kit's veins. He looked forward to the fight. To do something. 'Shall we have at it, here and now?'

The mountain shoved Hattie away from him. Kit breathed again. 'If you wish.'

'Kit…' Hattie was suddenly very afraid '…he has a knife.'

'Go, Hattie. Get help. This shouldn't take long.' He turned his head slightly and felt the first punch graze his temple. 'You shouldn't have done that. I don't mind a fair fight, but not an unfair one. We start when we start and not before.'

He landed a punch squarely in the fat farmhand's middle, brought his knee up and connected again. The man countered with a wild stab, but the knife missed by a hairbreadth. Kit punched again, harder, and the man collapsed on the ground. When the man was down on the ground, Kit stamped on his wrist and the knife dropped from his grip. Kit kicked the knife away.

'Playing with knives can get you hurt.' Kit picked him up by the lapels. 'Are you ready to begin our fight?'

The man grunted and wildly flailed his arms. Kit landed a blow on the man's jaw. The man gurgled slightly and lay back. Kit lowered him to the ground. It was easier than he thought. Kit dusted down his breeches and turned his back on the prone man. 'Does anyone else have a quarrel with me?'

The three men looked at each other and began to back away. Cowards.

Kit gave them a look of utter contempt. 'Next time, give the ladies more respect.'

'I ain't finished yet, Londoner.' A fist came out of nowhere, landing in the middle of Kit's back.

Kit crouched and began to fight in earnest as blow after blow rained down on his head. Somewhere in the distance, he heard the sound of a parish constable's whistle.

The world turned black at the edges and a sharp pain went into his jaw, swiftly followed by a pain to the back of his head.

'All my fault, Hattie, I didn't mean to frighten you,' he murmured. The world went black.

Hattie swallowed the scream and rushed over to where Kit lay in the dirt, heedless of the way her skirt swept into the thick mud, ready to defend him, now that he was defenceless.

She put her hand on his chest. He was still breathing. The attackers had either run off at the sound of the whistle or lay on the ground, groaning. The fight was over. Kit had won, but at what cost? He couldn't be seriously hurt because of her folly, could he?

Hattie offered a silent prayer. She didn't care what happened to her reputation or anything else as long as Kit was all right. This entire mess had happened because of her pride and her fear. She knew where the blame lay and she wanted to make amends. A shiver went through her.

'Come on. Kit,' she said. 'We need to get you to the doctor.'

Kit mumbled incoherently and failed to rise.

'Here now, what is going on?' a burly parish constable demanded, bustling up. He gave another loud toot on his whistle. He started in surprise. 'Mrs Wilkinson, what are you doing here? Messed up in this nonsense? It isn't a sight for a lady such as yourself. Where is your family? Someone should be looking after you. It ain't safe around here. Here is where the gaming happens. And the cockfighting. Your brother-in-law should have known better.'

Hattie heaved a sigh of relief. Mr Jessop was the parish constable for St Michael's, rather than being from one of the other parishes. It made things much easier. She stood up and faced him.

'I made a mistake and turned the wrong way. Thankfully, my guardian angel was looking after me and sent a protector.'

'Where is he?'

'There on the ground. Sir Christopher Foxton.'

Mr Jessop gaped. 'Sir Christopher Foxton? He is involved? This is bad, very bad.'

Hattie noticed the other men turn white and start to edge away. A group of farmhands stood solidly behind Mr Jessop, preventing them from leaving.

'These men attacked me and Sir Christopher defended my honour, Mr Jessop. What you see is the aftermath of battle, which I am delighted to say Sir Christopher won.' Hattie rapidly explained the situation, giving an account that was accurate in all the particulars but skated over some of the details. There was no need to tell the constable about the quarrel which preceded the event. All he had to know was that Sir Christopher had defended her honour with great vigour.

'In broad daylight?' The parish constable's eyes widened. He drew himself up. 'What is the world coming to? You should have stayed to the main part of the fair, Mrs Wilkinson.'

'They were insensible with drink.' Hattie

pressed her hands together and tried to keep her limbs from trembling. 'It is lucky Sir Christopher happened by when he did.'

'Do you wish to press charges?'

Hattie regarded the patch of spreading red on Kit's chest and the way his face was swelling. A primitive urge to see the men hanged filled her. She pushed it away. 'You must do as you see fit, Mr Jessop. It was a fight, but it is also the day of Stagshaw fair. You will have to speak with Sir Christopher when he is in a better state.'

'I see, Mrs Wilkinson. No doubt there will be a few sore heads in the morning. A spell cooling off over in Hexham gaol will do them good.'

'I wish to get medical help for Sir Christopher before anything else happens. Sir Christopher's well-being is the most important thing.'

Kit mumbled something. Hattie bent down. 'What is it you want to say?'

His fingers curled about hers. 'Don't leave me,' he murmured in a broken whisper. 'Please stay…please, I beg you.'

Hattie's heart flipped over. She smoothed a lock of hair from his forehead. He'd risked his life for her. All this had happened because she had decided to take offence at his flirtatious comments, comments which were not meant to be taken literally. She had behaved worse than an aged maiden aunt. He wasn't asking her to stay for ever, just until he recovered. 'Yes, I'll look after you. I promise. I've no intention of leaving you.'

He gave a crooked smile and closed his eyes. 'Good.'

She held his hand, waiting until he became calm and his breathing regular. After what Kit had said, her decision was surprisingly easy. It didn't matter that Stephanie would be terribly shocked. Stephanie would get over it. One simply did not turn one's back on someone who had risked his life for her.

'His lordship can't stay here,' Mr Jessop said. 'It's not right.'

'I will take Sir Christopher back to the Dower House where he can be properly nursed.' Hattie stood up. 'I would appreciate the doctor arriving there as soon as possible. I will want several stout men to help me to get him into the governess cart.'

'Back to your house, ma'am? Are you sure that is wise?'

'I pay my debts, Mr Jessop, and I owe this man a huge debt. You send Dr Gormley to me once he has been found.'

'It is fair day, Mrs Wilkinson.' Mr Jessop rocked back on his heels.

'You may try the ale tent or, failing that, machinery exhibition. The good doctor is as fond of inventions as the next man.'

Hattie waited, trying to keep her gaze steady. Surely Mr Jessop was going to assist her, rather than throwing up roadblocks?

Mr Jessop nodded and gave the orders. 'It is my profound regret that this happened. We run a clean fair. It must be ten years since anything of significance has happened.'

'I know you do. It wasn't your fault.' Hattie bent down and shook Kit's shoulder. 'Kit, can you walk or do you need to be carried?'

'Give me your shoulder, Hattie, and I'll walk. I can do anything if you help me. I can do more things if you'd kiss me.' The words were a bit slurred and Hattie wondered if he'd hit his head in the fight. The Kit she was used to would never say such a thing.

Mr Jessop, she noticed, had studiously averted his eyes. So much for her hope to keep anything with Sir Christopher private—the gossip would be all over the fair within minutes. 'If you are sure you don't need us for anything else, I will get him back to my house. I believe he has hit his head.'

'I'll help you, ma'am, in case he falls like,' a thin farmer said. 'Way aye, I saw the whole thing and one of them brought a walking stick down on his head. 'Tweren't right, that. The man's a hero. It weren't many men who'd do something like that.'

'We will haul this lot up in front of the magistrates come Monday morning,' Mr Jessop declared.

'I will be happy to give evidence,' the farmer said. 'And me lad as well.'

Hattie felt the tears well up. She hadn't expected any assistance and now it seemed people were queuing up to support her.

'Let me know if his condition worsens,' Mr Jessop called out as she started the slow march towards her governess cart with Kit's heavy weight leaning on her shoulder.

'Obviously.'

Was what she was doing the right thing? Hattie gave a small shudder when she thought about Stephanie, but that couldn't be helped. She'd given Kit her word and she intended on keeping it. They were friends.

Please let him be all right. That was all that mattered.

Chapter Eight

Kit woke with a start from confused dreams about Hattie, his uncle and various jumping-jacks. A single candle shone by the bed and there was an engraving of some biblical scene hanging on the opposite wall. The room was small and austere, a sickroom and utterly unfamiliar.

His entire body ached and his right eye was swollen shut. And he was dressed in a voluminous nightshirt, unlike the sort he normally wore. His head ached like the very devil.

He searched his mind, trying to figure out how he'd arrived here. The events of the afternoon came flooding back. As far as bright ideas went, taking on four men was not one of his better ones. But try as he might, between landing the first punch and to just now, his mind was a blank.

He put a hand to the back of his head, probing. A huge pain shot through him, blinding in its intensity. He'd obviously banged his head. But beyond a few aches and pains, he would survive. There was no reason to stay here, helpless and at the mercy of some unknown quack.

He swung his feet over the side of the bed and started to push his protesting body to a stand.

'Oh, no, you don't. You are to stay in bed and get well.' Cool hands pushed him back down on to crisp linen sheets. He turned his head in case his fevered mind had conjured her up.

The candlelight made her blonde hair shine and highlighted the hollow at the base of her throat. An angel. No, an angel would not wear a sprigged muslin. An angel would be dressed in flowing robes. It was Hattie in the flesh and blood. Her sewing had fallen to the floor as she stood to enforce her command. The sheer domesticity of the scene made him want to weep.

He rubbed his left eye and tried to open his right to make sure he wasn't dreaming. He could not remember the last time when someone volunteered to look after him. Since an early age, it had always been someone who was paid and done out of duty, rather than for any other reason. A sense of great humbleness filled Kit. Hattie had done this for him.

'Where am I?'

'At my house.'

'Your house?' Kit searched his mind, but the big black well prevented him. 'What am I doing here? The last thing I remember is getting into a fight with a stubborn drunk.'

'You are to stay in bed until the doctor says that you can rise.' She crossed her arms and glared at him. 'I'd be grateful if you obliged me in this if nothing else.'

He tried to catch her hand before remembering how she'd walked away from him and settled for clutching the sheet instead. He refused to beg. He had deliberately driven her away.

'Hattie? Why am I here? How? You live miles away from Stagshaw. The last thing I recall is the fight near the cockpit. And that drunk with his paws on you.'

'Not too far.' She turned her face from him, revealing her slender neck. 'I had them bring you to my house. It seemed the best place. A bit closer than Southview. I was being practical after…after the fight. You couldn't be left on your own, waiting for the doctor to show up.'

'I thank you.'

'It was the least I could do in the circumstances. I'd do it for any wretch who risked their neck to save me.'

Kit swallowed with difficulty. She'd had him brought here out of duty. 'Why?'

She stood up without speaking and moved over to the right, away from his vision.

'Why, Hattie? There must have been a dozen other places I could have gone.'

'You were injured trying to save me. It seemed to be the Christian thing to do. I could hardly count on your valet or Mr Hook to look after you properly.'

'Beggars can't be choosers. I shall put my faith in your nursing skill.' He hated how his heart thumped. He knew it for a lie. He couldn't think of anyone he'd rather have nursing him and it frightened him. She'd forgiven his outburst without him doing anything.

'It is good of you to accept what is going to happen.'

'You haven't given me much choice.' He lay back on the pillows and breathed in the lavender scent. The smell reminded him of when he was a young boy in his room back in Hampshire, safe and secure without a care. He could almost picture the scene with the fire blazing and his nurse sitting, knitting socks, while a kettle hummed in the background.

'You were in no fit state.'

'My head pains me.' Kit tore his mind away

from the memory. He always swore that he'd never voluntarily think about his childhood, and certainly not with a great longing. He must have hit his head far harder than he'd thought.

Hattie laid a cool cloth on his forehead. 'Is that better?'

A warm glow flooded through him. Despite her words dismissing him earlier, Hattie had stayed by his side. More than that, she'd obviously insisted that he was carried to her house. She'd publicly declared their friendship, after telling him that they were finished. Women were a different species entirely. He reached out his hand. 'You need not have done that.'

'Allow me to make my own decisions. I prefer to have my conscience at rest than worrying over your health.'

Kit struggled to upright. He clutched the blanket to his chest and tried to make sense of the turn of events. Nothing, simply flashes of voices. However, with each breath, he found himself more distracted by the way Hattie's hair curled about her shoulders and the shadowy place at her throat. 'Did you undress me? How did I get this nightshirt?'

A merry peal of laughter filled the room. 'You may stop looking shocked. You would think you were unused to a woman's attentions. It is not as if I haven't seen the male form before.'

'Hattie!' He pulled the collar of his nightshirt up.

'The doctor did it for me.' She shook her head. 'He wanted to examine the wound to your chest, but it turned out to be just a light cut. But your shirt is ruined. I found one of my late husband's nightshirts. It seemed sensible. Sleeping in one's clothes is hardly advisable at any time, but particularly not when one has been injured.'

He collapsed back against the pillows. He should have expected respectability from her. It was wrong that he'd briefly hoped that she'd been unable to resist taking a peek. 'The ruffian managed to miss. Sometimes my luck astonishes me. He must have been unable to see straight.'

'There was a deflection, something was in the way.' She sobered and her teeth worried her bottom lip.

'Out with it. Let me know the worst.'

'I'm afraid the jumping-jack took the brunt of one knife blow and then you managed to twist the knife out of his hand.'

Kit fell back amongst the pillows. Had the jumping-jack not been in his breast pocket, the knife would have sliced through his chest. A cold shiver went through him. 'Obviously a good-luck charm. I intend to keep it.'

'I'll get it for you.' She handed him the remains of the jumping-jack and shook her head. 'I don't think it is worth saving.'

'I must be more sentimental than you.' He smiled up at her. 'I think it is worth keeping.'

'That is your choice.'

'I shall treasure it always. Generally I take better care of my gifts than this.'

Her lips parted as if she was about to say something, but thought better of it. 'You need to rest. The doctor left some more laudanum for you.'

Kit shook his head. He felt as if he had been run over by a cart and then stamped on, but he could manage. If he drank the laudanum, the dreams about his childhood would start again— a figure in a blue dress smiling down at him, laughing at her boy, asking him to be brave.

He forced a wry smile and hoped Hattie would believe him. 'I dislike having my wits clouded. I've endured worse pain.'

'It is here if you change your mind.' She put a small glass beside the bed. He was aware of the intimacy and how her hair fell about her shoulders.

Gingerly he felt his jaw, sore but unbroken. He

wanted her, he wanted to feel her move under him and catch her soft sigh in his mouth as she surrendered to the heat and passion. But he also wanted to hear her laugh, see her smile and above all he wanted to talk to her.

'Is there some reason why you are nursing me?' he asked in case she decided to leave.

'Instead of Mr Hook?' Hattie leant forwards and tucked the bedclothes about his body. Impersonal, but intimate at the same time. Her round gown gaped slightly and he caught a glimpse of the shadowy hollow between her breasts.

He tore his mind away from such thoughts. Hattie nursed his broken body out of compassion and duty. The fact that he noticed her considerable assets showed him that death would have to find another victim. He'd recover. It was merely his blinding headache that bothered him.

'If you like, Rupert could have done it.'

She laughed. 'He appeared distinctly ill at the prospect of blood. I'd no wish to torture him.'

'And Johnson, my valet?'

'Your valet was no use. Last seen in the ale tent, according to Mr Hook, rather the worse for wear.'

Kit silently blessed Rupert's quick thinking. If they had found Johnson, he would not be here. And despite everything, he was glad to be here.

In this room. With Hattie. He valued her friendship. He groaned, remembering the taste of her mouth. He wanted to taste it again, particularly now.

At her look he said, 'I gave him the day off. It is his to use as he pleases.'

'You are a generous employer.'

'I can afford to be. Johnson's ability with boot polish and the starching of neckcloths is second to none.' He watched her, waiting for the slightest hint of what she was thinking, if she was aware of him as he was of her. 'No doubt he will turn up early in the morning with a suit of clothes. Johnson takes his job very seriously.'

'It is good to know. I will leave a note for Mrs Hampstead so she isn't surprised.'

'You still haven't said. Why did you insist on bringing me here?'

'You saved me from those drunken men and I'm determined you will be nursed with all care and attention.' She dipped her head. 'Too many people in my life have died who were not nursed properly. It was time to make sure it didn't happen again.'

Her husband. It was painfully simple to guess who she wasn't naming. Kit hated the twinge of jealousy he felt for Charles Wilkinson, the hero of Talavera. He had to be slipping. He prided himself on not caring about anyone's past or who they had loved. It was only the present that interested him. Ever. Except Hattie's past interfered with his present. She had the capacity for life.

He breathed in and his ribs ached.

'Then I'm grateful,' he said stiffly. 'You mustn't feel you should sit up with me. It will take more than a few knocks on my head to kill a reprobate like me.'

'You always insist on painting yourself blacker than you are.'

'I will not have you thinking I am better.'

'It was my fault that you were involved in the fight. I do pay my debts, Sir Christopher, and I owe you a great one.'

Kit watched how her slender fingers moved in the candlelight. She no longer wore a wedding ring. 'I enjoyed the fight for the most part. It suited my mood.'

'You enjoyed it?' She blinked rapidly. 'How could you enjoy something like that?'

Kit closed his eyes. It had felt good to work off his excess anger. He wanted to show her that he could do something for her and he had. The bruises and cuts were superficial. 'There's a certain amount of satisfaction in seeing someone get what they thoroughly deserve. He should never have done that.'

'But you are hurt. You didn't have to.'

'What would you have used—your elbows?' It was far harder to remember how Hattie looked, than to think about the way his hands and face hurt.

Her jaw became set. 'I can look after myself. I've been doing it for a long while now.'

'And I've been worse.' He forced his face into a ghost of a smile. 'Nothing appears broken. I will mend.'

'You will mend because I intend on making certain that you do.'

'Well, I feel that my presence is an imposition. And you even have me dressed in one of your husband's nightshirts.' Kit hated that he sounded so ungrateful.

'He never wore it.' Shutters came down on her eyes, instantly hiding her soul from him. 'Somehow, I never could get rid of the linen. I found it when I got out the sheet for the bed. It seemed the ideal opportunity to put it to practical use.'

It annoyed him that even after all this time, she still mourned her late husband. He was under no illusion that when he left a woman, within a few months she had forgotten him. Sometimes the bed they had shared was barely cold before another entered it.

He certainly made no effort to remember any

of them. There might be tears for a little while, but ultimately they both went on their respective ways. It was the way it had to be. Remembering never did anyone any good.

Kit refused to think about the little boy he'd been, crying for a mother who never came. A mother who never came not because she was dead and living with the angels, but because she had left, unable to stand living with him. He had crouched down on the landing when his nurse thought he was in bed and had heard everything, seen everything. Silently he had willed his mother to glance up at him and stop. She kept walking with a handkerchief pressed to her face. She had been the most beautiful thing in his life and then she was gone, no more than a memory.

'You must have been very close.' He choked out the words, tearing his mind away from the unwelcome thought. He must have hit his head far harder than he'd considered. Normally he had no trouble in forgetting his mother. The illusion of her exquisiteness and delicacy had been well and truly shattered when he discovered a pile of old newspapers, complete with the criminal conversation trial of his mother, detailing her lovers. 'That much is clear.'

'Why would you say that?' Hattie clenched her hands together so tightly he could see the white knuckles. Her eyes glittered in the candlelight.

Silently Kit prayed that there wouldn't be tears. He hated tears. He'd lost count of the crocodile tears various women had shed in order to gain some trinket or another.

'You always look away when you speak about him.'

'We weren't close.' Her hesitant voice trembled with barely suppressed passion. 'I found out after he died that I never really knew him at all.'

'I'm sorry.' To his surprise, he meant it. 'A wife should know her husband. They should not have secrets.'

'Don't be,' she snapped and then appeared to recollect where she was. She sat up straighter and smoothed her sprigged muslin. She continued in a self-deprecating tone. 'I used to be very naïve and believed because a man told you that he worshipped the ground you walked on that he meant it.'

'He didn't?' Kit put his hands behind his head. The news that Charles Wilkinson was not a paragon made things easier.

Hattie was silent for such a long while that he wondered if she'd fallen asleep. Then, when he was about to whisper her name, she slowly began to speak.

'He had an adored mistress and a scattering of illegitimate children. Born before and after our marriage. I was the socially acceptable wife.' Her hands shook and she clasped them together until her knuckles shone white as she choked out the words. With each trembling syllable, the words sped up until they became a raging torrent. 'He feared if he married the woman he truly loved that his father would cut him off without a penny. It would not have been so bad if I had known how he felt, but I had no inkling. It came as a great shock.'

She finished on a half-laugh combined with a sob.

A coward. Powerful and primitive urges filled Kit. He longed to wring his neck for making a woman like Hattie suffer.

'So it was an arranged marriage?' he asked, trying to understand why someone who was so passionate had opted for something as bloodless as an arranged marriage.

'It was a marriage because he took me out to a summer house and whispered sweet nothings, swearing eternal devotion.' A single tear tracked down her cheek. She brushed it away before he could capture it. 'I was in love with the romance of it all. My husband knew the right words to woo me. I only discovered the truth after it was far too late.'

'On your wedding night?'

Her throat worked up and down. Her entire being vibrated with anguish. 'Worse, after he died. Stupid fool that I was. I swallowed his lies whole, never questioned. He was away, fighting, most of the time.'

'You never questioned or you didn't want to question?' he enquired.

She gave a sickly smile. 'It made it easy to keep my illusions. I lived for his letters. They were so sweet and so full of promises.'

'Were you in love with him?' He held up his hand, appalled that the question had slipped out. 'That was bad of me. I apologise. I have no right to ask.'

She turned her blue-green shimmering eyes to him. 'Sometimes I wonder if I ever loved him or just the idea of him,' she said in a deadly calm voice which contrasted with her earlier anguish. 'When I found out about his perfidy, I discovered that I couldn't tell anyone about the truth of the marriage.'

'Why?'

'I've my pride. I paid his debts and settled his other loose ends in the most expedient fashion. Then, Stephanie needed help and so I gave it, selfishly gaining a new start to my life where no one could pity me.'

'And no one knows about it? Not even your sister?'

'You know now.' She wiped her eyes with fierce fingers. 'I didn't want you to have some mistaken idea about my marriage. Or how I might feel about my late husband.'

Kit's heart leapt. Her marriage was far different from the one he'd imagined. He wasn't competing against some perfect ghost, but rather she'd been damaged in some way because of her late husband's heavy-handedness. It put the kiss they had shared in an entirely different perspective.

'I'm sorry,' he said. 'I had no idea.'

She dipped her head. Her hands were folded in her lap. 'You can't lose something you never had.'

He watched her without saying anything, but he could see she was teetering on a knife's edge. He doubted that she would have shared this information even a few hours ago. The fight had changed everything. He was very glad it had. The minor discomfort of a few bruises and pulled muscles was nothing compared to the relief of not competing against a ghost.

'What would he have wanted for you?'

'What he would have wanted is no concern of mine.' She shook her head. 'Stephanie keeps telling me that he'd have wanted me to marry. Charles Wilkinson was a dear friend of my brother-in-law's. Every time she brings the subject of remarriage up, I become more determined to stay a widow.'

'You are allowing him to define you.'

'I beg your pardon.' Her nostrils quivered like she was a wild deer, catching the scent of a hunter.

'You devoted your life to making Charles Wilkinson seem respectable. Why on earth did you do that?' Kit asked, keeping his voice soft and steady. He wanted to release her from the prison she'd encased herself in. Misplaced guilt. She had sealed herself off from love and desire. She denied her passionate nature. 'Where has that led you? Are you any happier for it?'

'Since when did my happiness become any of your concern?'

'Since I decided to fight for you. What happened, happened, Hattie. You can't change it, but you can stop allowing your life to be defined by it. It is not good to live in fear. You are a passionate woman. Why must you shut yourself off from life?'

'I will accept that you have no idea what you are saying due to the laudanum.'

Before Kit could protest she stood up and walked out of the room. Kit clenched his fist and slammed it down on the bedclothes. Since when did he break his rules about non-interference? It was better to allow her to go. Her life was nothing to do with him. She should be able to lead the sort of life she wanted, even if it was limited.

He should be thanking his lucky stars for the narrow escape. There could never be a future with her. He shuddered with the memory of the taunts he'd suffered, and the way respectable women had turned away from him in his youth after they had found out The Scandal.

Hattie laid her fevered cheek against the cool plaster of the hall and attempted to regain some measure of control. Her hand trembled so much that the wax spilt, burning her wrist. She set the candle down on the floor and forced herself to breathe in deeply.

She had made a mistake, a colossal mistake. She'd vowed never to speak about her husband's betrayal. Ever.

Now she'd confessed the bald truth to a man who was little more than a stranger, simply to keep from confessing how she felt about him!

What was worse—he'd said the things she had known in her heart. Every single word was true as much as she might wish it were a lie. She had allowed herself to be defined by Charles and what he'd done. She had hated what he'd done to her, but everyone considered her to be the grieving widow. How could she besmirch the memory of a hero? She'd used it as a way to lick her wounds for years but it was hypocrisy of the highest order. She had stopped living. Her dreams were just that—dreams.

Neither did she want everyone to know of her humiliation. Even now that burning sense of shame filled her. She hadn't been able to keep her husband happy. He had secretly laughed at her feeble attempts. His mistress had taken great delight in showing her the letters. She knew nothing about making love. Sensible and unattractive, lacking any real fire or passion. She'd longed to scream that he was wrong. But how could she when she had lived her life without passion?

Hattie hugged her arms and sank down to the floor. She wanted to feel passion, the real sort, the feeling-utterly-alive sort that she had felt when Kit kissed her at the Roman ruins. She had never had that all-consuming feeling before. She wanted to be alive, instead of existing.

When she had discovered the mistress's address, she had visited her. Hattie had not wanted Charles's miniature, but throwing it on the fire had seemed less than charitable. She had packed it up along with a few personal items so that the children would have something to remember their father by. Afterwards, Hattie had been sick in the street. The obvious love that woman had for Charles contrasted with her infatuation and fantasy of the perfect marriage.

All she'd wanted to do was to run away and hide. And she had—all the way to Northumberland. She'd been successful as well.

Undone by a man's nightshirt. How pathetic was that?

Hattie pressed her hands against her eyes and tried to control the shaking in her limbs. She refused to cry after all this time. Not again and most definitely not over him.

It had been a mistake to insist that Kit return to the Dower House, rather than allowing the doctor to look after him. And then she had further compounded the mistake by sitting up and watching him sleep.

What he must think of her! She hardly knew what she thought of herself! All she knew was that she could not have gone on with the pretence that somehow she had loved Charles with a deep and unyielding love when he'd asked.

She wanted to cleanse the knowledge of him and their marriage from her soul. She wanted to live her life rather than being defined by the old one.

Hattie stood up straight, and brushed the tears from her eyes. 'I'll live. Whatever happens. No one is going to laugh at me again. At the same time as writing me letters of sweet promise, Charles mocked me in those to his mistress. She showed them to me. Sometimes even now, I wake up in a sweat remembering the phrases. That stops now. I start living the life I was meant to.'

She picked up the candle and started down the hallway to her room. Kit did not need her to play nurse. She was through with being pathetic. She would be strong and aloof. She'd do her duty. And then she'd start to follow her dreams.

'Hattie? Harriet? Wait.'

She continued to walk towards the stairs, pretending she had not heard him call. The great Kit Foxton could survive the night without her panting over him, like some love-starved widow.

'Wait.' The note of despair tore at her heart.

She half-turned and saw him standing in the doorway of the sickroom with tousled hair and a shadow of beard on his chin. The voluminous white nightshirt revealed his muscular calves and bare feet. And where on any other man it would have looked ridiculous, somehow, on Kit, it highlighted his absolute masculinity.

'You were supposed to stay in bed.'

'You were supposed to stay by my side.' He gave the semblance of a smile. 'Looking after me. My nurse flees—what choice do I have but to go after her?'

Despite her misgivings, a hot spark smouldered its way around her insides. She wanted to touch his skin and see if it was silky smooth. If she took one step towards him, she'd be in his arms. She curled her hand into a tight fist about the candlestick and turned away from the enticing picture.

'It is late. Back to bed with you,' she said over her shoulder. 'And if I don't get some sleep, I will be in no fit state tomorrow. Tomorrow is sure to bring a steady stream of visitors, well-wishers and the downright curious. Your exploits will be picked over for days to come. The talk of the village.'

'I prefer to think of it as heroics. Don't disabuse me of the notion.'

'Heroics, if you must, but now is not the time for you to be up.'

'I wouldn't be if you acted sensibly and stayed. I believe I offended you. It wasn't my intention.'

'It is nothing to do with you. Nothing at all. I'm tired. I need to rest.' Hattie concentrated on keeping the candle steady. 'If you need someone, I'll wake Mrs Hampstead.'

She hoped he thought her voice stern and unyielding. To her ears, it sounded hopelessly breathless.

'Come here.' His voice allowed for no refusal.

Hattie took a step towards the stairs. Her stomach tensed. If she started towards him, she'd be in his arms, begging for his touch. And she already knew that was a hopeless cause. 'That wouldn't be a good idea.'

'I've gone beyond what you consider a good idea or not, Harriet.' He ran his hands through his hair. 'Come here. Let me see your face. All I can see is the light from the candle.'

She wiped the back of her hand across her eyes and straightened her skirt. He was too far away and the candlelight hid her upset state. 'No one calls me Harriet.'

'I know. It is why I am doing so.' He held out his hand. 'I've no wish to frighten you. Come back and talk to me.'

'Why should I?'

'I had no idea about your husband's betrayal.

I thought your prim reserve was from a different cause. I'm sorry.'

'It served my purpose.' Hattie raised her chin. 'It is the first time I could speak of it.'

'Are you crying over him?'

'I shed my last tear for him a long time ago.'

'Then why the tears?'

'Because I've wasted my life.' When she said the words, she knew she meant them. They had sprung from a place deep within her. She'd wanted to erase all trace of Charles from her life, but she hadn't done. For too long she had been hiding, fearful of the long shadow. 'It is not what I wanted. I had so many plans. I've done none of them.'

His hand closed about hers and gently took the candlestick from her. 'You will burn your hand.'

'I already have.' She gave a shaky laugh. 'It is fine. I won't set the house on fire.'

Rather than letting her go, he pulled her to his hard body. 'Silence. Perfect silence.'

He bent his head and captured her lips, demanding a response. Hattie opened her mouth and tasted the sweet interior.

A deep and dark fire welled up inside her, blotting out everything else. She twined her hands about his neck and held him close, allowing her body to say things that she didn't dare.

His mouth travelled over her face, softly nuzzling her cheeks and temple. 'Hush now.'

A soft moan escaped from her throat. With the last vestige of common sense, she put her hands on his shoulders and created a space between their bodies. 'I ought to go.'

'Why did you bring me here?' he said, sliding his hands down her back and cupping her body to his.

'I told you. Because I wanted to make sure you lived. You saved me and my honour.' Hattie kept her head up and looked him straight in the eye, attempting to ignore the fire blazing in her nether regions. If she wasn't hanging on to him, she'd fall. Her legs had become wobblier than jelly.

'It is poor excuse. We have gone beyond such things.' He traced the outline of her lips. 'Whatever you do, give solid reasons, rather than mealy-mouthed excuses.'

He placed a kiss in the corner of her mouth.

'Why do you think I brought you here?'

'Because you craved intimacy. You wanted more to your life than a solitary kiss in windswept ruins.' His fingers touched her face, gentle but at the same time wildly exciting. 'You wanted it as badly as I do. You have been driving me mad with longing, Harriet. The things I want to do with you.'

She turned her face to his palm. She was tempted to pinch herself to see if she was awake or if she had somehow fallen asleep and was dreaming. 'Did I?'

'You do.' He put his hands on her shoulders. His face turned grave. 'I'm not making promises that I can't keep, Harriet. You understand that. It is about living in the moment with no regrets. I can offer you a summer and that is all.'

'I'm aware of the rules of engagement, as it were.' She tucked her head into her chest, torn between a longing to put her head on his chest and listen to his heartbeat and the instinct to flee. He wasn't offering anything honourable, only pleasure and only for the summer.

There was nothing wrong with taking her pleasure. She was a widow, rather than a débutante in search of good marriage. Sir Christopher was notoriously single. With discretion all things were possible.

'A summer affair sounds intriguing, but we must be circumspect,' she said quickly before she lost her nerve.

He raised an eyebrow. 'Bringing me here is circumspect? The story will be all around the village before morning.'

'I brought you here because you were injured.' Hattie tilted her chin upwards to show she had considered the potential for disaster. 'I was doing my Christian duty. No one dare gainsay that.'

'You kissed me all the same. And shall do again, I wager.'

A single finger lifted her face so she was staring directly into his eyes. His lashes were far too long and pretty for a man, she thought abstractly. She wasn't in love with him, not in the way she had thought she'd been in love with Charles. She desired him and his touch. Her heart was safe, more than safe. Passion might burn white-hot, but it rapidly turned to ash. She knew not to want for ever with this man. She'd settle for living in the moment for this one summer. 'Then we are agreed.'

'Until the summer ends.' He bent his head and softly kissed her lips. This time, the kiss was less fierce. It was a gentle heart-stopping persuasion. His mouth pressed kisses against her eyes, her nose and trailed down to her ear. Hattie knew that Charles had never kissed her like this. These kisses were about giving pleasure and healing.

She twined her arms about his neck, pressing her body against his. Hattie opened her mouth and allowed her tongue to tangle with his. In that kiss, all her fears and regrets fell away and all she knew was the feel of his lips against hers.

Her hand mimicked his and slid down the length of his torso. Instantly he stiffened.

'Is something wrong?'

He groaned in the back of his throat and put her from him. His face contorted in pain as he rotated his shoulder. 'I'm sorry. It is worse than I thought.'

She clapped her hands over her mouth. She'd been so intent on assuaging her own anguish that she'd forgotten about his very real pain. 'You are hurt. You have no business being up and about. This should never have happened.'

'I'm very glad it did.' He gave a ghost of a smile. 'I couldn't pass up the opportunity. You must never cry alone in a corridor again.'

'You should have done. The last thing I wanted to do is to cause you to get worse.' She felt the hot tears prick the backs of her eyes. 'You are the one who is supposed to be recovering from a terrible fight. You shouldn't have to comfort me because of something that happened seven years ago.'

'Allow me to be the judge of that.'

'You are to get back in bed.'

'And you shall join me in a bit of bed-sport?'

Hattie knew her face flamed. 'Mrs Hampstead will be up soon. We need to be discreet.'

She found it hard to believe that she was even discussing the possibility...of an affair.

'I would love to make love with you, Harriet. Right here and right now, but...it wouldn't be wise. My body aches too much.'

'The last thing I want to do is hurt you.' She looped her arm about his.

'It was worth having that fight simply to have you kiss me properly. I intend to hold you to your promise.'

'Which promise would that be?' Her voice sounded hoarse and seductive, foreign to her ears.

He smiled down at her and then immediately winced, going pale.

'You are to stay in bed tomorrow and I will have no excuses.'

'You are a saucy wench, Harriet. Ordering me to stay in bed, while your mouth is cherry ripe.' He gave her a hooded look. 'What else do you intend?'

His using her full name made her seem special and different from the Hattie who had been at the fair, but she also recognised the teasing note. She had never been teased in this way before, or indeed felt comfortable enough to tease back. A ripple of contentment went through her.

'I thought all fallen women were bold,' she retorted.

'You haven't fallen yet… It is not anyone else's business. It will stay that way if we are discreet.' He twisted a lock of her hair about his fingers. 'Reputations can be protected. I intend to do all that is in my power to be discreet and to prevent speculation.'

'I know. You can't promise…but you will try.' Her insides twisted. Open her mouth and insert her foot. She wanted this. She wanted that dark heat from earlier to consume her. Charles's love-making had been perfunctory and tepid to say the least. Even his early kisses in the summer house had been respectful. If she had known what it was like to be kissed by a master, maybe she would have stopped it. Hattie squeezed her eyes shut. No regrets. Ever. 'After you recover…'

'After I recover, we will take up where we left off. I want you, Hattie. That wanting is not going to go away. Trust me.'

She half-opened her eyes. He was looking at her with an intent gaze, but she could also see the pain in the way he held his mouth. 'I trust you.'

He dropped a kiss on her nose. 'This is where you leave me. If you stay, I will want to make love to you and my mind may be willing, but my flesh is weak. When we make love I want to be strong. I want to give you pleasure. Immense pleasure.'

Her stomach tightened at the thought. He was interested in her pleasure, not just his own. She tried and failed to imagine having this conversation with anyone else. 'I...I don't know what to say.'

'Run along before I change my mind and do something we both regret.'

'I promised to stay.' The words escaped from her mouth. She swallowed hard and tried again in a calmer tone. 'At least allow me to see you back to your bed.'

'When? When did you promise?' The colour drained from his face, leaving him pale and tense.

'At the fair, you asked me.' Hattie blinked rapidly. Somehow she had made a mistake and she wasn't even sure what it was. She felt sick. If he hadn't requested her to stay, she'd never have confessed. She should have thought that it wasn't anything but a plea for the hurt to be gone. 'Surely you remember? You must remember.'

His gaze became troubled. Slowly he shook his head. 'Everything remains hazy. It remains a blank. You mustn't take what I said literally.'

'I brought you here because you asked me to stay with you.' Hattie's heart pounded. He didn't remember when he'd gripped her hand. It had seemed so important to her and he'd forgotten.

'I can take responsibility for myself tonight. I want you to dream of me in what little is left of the night.'

'And afterwards…'

He cupped her face with his hands. 'I want you, Harriet Wilkinson, never doubt that. I want to make long slow love to you and show you how good it can be between us.'

Chapter Nine

Kit woke in the early hours of the morning and lay, gazing up at the ceiling. His entire body ached from the fight, but also with desire for Hattie. It unnerved him.

He kept willing himself to remember all the events. He couldn't have asked Hattie to stay. He never did things like that. He never tried to compromise anyone else's freedom in that way or put demands on them. Asking someone to stay would mean he had feelings for Hattie and he always made a point to end a relationship then. He refused to allow himself to be hurt.

What was worse was that he distinctly remembered speaking about his father. Kit had spent several years forgetting about him, his quick fists, the never-ending stream of perfumed women and his refusal to allow them in his life. He took pride in the fact that his fortune had not come from his inheritance, but from shrewd business decisions.

In his mind he went over the kisses in the hallway. None of them was supposed to happen. He had gone out to comfort her and to make sure that she wasn't hurting. And he'd nearly ended up seducing her. He should give her up. But having tasted the pure honey of her mouth, he knew he wanted more. It had infected him the first time he'd kissed her at the Roman ruins. He'd thought the feeling would diminish, but it had only grown stronger.

He knew she'd only kissed him out of a need to stop thinking. But he was very glad she had.

Now he was going to have to consider how to put things to rights and conduct their summer affair.

Discretion was called for and, as much as he might not like it, he had to take the hard decisions now. When autumn came, it would end, but Hattie would need to be protected. For once he was going to do this right.

Hattie sat in the dining room, staring at her half-eaten breakfast. Moth lay under the table, waiting for crumbs.

She had gone to bed, but had lain fully dressed, waiting to hear the slightest movement from the sickroom. Mrs Hampstead had appeared about six and told her to sleep.

'I came as soon as it was practicable, Hattie. These scrapes you do get in. I declare you are worse than the children.' Stephanie strode in, every inch the outraged matron.

Hattie dropped her piece of toast and stared at her sister. Silently she thanked her guardian angel that Kit remained upstairs, asleep in the sickroom. She swallowed hard to get rid of the tightness in her throat. 'Stephanie. How good of you to call and at such an early hour. It is not even ten.'

Stephanie towered over like some avenging angel from the inquisition. The ribbons on her bonnet trembled. 'Is it true that you insisted on bringing Sir Christopher here after what happened? Have you taken leave of your senses? Never mind the village, the entire Tyne Valley and possibly all of Northumberland are speaking about the fight and the aftermath. Your behaviour, Hattie, has been much remarked on.'

'No, I had my senses fully engaged. Sir Christopher had just rescued me from what is delicately referred to as a fate worse than death. I had no intention of leaving him to bleed on the muddy ground. Would you have done that?'

'You owed him nothing.'

'We shall agree to disagree on that. I always pay my debts.' Hattie gave a small shudder as she recalled how the drunk had pawed her and how his fetid breath had smelt. She hadn't been strong enough to fight him. 'He saved me and was injured, probably badly injured. Doctor Gormley has diagnosed a mild concussion at best. What sort of person do you take me for to put some form of mock refinement before my duty?'

'Surely Dr Gormley would have taken him in?'

'It was two hours before Dr. Gormley was found in the ale tent. I do not think he could have seen straight to sew stitches. And you know that his housekeeper is rather too fond of whiskey to be fully trusted.'

'It would appear that I misjudged matters,' Stephanie mumbled, sinking down into a chair. 'You were attacked. He saved you. Of course, it was right and proper in those circumstances to behave in the manner you did. I will make the appropriate people know how proud we are of you. It should stop the worst of the gossip.'

'You have indeed.' Hattie crossed her arms. She clearly recalled the enlightening conversation she'd had with Portia and Livvy on the way to the fair. Stephanie's meddling and interference stopped now. 'You rushed in without waiting for an explanation, Stephanie. However, if I had decided to utterly ruin myself, that would have been my business.'

'You won't be ruined. I will force him to marry you if needs be,' Stephanie declared. 'You can count on me.'

'How?'

'I will think of something.' Stephanie's ribbons swayed as her face took on a defiant air. 'I'm not a woman without influence. Mr Parteger will ensure the right and proper thing is done.'

'You mean a duel.'

'If called upon, my husband will be happy to defend your honour.' Stephanie put her hand to her mouth. 'But I doubt it will come to that. Sir Christopher will see the sense in my argument.'

Hattie shuddered at even the merest suggestion of a duel between Kit and her brother-in-law. In her mind's eyes she could see her brother-in-law's rather rotund figure lining up to face Kit's rather more athletic form. She was torn between laughing and crying at the prospect. She leant down and stroked Moth's ears, regaining some semblance of control.

'I would hardly want Mr Parteger fighting

a duel over my reputation. Besides, it is utterly pointless and unnecessary. Nothing happened. How could it? Sir Christopher was insensible most of the time. You worry needlessly. Mrs Hampstead is here and you know what an ogress she can be. I remember when you were courting. You used to complain bitterly about Mrs Hampstead poking her nose into the drawing room.'

Stephanie readjusted the ribbons of her bonnet and gave a pained expression. 'Are you willing to give me an assurance that nothing untoward happened last night?'

'When have I ever done anything that was in the remotest way indiscreet?' Hattie sat back in her chair and waited, swallowing her other caustic retorts. Patience was required with Stephanie, not barbs.

'You have changed your hair. It is softer. Suits your face.'

'I thought I'd worn a crown of braids long enough. I like the ringlets.' Hattie tilted her head and regarded her sister through narrowed eyes. Stephanie had to be redirected before she started asking awkward questions. 'You are changing the subject, Stephanie. It generally means you are losing the argument.'

'You always look for the ulterior motive. I noticed it and I like it. I can also guess the reason.'

Stephanie reached over and squeezed Hattie's hand. 'I'm your sister. I care about you, but you need to be careful. Sir Christopher has a much different stamp than your dear, but now long-departed, Captain Wilkinson. You were always too reckless, Hattie, even as a girl. I can't help fearing for your reputation. I want to make it right for you.'

Stephanie was worried about her. She was tempted to tell her that Sir Christopher was a man of entirely different sensibility than Charles, but it would leave her open to questioning and, having faced one storm last night, she knew she couldn't face another. And she had to wonder how much Stephanie knew or guessed. Her husband had been a friend of sorts to Charles.

'Mrs Wilkinson was merely doing her Christian duty,' Kit's lazy voice said from the doorway before Hattie could think up a coherent answer. 'Surely no one would stoop so low as to accuse a woman who is doing her Christian duty of untoward behaviour?'

Stephanie gave a little panicked cry and ducked her head. Hattie saw him, standing in the doorway, dressed in his clothes with an intricately tied neckcloth. He carried his body stiffly as if badly bruised. Her heart gave a little skip and she was pleased that she'd changed into her dimity with the tiny blue flowers embroidered on it. Portia always declared that it was her favourite dress as it made Hattie look sparkly.

From Kit's grim expression as he bent down to greet Moth, she had to wonder how long he'd been standing there and how much he'd heard.

Stephanie cleared her throat several times, obviously having the same concerns as Hattie. Hattie fought the temptation to laugh.

'Sir Christopher, you are up… That is to say— this is a most unexpected development. But welcome. A welcome development. Dear Hattie is such a good nurse. Quite devoted to it.'

'Then you will agree I was in good hands.'

'Very good hands.' Stephanie turned several deeper shades of plum. 'You are dressed, Sir Christopher.'

'He could hardly come down in a borrowed nightshirt,' Hattie said crossly. Stephanie had no right to be quizzing Kit in this manner. And Kit had no right to be up. Her carefully arranged plans of going up to see him after breakfast when she looked fresh and lovely were in smithereens. 'Really, Stephanie, you do spout some nonsense.'

'My valet arrived very early this morning with my clothes. I believe the ride over from Southview did him good. Cleared his thick head. He spent rather too much time in the ale tent yesterday.' His smile failed to reach his eyes. 'He wished to make amends and brought fresh clothes.'

'You are able to move about?' Stephanie gasped.

'The doctor advised strict bed rest.' Hattie put her hand on her stomach and wished she hadn't eaten that square of toast. Kit was dressed as if he was preparing to depart. Did he regret their late-night conversation? Had she dreamt it?

'I don't care a fig for the doctor's advice.' His deep-grey gaze met hers. 'I do, however, care about your reputation. I came to the same conclusion as Mrs Parteger. It is commendable but unwise to have me as a guest when Johnson is more than capable of looking after me.'

'And your plans?' Hattie tapped a finger on the table top. Everyone had neglected to consult her. Surely, at twenty-seven, she was more than capable of making the correct choices?

'I shall journey slowly and sedately back to the Lodge in my carriage.' He gave a crooked smile. 'You may direct all well-wishers there, but you must under pain of death retain any strengthening concoctions such as calves'-foot jelly. The very thought turns my stomach.'

'Allow me to be concerned about my reputation,' Hattie said between gritted teeth.

'Nevertheless, my mind is made up. Johnson should be returning with the carriage within the hour.' He inclined his head. 'I do hope there is some chocolate. I would hate to leave without partaking of breakfast. I trust that meets with your approval, Mrs Parteger?'

Without waiting for an invitation, he came in and took a seat opposite Hattie. She carefully poured him a cup of chocolate. He took it, but made sure their fingers briefly touched.

'Did you pass a comfortable night?' Stephanie asked.

'Mrs Parteger, the doctor gave me laudanum to make me sleep. I remember little, except I woke completely refreshed and a new man. One might say that the fight did a powerful amount of good.' He saluted Hattie with his cup of chocolate. 'Improved my mood no end.'

Hattie took a hasty sip of her coffee and burnt the roof of her mouth. He couldn't have forgotten their kiss? She had made a positive declaration and now he'd forgotten it. How like her luck. She tried to think about how to best approach the matter, but her brain seemed to move at the speed of congealed porridge.

Voices were heard in the hall and Moth gave a series of sharp barks before racing to the dining-room door and then back to Hattie.

Kit put down his cup. 'Ah, here is Johnson, and Rupert as well. Their timing is impeccable. My stay was short, but most enjoyable, Mrs Wilkinson. Mrs Parteger, you will understand that I wish to get home as soon as possible. I do hope you will be at pains to point out that Mrs Wilkinson has behaved correctly in all circumstances.'

'Shall I see you out?'

'It is not necessary. I have everything in hand. Pray stay seated and visit with your sister. I can see my own way out.' He gave an approximation of his smile. 'Until next time, Mrs Wilkinson. Mrs Parteger.'

Hattie sat completely still until the voices had receded. He had gone just like that. No searing look or even a promise to call when he was better.

'I declare Sir Christopher is a gentleman—putting your reputation above his own comfort and consideration.' Stephanie reached for the coffee pot, a sure sign that she intended to stay a while. 'At last someone in this sorry affair thinks about reputations and the impact their actions may have on others. I declare you have no more sense than a gnat, Hattie. Livvy is due to make her début next season. The last thing you want is for your exploits to become common fodder for the gossips.'

'He certainly did that.' Hattie hated the way the butterflies in her stomach started. Surely he could not have forgotten about last night so quickly? They spoke at such length. It was impossible and if he had, how could she face him knowing that she had once divulged those secrets to him?

Stephanie dabbed her eyes with a lace handkerchief. 'Here I was a bit concerned about Mr Hook, but with an example such as his guardian, I know that he will behave with the upmost propriety.'

'You are resigned to Mr Hook now? Or do you think Livvy will do better in London?'

'Mr Hook's relations with Livvy are not something I entirely want to discuss. Rather I want to speak about your gloves.'

'Which gloves this time?' Hattie rapidly considered all her pairs of gloves. She knew where they were.

'It was so kind of you to buy Livvy that pair of butter-yellow gloves. They are far too expensive.'

'I bought Livvy a pair of gloves?'

'She tried to tell me that they were yours, but you never buy frivolous things like that. You are always so practical, Hattie. Charles always said that it was one of your more admirable qualities. I will confess that I failed to see it until after his death, but there you go. A sister is always the last to notice.'

'I am pleased she likes them.' Hattie made a mental note to speak to both Mr Hook and Livvy about lying. It was entirely possible that Stephanie had become muddled, but Livvy had to understand the consequences. A tiny prickle went down her back. Unless... 'Did you say they were butter-yellow?'

'They must have been tremendously expensive.'

'They were.' Hattie pressed her lips together, remembering Kit's gesture to the stall keeper at the Hexham Tans stall. She should have intervened then. No matter what happened, she did not intend to accept gifts from him. It would make the relationship less equal.

'Is there any other news? Surely something else happened beside Livvy's mysterious pair of gloves?'

'Beyond Sir Christopher's injury?' Stephanie frowned. 'Mr Hook has agreed to give his lecture on newts. Apparently Mr Hook has decided that it would be best if they stay in the neighbourhood while Sir Christopher recuperates. That young man has a sound head on his shoulders. After you became separated from Livvy, he made certain that she was escorted back to me. I just pray he finds some confidence from somewhere or otherwise poor Livvy will be dreadfully disappointed.'

Hattie hid her smile behind her hand. It appeared that Livvy and Mr Hook were enjoying a romance, despite Stephanie's interference and she found that she wasn't inclined to stop it. It was no one's business and she had to trust that Livvy would be sensible. 'Is that so?'

'He is far too diffident. I doubt he has any idea about women.'

Hattie moved the conversation on to much safer topics. When she next saw Kit, she'd tackle him about the gloves. But whatever he had intended, the gloves now belonged to Livvy. Hattie quite looked forward to quizzing him about it.

The sickroom was immaculate. No sign beyond the tidily folded laundry that Kit had ever slept here. Hattie regarded it with distaste. She had come up immediately after Stephanie left, hoping for a little clue or perhaps a forgotten article which would enable her to visit him.

Hattie caught sight of her stricken reflection in the little mirror over the chest of drawers.

'What did you expect, my girl? You knew he

had suffered from a concussion. He probably doesn't even remember.'

The irony did not escape her. How could she go to him and ask? What did one say—when you were suffering from a concussion, you promised to make love to me? Will you do so now? The mere thought made her feel sick to her stomach.

A great wave of tiredness came over her and she stumbled to her bedroom. Everything would be clearer after a sleep.

She put her hand to her head as a wave of dizziness passed through her. Whatever happened, she was not going to humiliate herself again. She was going to retreat and lie down.

There, propped up on the middle of her bed, was a single red rose and a note. Hattie's tiredness melted away.

With trembling fingers, Hattie undid the sealing wax and opened to the note.

Summer house in your garden. Four p.m. Tomorrow. If you are still willing. Kit.

Hattie sank down on the soft bed. He'd left her a note where only she would find it.

She pressed the note to her lips, trying to think. He'd given her an option and had preserved her reputation in case she changed her mind.

Hattie tightened her grip on the paper. Retreating was the last thing she wanted to do.

She'd be naïve if she thought she was anything but a distraction. She knew the boundaries going in. This was not about love or finer feelings. She'd had all those words from Charles and had believed them. This was about proving her independence.

She could stop living the life that Charles had chosen for her now. She had a choice and she intended to take it.

She gulped twice. What did one wear to a seduction?

The garden was bathed in warm golden sun the next afternoon. Hattie had sent Mrs Hampstead to Highfield on the pretext of helping Livvy get ready for the dinner party the Dents were giving. She claimed tiredness and the wish to have some peace after the turmoil of the last few days. Mrs Hampstead had taken Moth with her so that Hattie could sleep properly and undisturbed.

A life of half-truths had begun, Hattie thought with a wry smile. Perhaps it said something about her that they sprang so easily to her lips. She had been certain that Mrs Hampstead guessed, but she accepted Hattie's rather garbled explanation.

At first, Hattie considered that no one was there, but then she saw movement in the shadows.

'Kit?' she called softly, wondering precisely how one went about this new life of sin.

When she had gone to the summer house with Charles, he had led the way, insisting that she could see the fireworks better from there. She had been far too young and in love with love to question him. It had seemed a dream that someone so handsome and at ease with society, not to mention brave, should be interested in her. She had never thought about it until far too late. Then, looking back with the benefit of hindsight, she had seen the signs—the unexplained absences, the moodiness, the perfunctory lovemaking. It was not going to happen again. This time, she wasn't going to give her heart.

He appeared in the doorway. He was simply dressed and bareheaded. The bruising on his face was starting to come out and gave him a decidedly roguish appearance.

'You made your decision.'

'It was painfully easy.' She held out her hands. 'I'm not certain about what happens next.'

He crossed the short distance between them. His fingers touched her jaw. 'We go slowly. It happens at the pace you want it to happen.'

'I sent Mrs Hampstead to Highfield. We have about two hours before she returns, I imagine.'

He cocked his head to one side. 'And that will be long enough?'

'More than ample. I want to do everything in my power to prevent Mrs Hampstead from guessing.'

'Mrs Hampstead is no fool.' His face sobered. 'You will need her as an ally rather than as an enemy. On another note, while we are together in public, we must not take chances.'

She refused to think about his words—*while we are together*. He had played this sort of game before, but she was a novice. The future was going to happen whether she wanted it to or not. She had stopped believing in for ever a long time ago.

'I know.' She moved closer to him. Her hand touched the broad cloth of his coat. 'But...' she stood on her tiptoes and brushed his lips '...I understand the rules, perfectly.'

He put his hands on her upper arms and held her from him. He searched her face. 'Why are you doing this? Is it because you want me or because you want to get back at some man who has been dead for seven years?'

'It is because I want you. What I might have felt for Charles vanished years ago. I am tired of living in fear. I want my life back.'

He lowered his mouth and drank from her

lips. The kiss teased her senses and increased in urgency. Hattie twined her arms about his neck and pulled him closer. Her body arched towards his.

It was as if she had been encased in ice and his breath was setting her free. She mimicked his actions and slipped her tongue into his mouth, revelling in her new-found power.

His hands roamed down her body, arms, shoulders, sides. The light touch sent a series of tremors coursing through her body. He stilled when his hand reached her bottom.

'What are you wearing under that dress?' he rasped.

'Nothing. I came dressed for seduction.'

He gave a husky laugh and pulled her closer, leaving her in no doubt of his approval. 'Once you make up your mind, you are very determined.'

'I like to think it is a good trait.' She reached up and brought his head back down to her lips. 'I hope you think so, too.'

'Definitely.'

They stood there, kissing until Kit gently eased her back into the shadows of the summer house. She saw he'd brought a blanket and pillows. In the corner sat a basket full of food and wine.

'I also wanted to be prepared.' His breath caressed her ear. 'Food or passion first?'

'What do you think?' She brushed her lips against his. A liquid heat bubbled up within her. 'But why the pillows?'

'The hard ground does nothing except give one backache. This is about pleasure rather than discovering muscles you didn't know you had.'

She mutely nodded. A reminder, if she needed it, that he was used to trysts of this nature whereas she was a mere beginner. Above all things she didn't want to disappoint him.

'My ignorance is astonishing.'

'You are doing fine.' He kissed her temple. 'More than fine. Go with your instincts.'

'I feel awkward,' she admitted.

'May I?' he asked and gently took the hairpins out of her hair, allowing the mass of unruly curls to fall down about her shoulders. 'I have wanted to see it loose.'

'I normally wear it in braids because otherwise it goes wild.' Her voice sounded husky and thick.

'It is very passionate hair. It has a mind of its own.' He ran his hands through it, winding it about his hands. 'So many different colours.'

He pulled her to him and recaptured her mouth. His tongue played with hers, twisting and tangling. The fire in her belly grew more urgent. Her body moved against his, seeking his. She moaned in the back of her throat. Give in to your instinct, he'd said, and her entire being screamed that she wanted to touch his skin. Her fingers worked his neckcloth, revealing the strong column of his throat. She touched her lips to the base of his throat and felt his heart thrumming.

She pushed at his coat, wanting to see more and hoping that he'd understand. He gave a soft laugh and divested himself of his coat, waistcoat, shirt and trousers until he stood before her, naked. His skin gleamed golden in the afternoon light. A sprinkling of dark hair covered his chest with a line leading down to his erection. Firm. Rigid. Visible proof if she needed it that he wanted her. A primitive hunger surged through her.

She reached out and touched his warm chest, felt the nipples pucker beneath her fingertips.

'Can I see what lies underneath?' he asked, and at her wordless nod, quickly removed her dress.

She stood before him, dressed only in her stockings, garters and dancing slippers. She stepped out of the shoes and resisted the temptation to cover her nakedness. His appreciative gaze roamed over her. Slowly he reached forwards and undid one garter and then the other. With infinite patience he rolled the stockings down. She sank down to the blanket before her knees gave way. He removed the stockings, rubbing the base of her foot with his knuckle, sending ripples of pleasure cascading through her. Then he positioned himself between her legs, looming over.

He reached out his forefinger and traced a circle around the dusky rose of her nipple. 'Exquisite.'

Where his finger went, his mouth swiftly followed. He captured one nipple, suckled, released and took the other one in his mouth. Her back arched upwards. She dug her hands into his thick crisp hair, holding him there.

He moved his hands downwards, sliding them over her curves until they reached her nest of curls. There, he slipped a finger into her folds, seeking her innermost centre.

She gasped as his finger found the hardened nub. No one had ever touched her that intimately before. Always she had stayed rigid, afraid to move, but the liquid heat which filled her made that idea impossible. Her back arched upwards, inviting his fingers to probe deeper.

'Relax,' he breathed into her ear.

'I'm trying not to move,' she cried in desperation. 'It is the correct way to behave.'

He gave a husky laugh. 'I want you to move. I want you to enjoy this. Stop thinking. Listen to your body. Touch me. Here.'

She reached out her hand and ran it down the planes of his chest, following the line of hair until she encountered his arousal. Hot. Velvet smooth, but hard. Her hand closed around it as his fingers slid in a figure eight in her folds. Wave after wave of heat washed over her.

'Lie back. Enjoy.' His rich voice rippled through her.

Her hands grasped his shoulders, tugging, hoping he'd understand her wordless plea.

Slowly, slowly he wedged her thighs wide. The tip of him nudged her inner core. At her nod he drove himself forwards, impaling her willing flesh.

Her body opened and swallowed the entire length of him.

He lay there, joined and unmoving. He looked down at her and smoothed a tendril of hair from her forehead. He lowered his mouth to hers. His tongue penetrated, demanding a response as it teased and provoked. Her hips began to move, seeking relief from the increasing need that welled up in her. He responded, withdrawing and then driving deeper.

Then the world burst around her and he caught her cries in his mouth.

As she floated back down to earth, she stroked his cheek. 'Thank you.'

'My pleasure.'

She moved her hips slightly and felt him respond deep within her. No one had told her that being wicked could feel this good. She wanted it to continue. She wanted to make a memory and keep it with her for ever.

'Shall we try it again?' she whispered, ignoring the faint prickle of worry that this could not last.

Chapter Ten

A cold wet nose snuffled into Kit's shoulder, waking him from a sound sleep. He started, turned his head and saw Moth's brown eyes peering at him and Hattie. The summer house had sunk deep into twilight's shadow. Hattie's bottom curved into him and her hair spilled out across the both of them. Kit found it difficult to remember the last time he had felt this contented or relaxed.

Normally after a spot of bed-sport, he was full of energy and found the first excuse he could to leave. This time, he'd stayed, fallen asleep and now they had to face the possibility of discovery. And it was his responsibility.

'Harriet,' Kit murmured, his breath caressing

her ear. The last thing he wanted was her to be startled and scream. 'Moth's here.'

Hattie mumbled slightly in her sleep, pushing him away. They had made love twice more after the first time. Her passion and inventiveness had surprised and delighted him. One time was not nearly enough. He wanted to explore her hidden depths. He wanted to catch her cry in his throat as she trembled on the brink of passion. And now she slept.

Moth sat down and gave a sharp bark before licking Kit's shoulder. There was an urgency to the little dog's movements.

'I understand, Moth. We have to move. Your mistress needs the veil of propriety.'

He shook Hattie's shoulder. Harder. 'Hattie. Time to wake up.'

Her eyes blinked open. He smiled down at her and she jumped. Startled. Kit clasped his hand over her mouth, stifling the cry.

'Quiet now.'

She gave a brief nod and he removed his hand.

'It wasn't a dream?'

'No dream. A much-desired reality.'

She sat up, moving away from the safety of his arms. Her blonde hair fell wildly about her shoulders, providing a soft veil over her chest. She wrapped her arms about her waist and turned her back towards him.

'It was wrong of me to fall asleep.'

'It happened.'

Moth immediately went to her and rubbed her head against Hattie. 'I didn't mean to sleep. I only intended to close my eyes for a moment.'

'Now Moth is here. Will anyone else be looking for you?' Kit pulled his trousers on and reached for his shirt, trying not to think about the consequences if they were caught. He would have to do the decent thing, but right now he prayed to anyone who might be listening that it would not happen.

'She wasn't supposed to be here. Not for a long while. Mrs Hampstead was going to stay at Stephanie's for a couple of hours.' Hattie scooped the little dog up and held her against her chest. Moth endured it with a scrunched-up face before wriggling to escape. 'I only meant to close my eyes for a moment. I must have drifted off. Goodness, how long were we there?'

'It happens after vigorous activity.'

'That is one explanation. How…how long did we sleep?'

He gestured towards the garden where the shadows were deep, but the darkness had not really begun. The last rays of the sun remained red-orange. 'It remains twilight. Barely any time.'

'Twilight comes much later in Northumberland. At this time of year, it never gets properly dark.' She stuffed her fist into her mouth. 'What are we going to do?'

'It is up to you. Your house. Your rules. Panic never solves anything. Keep a cool head.'

He reached down and retrieved the crumpled gown from where he'd tossed it earlier and handed it to her. She wrinkled her nose as she examined the now highly creased gown.

'It looks precisely like what has happened to it.'

'It could be worse. It isn't grass-stained or torn,' he said, trying to be encouraging. 'Will Mrs Hampstead come out into the garden, looking for you?'

She clapped her hand over her mouth. 'I hadn't considered it. I told Mrs Hampstead that I might take a turn about the garden before bed. It will have to do as an excuse. Do you think she will accept the excuse?'

'It happened.' Kit caught Hattie's elbow and turned her towards him. Her eyes were wide with fright and panic. He gently lifted her chin so he was looking directly at her. 'I'm glad it did. It was delightful to wake up in your arms.'

She turned rosy in the dying sun. It pleased Kit that even after everything they had done, she remained innocent.

Her frantic hands tried to twist up her hair and singularly failed. 'Thankfully it was only Moth. I suspect Mrs Hampstead would have fainted. And it doesn't bear thinking about if it was Portia or Stephanie. I meant what I said, Kit. I have no plans to marry again. This must be a summer romance.'

Kit experienced an unexpected pang of regret that it was not either of them. It would have solved a problem. He knew with Hattie that he would do the honourable thing, if it came to it. It surprised and slightly unnerved him. He had never experienced regret like that before.

Kit pushed the thought away immediately.

He had no need of a wife, even one like Hattie. He had to keep perspective. Like him, she had no desire to stick her head in the parson's noose. Their affair would last for the summer, no longer.

He was in no hurry for autumn, but some day Hattie would get possessive and throw a tantrum as so many of his mistresses had done before he'd learnt. Time limits at the start saved heartache at the end.

Far better to cause a little hurt than to experience the great searing pain of one's heart breaking or having her discover that he was actually like his father—cruel and unlovable.

'Until the summer's end, then,' he remarked when he was certain he had his feelings under control. 'Unless you have regrets?'

'It is far too late for regrets. Far too late.'

He released his breath. 'You can only regret things you haven't done.'

She glanced at him over her shoulder, her hands pausing in their task. It was all Kit could do to keep from hauling her back into his arms. Instead he bent and picked up several of the scattered hairpins and held them out to her. She smiled her thanks.

'And I enjoyed myself far too much,' she said quietly. 'Whatever happens, thank you for that. I thought it was me, but it wasn't. I know now why people are so fond of the act.'

'The person matters more than the act.'

'Thank you for saying that.'

He reached out and straightened the folds of her gown. Once again she appeared prim and proper, reminding him of the night they had first encountered each other. He had what he wanted from her then, but it did not matter. This was not about teaching her a lesson in love. He desired her and her alone.

'You look well kissed,' he said, lightly touching her cheek.

She dipped her head. 'I shall take that as a compliment. But Mrs Hampstead will refrain from enquiring. I will tell her that I was gathering late roses and dropped off in the summer house.'

'Second thoughts? I thought you were determined to carve a new life for yourself.'

She worried her bottom lip. 'Because it is far too new and I have no wish for speculation. I've no wish to force you to do something you might regret.'

'Allow me to look after myself.'

'I knew I could count on you.' She gave a few final twists to her hair and patted the side of her gown, signalling to Moth to follow. 'Until the next time, Kit.'

'I look forward to it.' Kit knew that any further meeting had to come from her. If he pursued, it would look like he cared. And he wasn't ready for that. 'And, Harriet...?'

'Yes, Kit?'

He smiled at her, enjoying the way her gown accentuated her curves. 'Make it soon.'

'I will try my level best.'

She clicked her fingers and Moth trotted along behind her. Kit watched until she had gone into the house and lit a lamp in the drawing room. He saw her speaking to Mrs Hampstead and laughing. She was safely back in her world without a stain on her character. He'd kept his word.

Kit leant against the doorway and closed his eyes.

'I wish you had come to dinner at the Dents. Doctor Hornby was there and everyone wanted to hear about your exploits. You are quite the heroine,' Stephanie said when Hattie stopped by Highfield the next morning.

In the depth of the night, Hattie had resolved to continue about her routine as if nothing had happened. She had determined that today would be making jam and doing things about the still room. She found making the preserves, flavoured vinegars and chutneys ultimately satisfying. She had discovered a real talent for the enterprise when she came up to Northumberland. Her elderflower cordial might be prone to exploding, but she knew her damson gin was some of the best in the county.

Above all, she wanted to avoid visiting, in particular seeing Mrs Reynaud. If anyone was going to guess about the affair, Mrs Reynaud was the most likely candidate. Her eyes were so sharp. She'd even guessed about the kiss at the Roman ruins. And everything was far too new and precious. Hattie needed to decide if she wanted anyone else to know, but for now she wanted to hug the news to her chest like some glorious secret.

'I take it that Sir Christopher and Mr Hook were absent?'

'Obviously.' Stephanie rolled her eyes heavenwards. 'A fight like that is not something you simply get up and walk away from. Mrs Dent agrees that you were reckless, but did what you did out of pure Christian spirit. If your reputation wasn't so spotless, questions might be asked, but you have been on the shelf for so long, there is little danger of anything untoward happening.'

'I don't very much care what Mrs Dent thinks.' Hattie crossed her arms. On the shelf, indeed! 'She has a mouth like the Tyne and speaks before she thinks.'

'Hattie, what has got into you today?' Stephanie frowned. 'You are not usually rude. Of course you care about what Mrs Dent thinks. She is our close neighbour and a powerful force in Tyne Valley society.'

'She is looking to marry off her eldest daughter.'

'Livvy is more than a match for her.' Stephanie tapped a forefinger against her mouth. 'Come to think of it, Mrs Dent was awfully curious about Mr Hook and his habits. She has heard about the proposed lecture.'

'I thought you were not interested in Mr Hook for Livvy. Livvy must have a title and all that.'

'Mr Hook has asked Mr Parteger if he will help with the final preparation. Mr Parteger is reluctant. There is no good encouraging him, Mr Parteger says, as there is no title.'

Hattie leant forwards. She had been racking her brain all morning as she picked strawberries about how she could go about contacting Kit and the answer lay before her—the lecture preparations. 'But it was your scheme.'

Stephanie heaved a long drawn-out sigh. 'I swear my husband does not appreciate any of my schemes. I have had to ask the Colonel.'

Hattie glanced over to the firmly closed library door. 'I believe he likes a bit of peace, Stephanie. He doesn't see the same urgency as you and he has never been terribly social.'

'You know I was pregnant with Livvy when I was just a bit older than her. It scarcely seems possible.' Stephanie put her hand on her stomach. Her face crumpled. A single tear ran down her cheek.

'What is wrong, Stephanie? You are practically in tears.' Hattie covered Stephanie's hand with hers. 'Was Harold cruel? He doesn't mean to be cutting. He does want the best for Livvy.'

'I fear it might be happening again. I have been ill every morning for the last week. If it had not been for the fair, I'd have stayed in bed, but someone had to support dear Mr Parteger. He expects me to be there for him on that day of all days. Then you went and recklessly endangered your reputation with rescuing Sir Christopher after that dreadful fight where you needlessly exposed yourself. No one cares about my nerves.'

Hattie closed her eyes. Stephanie pregnant. Again. She had half-hoped to suggest to Kit that they travel or arrange to meet abroad. And she'd even toyed with going down to London next spring for the entire Season…if their affair lasted that long. However, if Stephanie was pregnant, it would mean a baby in the late spring, and she knew how much Stephanie counted on her help.

'We shall cross that bridge when it comes.'

'But Livvy and her Season. It has been promised. Livvy is over the moon with excitement.' Stephanie dabbed the handkerchief to her eyes and gave a rather pathetic sniff. 'I will need you here. No one understands me and my babies like you do. But I dislike the thought of Livvy being without support and guidance.'

'I could go.'

'Of course you could go, Livvy respects your opinion, more than mine. But…how am I going to run the house? You are my sister and the only person that Harold truly tolerates.'

Hattie sighed. She knew that she had to stay, if only to ensure her brother-in-law's sanity. It did make things easier. If Kit asked, she'd explain. And if he didn't, she was safe in the knowledge that she could not have gone anyway. She curled her fists.

'Mrs Hampstead could stay with you. She is far more useful than I on such matters,' Hattie said more in hope than expectation. The colour drained from Stephanie's face. 'But Joyce should be willing to sponsor Livvy. Livvy and Joyce's eldest niece are close in age. It will give her someone to have as a friend. These affairs can be awfully daunting if you have to go alone.'

Instantly Stephanie's countenance cleared. 'You are right of course. It is about time our sister-in-law did something for this family. It is not as if they are troubled by us much.'

Hattie squeezed Stephanie's hand. Remorse washed over her. Stephanie always dreadfully suffered in the first few months of a pregnancy. What she was asking was not too difficult. It was simply that for once she wanted a little time to live her own life. She pushed the thought away.

'You must concentrate on the new life. I will make sure everything runs smoothly.'

'You are so good to me, Hattie. I couldn't ask for a better sister.'

'I try.' Hattie nodded towards where the baskets of strawberries stood. 'I have an appointment in the still room. It is that time of the year. Jams, jellies, tinctures and a wide variety of gins await preparation. It gives me an outlet for my energy.'

Stephanie put her handkerchief to her face. 'I can't bear the thought of the jam bubbling, particularly not now.'

'You always did prefer the eating of jam to the making of it.'

Stephanie had the grace to blush.

Kit rode his new stallion, Onyx, hard. He enjoyed the freedom and excercise after weeks of inactivity.

When he woke up this morning with the memory of Hattie's mouth moving under his, he resolved that he'd stay away for a little while. The last thing he wanted was to get involved in her life or for her to start to depend on him. He knew what women could be like. The rules of engagement were strict and developed after years of practice.

He reached the ridge above Pearl Cottage. He looked down at the little house with its curl of smoke. Something struck in the gut. His tenant, Mrs Reynaud, was down there in that cottage but her identity remained a mystery.

He had spent the majority of the day going through his uncle's papers while he tried not to think about Hattie and what she might be doing. As he suspected, the woman who had rented the cottage did not go by the name of Reynaud, but another name altogether: Smith. The tenancy agreement was odd to say the least and his uncle had ensured that Mrs Smith could never be thrown out of the cottage. According to his estate manager, the quarterly rent was always paid on time from a London bank. His Uncle John had overseen the details personally.

Kit bent down and patted Onyx's neck. The horse blew out his breath.

'Who is she, Onyx? And why did my uncle let the house to her in that fashion? What was she to him? A mistress? A former love?'

Onyx pawed the ground and tossed his head.

It would be easy to turn the horse's head towards the cottage and visit. He just couldn't shake the suspicion that this woman might be his mother—hidden away from her shame by his kindly uncle for all these years. He wasn't at all sure what he felt, but as he watched the door a bent figure came out. Nothing. She was too far away. He closed his eyes and tried to conjure his mother's features. They were a blur, an impression really. He recalled a scent of night jasmine, but nothing real and substantial.

A great part of him wanted to know the truth. He deserved to know what his uncle wanted hidden. Had his uncle defied his father?

Silently he willed her to look up and acknowledge him. Take it out of his hands. He'd go down if she so much as waved.

The woman stretched and went back into the house without looking towards him.

Kit curled his hands about the reins. Did he truly want to know who the woman was? How would he cope if it really was his mother?

She knew where he was. He refused to beg. He was not going back to that little boy on the stairs, silently pleading with his mother to turn around and stay, not to leave him. He had left the past behind him.

To hell with his rules. He needed Hattie. He needed her to make the past vanish. His life was about the here and now and the past was kept in a little place marked Do Not Open.

Kit spurred his horse towards the Dower House and Hattie. Solace.

Hattie put her hands on her back and stretched. The scent of strawberries perfumed the still room. There was something supremely satisfying about making jams and preserves. And the entire process kept her mind off Kit and the fact that neither had arranged for the next meeting.

She carefully poured a bit of the bubbling liquid onto a cool plate.

'Mrs Hampstead said I would find you out here, but she neglected to say how delightful you'd look in your apron and mob cap.'

Hattie jumped and the plate crashed down on to the flagstones. 'Kit!'

She spun around and there he stood, dressed in riding gear. His highly polished black boots contrasted with the tight-fitting tan breeches. His top hat was rakishly tilted on his head. His grey eyes sparkled.

'I came to see if you'd like to go for a ride with me, but if you are busy...'

'I am making strawberry jam. It won't take long, but it has restored my mood. Stephanie was here earlier...' Hattie found she couldn't frame the words. To explain about her disappointment would mean having to explain why and that she had started to make castles in the clouds. She clenched her fist around the spoon. When she next saw him, she had wanted to be properly dressed, not in her oldest gown with a voluminous apron tied about her waist and the awful mob cap. How could he think she looked delightful? She looked a fright.

'I've never seen anyone make jam before.' He stepped into the small room, filling it. 'It is fascinating. You have a bit of jam on your cheek.'

Hattie gave a light laugh and scrubbed with her hand. 'All gone now. I'm a messy cook.'

'Is jam-making a messy occupation?'

He was exaggerating. How could anyone not have seen jam being made before? The preservation of food happened in all sorts of houses and it was the responsibility of the lady of the house. It was criminal to allow produce to go to waste. Stephanie might not enjoy the process, but she did lend a hand when called upon, particularly when it was the wines or other types of alcohol. 'You must have had a deprived childhood.'

His mouth turned down and the light faded from his eyes. 'An unusual one.'

'Surely your mother…'

'My mother was not part of my life after my fourth birthday.' His tone indicated the subject was closed.

'An aunt or another relative, then?' She gave a little shrug and moved the steaming pan off the stove to show she wasn't hurt by his refusal to talk about his childhood. Was his mother dead or had she just left? Hattie hastily bit back the question. Some day she'd question Mrs Reynaud, who knew of the family and their history if he never confided in her, as she was curious. But not now as that would be like spying. Silently she willed him to tell her.

'No, no one like that. My father's taste ran to other sorts of women.'

'A pity.'

With a practised eye, she began to pour the gleaming red liquid into the jars. Over the years she'd discovered Livvy and Portia were more likely to tell her secrets if she appeared to be doing something else.

'My father disliked having women in the house.'

That simple statement combined with the jumping-jack explained so much. Her heart bled for the little boy who was never scooped up or petted or given treats. 'How awkward.'

He gave a short laugh. 'My father enjoyed being awkward and contrary. It was his favourite sport. He liked it even better than the horses.'

'And you are nothing like that,' she teased.

'You never force anyone to anything they wish to avoid like waltzing.'

'Waltzing with you was an unexpected pleasure.' The grey in his eyes deepened. 'I've discovered many pleasures with you.'

'Very charmingly put.'

'I try my best to be charming. I learnt from his example that it is easier to get your way when you are.'

'I shall remember that.' Hattie concentrated on the liquid. He hadn't liked his father and his mother had gone from the household by the time he was four. He would have used the word— dead. She wasn't sure why that was important, but she knew it was. She had to wonder if Mrs Reynaud knew anything or indeed if she would be willing to confide. All Hattie knew was she had to try. She wanted to unlock his secrets, but she also knew that if she pressed too hard, he'd turn away from her.

'Did it take you long to learn how to make jam?'

'Preserving is easy to do once you know how,' she said, allowing him to change the subject. 'There is something satisfying about seeing rows of jars and bottles. I can't cook, but I can preserve.'

'Why do you do it?'

'And not leave it to the servants?' Hattie leant back against the small wooden table. He appeared genuinely interested. 'I like to do it. I find it leaves me free to think as I work.'

'Are you finished?'

'For now.' She tilted her head to one side, assessing him.

His body was perfectly still, but coiled like a spring. She wanted to go to him and see if what they had experienced yesterday afternoon remained or if it had burnt out after one joining.

Her stomach knotted. She had imagined that he'd stride over to her and kiss her as they were alone, but he just stood there. She balled her fist, wishing she knew more about how one actually conducted an affair. And there was no one she could ask! Stephanie would collapse in a fit of vapours even if she so much as hinted at having an affair.

To break the tension, she attempted a light laugh. 'You should have a taste. Dip your finger into the pot. It is one of the perks for knowing the cook.'

He stood watching her without moving. 'You do it. First.'

'Do what?'

'Stick your finger in the jam. Show me how it is done.'

'Don't tell you never have…' She rolled her eyes. 'Didn't you used to go and sneak biscuits from the cook?'

His face became shuttered. 'No, I never did. My father had simple tastes.'

Hattie ground her teeth. She hated to think of the lonely little boy he must have been. She stuck her finger in the cooling jam and held it out. 'There, see. It is simple.'

He captured her wrist and brought the finger to his mouth, suckling. The faint tugging at her finger made her insides skitter. He withdrew and wiped his hand over his mouth. 'I see what you mean. Thoroughly enjoyable.'

'That, Kit, was beneath you.' Her cheeks flamed. She was such a novice at things like flirting with one's lover. Even the thought felt wicked.

'But hugely enjoyable. Strawberry-flavoured Harriet. Definitely a good taste.'

She attempted to remain calm. They were alone and no one had seen. 'I'm pleased I have broadened your education, but you acted like you knew what you were doing.'

'Once you have the mechanics down, the rest falls into place.' He leant forwards so their foreheads touched. 'Your skin smells of strawberries.'

'That is hardly a revelation.' She tried for a sophisticated laugh. This meeting in the still room was not how their next encounter was supposed to go. 'Your charm is slipping, Kit.'

He softly kissed her temple. 'I have a confession. I was going to wait for you to contact me, but decided not to. Will you come out on a ride with me now?'

'You decided not to wait.' She leant back against his arms, staring up into his face. She wanted to believe that she was the only one he'd ever behaved like that with. That she was the only one he pursued.

She had been prepared not to hear from him again, except for a polite note and some little token of false esteem. The fact was he was here with such an eager expression, asking her to go horseback riding with him, looking like he desired her.

She was acutely aware that her hair curled in damp tendrils about her face and her apron was hopelessly stained. Not quite the picture of effortless perfection he required from his women. She gave a wry smile. 'A pleasant thought but…'

'You do ride?' he tilted his head and looked at her with his deep-grey eyes.

'I am a passable rider. I used to be better and

take all the jumps, but someone needed to look after my nieces and so I feel my skills are rusty.'

'We shall have to make you a better one. All you are lacking is practice.'

'I suspect you are the sort of person who attempts the largest jumps and thinks about the consequences afterwards.'

His face became carved out of stone. 'I always think about the consequences. I know the price of failure.'

'Your father...'

'My father insisted I learn.' Kit frowned. 'He disliked it if I showed fear. The fear of his temper was far worse than my fear of heights. He left me up a tree once overnight until I developed the courage to climb down.'

'How old were you?

'Five.'

Righteous indignation filled Hattie. How could anyone have been that cruel and unfeeling? She wished the man was still alive so she could give him a piece of her mind. One simply did not do things like that. 'It was wrong of your father.'

'It helped me to learn. He worried that I would be weak, that I had bad blood like my mother.' He gave a self-deprecating smile. 'There are some who say that Eton is a hard place. When my uncle took me there, I found it a paradise beyond my wildest imaginings and never wanted to leave. That suited my father.'

Hattie shook her head in astonishment. When she had been sent to school as a young girl, she had been homesick for weeks, even though Stephanie had been in her final year there. She had lived for going home at the holidays. But Kit was right. He had been better off at school.

Hattie put her hand on his arm. He shrugged it off.

'What your father did was inexcusable, but it can't rule your life,' she whispered.

His face instantly fell and then he covered it up again with a bland mask and she knew she had overstepped the mark. 'It doesn't. I live my life with style.'

'You are certainly proving a worthy mentor to Mr Hook.'

'I had little choice in the matter.' His mouth twisted with self-loathing.

Hattie reached out and covered his hand with hers. 'People die when they are meant to. You did not fire that bullet. And I suspect you would have taken it if you could have, but you didn't. You have no idea what attracted the marksman to your friend. You can't torture yourself with "what ifs".'

'I will attempt to remember that when I wake up in a cold sweat, knowing that I begged him to change places with me.'

She stared at him for a long time, suddenly understanding. He blamed himself. 'Do you expect me to turn away with loathing? Is that why you failed to say anything earlier? I won't. I do know something of war. My husband fell in battle.'

'It wasn't any of your business.'

'I'm pleased you lack any ounce of self-pity.'

'Irony is not one of your strong points, Harriet.' He gave a sardonic laugh.

'And you are doing a decent job with Mr Hook,' Hattie continued relentlessly onward, not allowing herself to become discouraged. He had to see the good that he was doing and that he wasn't like his father. 'I'm impressed at how he has immersed himself in the study of newts. Even Portia is won over. He does know more than she does.'

He stared at her for a long moment. 'Shall we go for this ride or do I find another companion? Surely in the country, you can ride without a groom?'

'I would be delighted to go with you. Or rather to meet you. It is best if we happen to meet rather than ride out together. I have no wish to raise suspicions.'

'You can be overly correct at times, Harriet.'

'You don't have to contend with Stephanie.' Hattie wiped her hands on a towel. Her heat thumped loudly in her ears. She was going to go riding without a groom. She was going to escape from the Dower House and her responsibilities. One ride and that was all. She could stop any time she wanted to.

'Let me find my riding habit. And my horse is a bit slow, but she gets there in the end.'

He touched her cheek. 'That's all I can ask.'

Chapter Eleven

The horse auction was out near Yarridge and the Hexham race course hummed with activity. While Tatterstalls would have been Kit's first choice for purchasing a horse for Hattie, he doubted if she would consent to a journey down to London. He refused to think about how much time they could spend together away from the watchful eye of her sister and housekeeper if she had a mount of her own. Even getting her to come here had been a trial. Mrs Hampstead had shared her carriage, but thankfully had decided to stay at the refreshment tent, rather than look around at the horses. A groom trailed at a respectful distance.

Yarridge and its selection would have to suffice…for now.

Kit ran a practised eye over the stock available for auction, picking out several which might do for Hattie.

'Be careful where you step,' he said, catching Hattie's elbow and helping her around the pile of manure. A pulse of heat went through him.

'I am well aware of what a stockyard is like. Have you spotted which horse I should bid on? Or am I allowed the privilege of deciding that?'

'I am here in an advisory capacity only. Far be it from me to trample on your ideas.'

After their first ride, he had decided she needed something better so she could keep up with Onyx. He offered to get her a horse, but to his surprise and annoyance she refused, insisting that it was to be her horse. Gifts were not permitted. He wanted to spoil her, but she wouldn't let him. Normally he liked to keep the women he was seeing out of his daily life, but he found himself thinking about her at odd times of the day and storing up little stories so that he could relate them to her on their rides, particularly about Rupert's attempts to master newts and his sudden liking for the circulating library, a place Kit had never known him to visit before.

'There are more horses than I had considered there would be.' She clutched her reticule to her chest and skirted around a cart. 'I want a horse which can ride, looks good and has a reasonable temperament but where do I start? Who can I trust?'

'You can trust me.' Kit tucked her hand in his arm. 'Accept my verdict. Despite his many faults, my father did have good eye for horse flesh and he made sure I learnt. The patience he had with horses was amazing.'

Hattie merely raised an eyebrow at his words, but her face took on a fierce aspect. Kit shook his head. She looked like she wanted to do battle for the boy he'd once been.

'I'm far too independent now to allow someone free rein.' Her laugh sounded forced. 'You tell me what to look for and I will see if the horse has it. What is wrong with that bay?'

She pointed towards a showy bay which was prancing about, definitely changing the subject away from his past. Kit frowned. Normally it was his choice to keep his past separate. He had wanted to share, but she refused.

He always said that he preferred independent women, but Hattie carried her independence that bit too far.

'Can't you see me on that horse? We would practically fly over the walls.'

'You and how many other people? The owner

means for that horse to be seen. It is the sort of horse that people buy for its beauty.'

'I like beautiful things.' Hattie developed a stubborn set to her jaw.

The horse reared up and pawed the air. All Kit could see was Hattie being crushed under the hooves. He shuddered and pushed the thought away. He turned, expecting to see Hattie cowering.

Hattie's eyes shone with admiration.

'That is a magnificent animal!'

'You like untamed animals.'

A mischievous smile lit her face. 'They have their uses. More than I thought.'

'You need a decent mount, Harriet,' he said, leading her away from the mayhem. 'Something reliable, but with a bit of spirit. The horse you have been riding plods, but that one would throw you as soon as look at you.'

'I'm amazed you can tell that with just one glance. High spirited, but I'm sure I can ride it with a bit of practice.'

Kit clenched his jaw. Not if he had anything to do with it. There was a balance to be struck— a horse who could keep up with Onyx, but not one which would harm Hattie.

'See how she throws her head about? She hasn't been schooled properly. Breaking your neck isn't part of this exercise. A novice rider and an unschooled horse are a disaster waiting to happen.'

'I doubt that will happen.'

In desperation Kit gestured towards the growing throng of people. 'See how many people are interested in her? Do you really want to compete against them?'

She withdrew her hand from his arm. 'I've no wish to pay over the odds for a horse. I want a horse with spirit, but not one that everyone else is competing for and therefore will cost me dearly.'

'Practicality in all things.'

'I learnt how to budget after my husband died.' She lifted her chin with a proud tilt. 'How can I tell the difference between a good horse and a bad one?'

'Look for the little clues—how they hold the bit, place their hooves or react to small noises—as well as the big items such as the way they move or their teeth.' He smiled down at her, preparing to be indulgent now that she'd agreed not to buy that horse.

She nodded seriously. 'Anything else?'

'My father used to say to look at the neck. You can tell a lot about a horse by the way it carries its head. It is probably an old wives' tale, but it has held me in good stead. There is something about a horse's neck.'

'Do you judge people in the same way?' She turned and Kit looked at her long swanlike neck. He wondered that he had ever thought her severe and lacking in beauty. Every time he saw her, he found something else to admire. Her charms might not be as on display as some, but he found himself thinking about her at odd times of the day, remembering different features.

'I like your neck.'

She laughed, a tinkling sound that filled the air with light. He could listen to it all day. 'I shall take that as a compliment.'

A horse crossed in front of them and he took the opportunity to move closer than strictly proper. 'I intend to show my appreciation later.'

'Is that a promise?'

'Of course and you know I never break my promises.'

He basked in her smile, but their current arrangement was unsatisfactory. Finding odd ways to meet and conducting their affair away from prying eyes was sensible, but he wanted to spend more time with her. He tried to tell himself that it was purely physical and, once they spent time together, he'd start to see her faults. He'd become bored or she'd become demanding. Right now the key to that was finding a suitable horse.

'We will find the proper horse for you today. Traipsing all over Northumberland is not going to happen. There will be more suitable horses over here.'

'Kit?' Hattie said, confused. Kit's mood had suddenly changed. He had to understand that the horse needed to be her choice, not his. He didn't answer, but continued to walk away from her.

She hurried after him. 'Where do you think you are going?'

A scrawny boy in rags leading a chestnut horse caused him to draw up and she caught up with him. His face appeared very serious.

'What is the problem?'

'I spied Mr Dent and wasn't sure if you wanted to be seen with me.'

She breathed a sigh of relief. He was considerate. 'Mrs Hampstead is sitting with a cup of tea and Harvey, my groom, is about ten paces behind. Everything is above board. I did think about that eventuality. Wherever you go in the Tyne Valley, you are sure to run into someone you know.'

'What about the grey?' He pointed towards where a large placid horse stood.

Hattie peered more closely at the ragged boy

and then the chestnut horse shook her head and she knew. She knew precisely what Kit meant by looking for the little things. 'I want the chestnut unless you have an objection?'

'The chestnut? But that one is a bit more spirited than I would like.' He put his hand under her elbow. 'You might like to take another look at the grey. I think the chestnut may have been mistreated.'

Her eyes narrowed. 'Why do you say that?'

He nodded towards the boy who soothed the horse with his hand. The horse calmed instantly. 'Instinct.'

'But horses recover from ill treatment.'

'Some better than others.' He nodded. 'It takes time and patience. The boy has a way with horses that most people can only dream about. All you have to do is watch him and see how he moves.'

Hattie's heart constricted at the sight of the boy's pinched face and the way his ragged clothes hung off his frame. 'Oh, Kit. He looks half-starved. Can you do anything? We ought to buy him a pie.'

She fumbled in her reticule.

'I was willing to buy the horse for you. The boy is another matter.'

'Buy the boy?' She stared at him in astonishment. 'Is this Sir Christopher Foxton, the man who does not get involved, talking?'

'It will take more than a pie to cure him. He needs a chance.'

'I want the chestnut, Kit, and I am paying. Sometimes you just know deep within your gut that a horse is right.' She glanced up at him. 'A pie is better than nothing. And he will have made a sale.'

'Shall we put the horse through its paces then? First things first, Harriet. The horse, and then we'll see about the boy.'

Kit signalled to the boy, who brought the horse over. Kit ran his hands over the horse's legs, examining every inch and talking to it softly. The way he moved over the horse reminded Hattie of how his hands touched her when they were making love, never unhurried or rough, but gentle and firm. The boy answered all his questions, becoming more animated as he realised that Kit actually cared about the horses.

'She will do,' he said finally.

Hattie let out her breath. 'Thank you.'

Kit spoke quietly to the lad, who raced back to his master.

'What did you tell him?'

'That you were a lady and interested in buying the horse for a fair price, rather than haggling. I know you will pay the price, but for once, Hattie, let me do the speaking.'

A rather overbearing farmer approached with quick footsteps and a greedy eye, and the bargaining began. Hattie was pleased that Kit took control and extracted a far better price than she thought possible. His eyes shone and she could tell that he was enjoying the process, whereas she would have been tempted to pay the first price.

'And now I will have the boy get us something to wet our whistles,' the farmer said, rubbing his hands together. 'You and your lady can surely spare the time to do that.'

'I am not his lady,' Hattie stiffly. 'We are merely…'

'Neighbours,' Kit supplied.

The farmer nodded as if he understood.

'Your boy?' Hattie asked as the lad ran off.

'The bastard son of my housemaid. His mam died when he were whelped and I have done my Christian duty by him.'

When the boy came back, he stumbled and spilled the tankard of ale. Hattie stifled a gasp as the man clouted him around the ear. Kit strode to the man and caught his wrist, preventing him from delivering the second blow.

'I don't think you want to do that.'

'Why not?'

'Mrs Wilkinson has just purchased that horse, but I want the boy. He has a way of gentling horses. It can't be taught, but it can be cultivated.'

The farmer frowned. 'He is mine, but good for nothing. Eats too much. Rarely minds.'

'Send him to Southview Lodge near Stagshaw. I will pay you twice the price of the horse.' Kit ignored Hattie's sudden indrawn breath. 'Better still, I will take him now. I can use a boy like that in my stables. It is an honest trade.'

The man held out a dirty hand. 'I ken a deal when I see it. John, you be a good lad to his lordship.'

Kit knelt down and looked the ragged boy square in the eyes. 'If you work hard, and are honest, I will promise not to beat you and to ensure you are taught an honest trade.'

The boy beamed back at him. Kit felt as if the world had lit up. 'Aye, that would be good, your lordship.'

'Take the horse, then. You see her back to this lady's house and get her settled, but you will be in my stables.'

'You will need the strap on him. He is a wilful lad.'

Kit turned towards the man and gave him an ice-cold stare. 'I sincerely doubt it.'

'You were magnificent, Kit,' Hattie breathed

as they walked back to the carriage with Mrs Hampstead trailing behind, holding the boy's hand.

'Most women of my acquaintance are impressed with jewels or new gowns. Trust you to be different. Luckily I considered this when I made the offer.' Kit waggled his eyebrows in an exaggerated leer.

Hattie pressed her lips together. He was making light of what he'd done, dismissing it as nothing, just as he'd done about Waterloo. 'Giving that boy a chance. Do you normally do things like that?'

'Please don't make me out to be a saint. It was a whim, nothing more.' Kit pushed the brim of his hat down, shielding his eyes. 'I'm currently a stable boy short. It is just that I took a chance. He might run off or not work out. Selfish of me more than anything.'

She glanced at him under her lashes. Whatever his motivations, Kit had done it and it wasn't a whim or an impulse. He'd done it because of what had happened to him as a boy. It amazed her that she'd been so wrong about him when they first met. There was far more to him than superficial charm. 'I trust your judgement.'

'You should have allowed me to pay for the horse, then.'

'You did quite enough with the boy. More than enough. I suspect you saved his life.' Hattie looked over towards where the young boy stood quietly chatting with Kit's coachman as Mrs Hampstead got into the carriage. Less than an hour, and she could already see a change in the boy. He stood taller, his shoulders were less hunched. 'You did a great thing, Kit. Don't belittle what you did. Allow me to think you a hero.'

His face became stony. 'What you are going to call this new horse of yours?'

'Strawberry.' She allowed him to change the subject.

'Strawberry?'

'For obvious reasons. The horse's colour reminds me of strawberry jam.'

'And all that goes with it?'

Their shared laughter rang out over the stable yard. Several people turned around and looked at them as if they were mad. Hattie relaxed slightly. It didn't matter if people saw them together here as they were properly chaperoned. 'If you hadn't been so concerned about the boy, I'd never have noticed the horse. I might have gone for the obvious one and paid over the odds. This one had hidden talents. All it needed was a bit of encouragement.'

His eyes twinkled. 'It reminds me of someone

I know. A tiny bit of encouragement and her full beauty was revealed.'

'I wonder who you might be thinking of?' Hattie enjoyed the warm feeling rushing through her. It was the less obvious compliments which made her feel utterly beautiful. 'Now when we ride, you will be the one who needs to keep up.'

'You seem awfully sure about that. Would you care to wager?'

She glanced up at him. 'Are we at the point of wagering?'

He slid his hand slowly down her arm until his fingers curled about hers and squeezed tightly. 'Yes, definitely.'

Hattie leant forwards in her saddle and urged Strawberry up the slope. She'd had her horse only a few short weeks, but she already saw a huge difference in her riding ability. Over the past few weeks, even though it was never specifically planned, she and Kit seemed to meet most mornings on horseback for a gallop across the fells.

Keeping her independence was important. Whatever happened long term with Kit, she knew she'd treasure Strawberry. Kit had wanted to give her this horse and that was enough. She hated that she clung to every moment they were together, hoarding them like they were precious jewels. If she started to accept gifts, it would change their relationship. Hattie knew that she could never be a kept woman. She never wanted to become like Charles's mistress.

Kit was the perfect companion. They spoke about everything. She learnt how the renovations for the house were going and how John the stable boy was working out. Her concern appeared to amuse Kit. Kit predicted that with a little schooling, the boy could go far, but he never said when or where it would take place. In odd moments, when she was on her own, it bothered Hattie as it was another sign that this was a summer romance, rather than anything permanent. But wasn't that what she wanted, too? All she would allow herself?

Besides, being involved in a summer's romance was an exhilarating feeling. Even Stephanie's complaints about her pregnancy and her increasing demands failed to dampen Hattie's enthusiasm for riding and for the clandestine affair. She rejoiced in the knowledge that it belonged to her and Kit only.

She reined in Strawberry at the top of the hill. Kit came thundering up the hill, a few feet behind her. 'You see, Kit, I could do it. I was able to take the wall and land correctly.'

'You made it to the top of the hill first…for once.' His grey eyes twinkled as he dismounted. 'You are fast becoming an expert rider. Only a week ago, you'd have avoided that wall. Today, there was no hesitation.'

'It felt like flying.'

'You should take care. The last thing anyone wants is for you to get hurt.'

'What are my winnings?' She slid off Strawberry's back and looped the reins around a branch. A buoyant happiness filled her. She had done it. She had actually jumped the dry stone wall and flown over the stream, things she never dreamt possible. And she wasn't going to allow Kit's sudden concern to dampen her triumph.

A dimple shone in the corner of his mouth. 'What were you thinking?'

She glanced about her. The ridge was secluded and private. She stripped off her gloves and hat, and placed them on the ground. She lifted her face to his. 'A kiss. No one is here. No one will spy on us.'

'My lady is demanding. A kiss it shall be.' He lowered his mouth to hers and brushed her lips. She wrapped her arms about his neck and drank from his mouth.

'You call that a kiss? Your hat kept hitting my

forehead.' Hattie knew her breath was coming a little too fast.

'A thousand pardons.' He took off his hat and tossed it neatly on top of hers before undoing his neckcloth.

'That's a bit better.' A deliciously wicked shiver went through her. There was something to be said for enjoying Kit's company. He was the perfect companion for playing and she had a hard time remembering when she'd last played so much.

He gave a husky laugh and pulled her body into his so that their pelvises touched. 'Perhaps I should allow you to win more often.'

'Only if I deserve it.'

'You definitely deserve to be kissed.' He pulled her more firmly into his arms. 'And for once no one is here.'

'I take it you wish to stay here for a while.'

'I might do...unless there is a call upon your time.'

'Do you think we dare?'

He placed his hands on her shoulders and looked down at her. His eyes crinkled in the corners. 'We can do what we want, but I suspect the grass will be itchy. And you will get seeds in your hair again.'

'Mrs Hampstead keeps her conversation to

domestic trivialities these days and Stephanie is utterly absorbed in her family. She never asks about how I spend my time.' Hattie bit her lip. She'd been thinking about touching him all morning while she was listening to Stephanie's complaints about how Livvy had suddenly become a bluestocking and was constantly seeking to go to the circulating library. She'd wanted to feel his skin under her hands and had stopped herself from saying something just in time.

Sometimes, in her wilder moments, she did wonder what her sister would do if she confessed to her indiscretion.

'You're wearing your serious face.'

'Stephanie gets worse. She keeps dropping subtle hints about me moving in with her until the baby comes. And I can't. The walls would press down on me too much.' Hattie knew it was another half-truth. If she had to move back there, all these clandestine meetings with Kit would have to cease.

He brought her hand to his lips. His eyes turned deep grey. 'I'd prefer a soft bed with clean sheets and a roof over our head, and hour upon hour to enjoy you without your sister calling on you at all hours. Someone will have to give way.'

'That is impossible, here. This is not London where you can be anonymous.' She glanced over her shoulder. Thus far, the gossip had been muted, but she knew the limits. Discretion rather than full-blown flaunting of the relationship.

When they met at social occasions, it was never by design but by happenstance. Hattie was always careful not to spend too much time speaking to him. She loved hugging the secret to her bosom.

'We're far too well known,' she said firmly. 'I shudder to think what would happen if knowledge of this became common currency. It would ruin Livvy's chances. I couldn't do that.'

'Have you thought about taking a trip?' He moved closer. A faint breeze tousled his hair, giving him a rakish air. 'We could travel to the Continent. There is no trouble with travelling now that the war is truly over. You could see the places you always wanted to—Rome, Vienna, even Paris.'

Her heart turned over. He wanted to go travelling with her. A brief vision danced before her eyes. She could visit all those places that she had read about, but it would be better because he would by her side, sharing the experience. It would mean what was between them was more than a summer's romance.

He was fast becoming as necessary as breathing. How had it happened? She cared about him.

More than cared for him, she carried him in her heart. Loved him. That was not supposed to happen. Everything she'd done had been based on keeping her heart safe and enjoying the physical passion. She knew it was a summer's affair, nothing more, something that would fade when the autumn winds came, but somehow her heart had forgotten that important fact.

The feeling nearly took her breath away, only to be immediately replaced with despondency. He had never offered for ever. He'd been clear about that at the start. He was everything that she thought she'd despise—a man who used charm and who could not be counted on. He was not the sort of man to love.

She knew how destructive one-sided love had been to her once. She turned her face from his and attempted to control her emotions.

'Hattie, are you all right?' His voice penetrated through her confusion. 'I'd expected you to smother my face with kisses. A trip to Europe this autumn. If you insist, we can take Mrs Hampstead as cover and pretend to accidentally meet.'

'Perfectly. I just remembered that Stephanie wanted help with the flowers this evening. She is giving a small dinner party before the Dents' musicale. I forgot to say no.'

'She makes too many demands of you,' he said flatly. 'You need to learn to refuse her sometimes.'

She shook her head. 'I could never do that. After my husband died, she was so good to me.'

'So good to you that you couldn't admit what had really happened to you.'

'It had nothing to do with her.' Hattie examined the grass. 'I promised her that I'd stay. She is expecting. She needs me. I don't know what I would have done without her after Charles died. I owe her this much. Perhaps it is best if we cut this ride short.'

She bent down to pick up her hat and gloves. Why when everything seemed fine, did he offer her something that she was scared about accepting? A trip with her to the Continent meant nothing to his ultimate future, but he was asking her to change her whole life, to give everything up and she wasn't ready for that.

He laced his fingers with hers, kept her there. 'You are saying that you don't want to travel. You fear it, just as you feared that stone wall. You cleared that wall without a problem, Harriet.'

'Some day I will…travel. I have it all planned out.' She took her hand from his. 'Like you, I don't go back on my promises.'

'That is because you are stubborn. The offer

is there, Harriet. I am going to the Continent this winter with or without you.'

A great hollow space developed inside her. He was asking her to choose and she couldn't. She wasn't ready. She needed time to think. 'I will let you know my decision. It needs careful consideration.'

'When?'

'Later.' She gave a shrug. 'How goes Mr Hook's preparation for the lecture? It is less than a week away now. Portia was asking this morning before she explained why the latest experiment with newts was doomed to failure. Livvy leapt to Mr Hook's defence. It made for a lively visit.'

'Stop trying to change the subject. You are unwilling to go away with me.'

'I can't go.' Hattie's heart tore into two pieces. He had to understand what he was asking. If she went, she would be even more in love with him. He wasn't offering marriage or for ever, but a trip, a way to pass the winter. When she returned, their affair would no longer be a secret—everyone would know who her travelling companion had been. She'd lose her entire way of life. 'But if you insist on an answer…no, not with Stephanie the way she is. Pregnancy doesn't agree with her. I'd never forgive myself if I wasn't there and you are wrong to press me. Arrangements would have to be put in place.'

'Some women would accept without a moment's hesitation.'

'I'm not those women!' Hattie's heart thudded. He had to understand how hard this was for her and how sudden.

'Then we know where we are. Forget I said anything.'

She hugged her arms about her waist, hating that the atmosphere had turned so suddenly. She'd been looking forward to making love in the late-summer sunshine and everything had gone wrong. It hurt all the worse because she knew she cared about him and wanted this enchanted time to go on for ever. She wanted to go to the Continent and see all those places she had dreamt about—to have him at her side would be heaven. But it would also be slipping further into an illusion that their relationship would last.

'I had best go. I've been neglecting my visiting and other duties.'

'Yes, you never hesitate to do your duty.' His mouth curled down.

'There is nothing wrong with doing your duty.' She put her hands on her hips.

'If you think that, we had best end it here as you will always find another duty to do.'

'You are putting words into my mouth. Did you only ask me so I'd refuse? So you have the excuse you were seeking to end our relationship?'

He caught her arms and dragged her against him. Her body collided with his. The fire which was never very far below the surface flared. 'I asked you because I want you with me. I'm not ready to end our affair. I'm not ready yet and neither are you. Shall I demonstrate?'

He ruthlessly lowered his head, plundering her mouth and feasting. It was a cold hard cynical kiss, one designed to punish her for refusing his invitation.

With only a token protest, she opened her mouth under his and allowed her body to tell him all the things she didn't dare. The kiss that started harshly became softer and more seductive, seeking rather than demanding.

She moaned in the back of her throat and squirmed against his body, seeking relief from the desire which was now raging out of control in her body.

'I want you,' he rasped in her ear. 'I want to enjoy you when I want to, not rushing around and hiding from prying eyes. That is the only reason I asked. Most of all I want you. Right here and right now.'

His lips trailed down her neck, making a fiery pathway. Pleasure rippled through her body as his hand roamed at will, sliding down her curves and caressing her over the heavy cloth. She silently wished that she hadn't taken such pains at dressing this morning.

As if he could read her mind, he reached down and bunched the skirt. His hand slipped under her skirts and parted her drawers, finding her moist core. His finger slipped in, stroked and played.

'I want you, too,' she said between gasps. A delicious vista opened before her. He'd always taken the lead in their love-making, but this time she wanted to be the one to be in control and in charge. 'I'm no longer a novice, but an expert. Allow me to ride you.'

Her hands slipped down his body and unbuttoned his trousers. His erection sprang free. She clasped it in her hand, feeling the velvet hardness. As he stroked her, she stroked him back, both of them using their hands to give each other pleasure.

'I don't know how much longer I can last.' He eased her down amongst the high grass. 'Ride me, Harriet. Ride me now.'

He lay back on the ground and she positioned herself above him, straddling his body. The moist tip of him nudged the apex of her thighs. She spread her leg wider.

Using her hand, she guided him to the very centre and slowly impaled herself. Rode him, controlling the movement. Up and down, going at her pace as he lay underneath her. She enjoyed the feeling of power, of bringing them to the brink and then slowing it down.

The weeks of riding had honed her muscles and she used them now to give him pleasure. Faster and faster until the wave crested, then crested again. Finally when she knew she could take no more, she clasped her arms around him and held him as he came to a shuddering climax deep within her, so deep it seemed like his seed was spilling directly into her womb. They were together, joined.

Chapter Twelve

Much later when they lay entwined in each other's arms, Kit smoothed her hair from her forehead. It amazed him that he once thought Harriet had no passion within her. His desire for her had grown rather than diminished. 'You are definitely an expert rider, now.'

'No longer in need of lessons? I think I have learnt lots about being wicked.' She stretched her arms above her head. 'It has been absolutely delicious.'

His heart gave an unexpected pang. Lessons in wickedness? Was that all she considered this? He knew they had agreed that it would be a summer's affair, but he had discovered that he wanted it to continue into the autumn and beyond. The thought shocked him. 'No more lessons. The pupil has outshone the master.'

'I shall take it as a compliment.' She moved her arm and Kit heard a faint tear. She wrinkled her nose. 'Oh, dear. More sewing.'

'I fear our exertions have ruined your dress.'

She pulled away slightly. 'It will mend and if Mrs Hampstead questions it, I will say that I acquired it riding. It is not less than the truth.'

A cold stab of fear went through Kit. 'Has she questioned you before?'

'No harm will come from today, I promise,' she said, pulling her sleeve a bit and rearranging the material so the tear didn't show as easily. 'Mrs Hampstead will not enquire too closely. She never does. Discretion rules all. We are safe.'

Safety. He rolled over onto his back, moving away from her. His body protested at the sudden space. He wanted to linger and relax in her arms. He wanted her to go away with him, but she had refused and it still hurt. Staying here was the worst of all possible worlds.

'There is always a chance of a slip. What then?' He forced his voice to be cold. 'A forced marriage? You know my feelings about marriage.'

'There won't be.' Her cheeks stained bright red. 'I've been careful.'

'Soon autumn will be here. It will be too cold for such things.'

'Are you really planning on travelling to the Continent so soon, then?' she asked quickly. 'I thought you might like to see Northumberland in the autumn. Stay a bit longer and stretch the summer out. Summer can sometimes last.'

He sighed and put his hands behind his head, staring up into the clear blue sky, rather than looking at her. Staying here with Harriet had its merits, but all it would do was to prolong the inevitable and increase the likelihood of discovery. Misery for all if he allowed it to continue.

'After Rupert gives his lecture, I have to go to London. It can no longer be avoided. I do have business interests that I have to look after. I've neglected them for far too long. Like you, I have responsibilities and people depending on me to make the right choices.'

The words caused his insides to twist. Normally when the time came for a parting, he looked forward to it. This time, he hated it. It was better now, though, while they remained friends. Rules were made to be kept.

Hattie smoothed her skirt down and hugged her knees to her chest. The silence grew deafening. He willed her to ask to come with him and give him some sign that she wanted to be with him.

'So soon?' she whispered. 'His lecture is tomorrow. Everyone is sure to want to fête him afterwards. He will be the toast of the Tyne for weeks to come. Surely you can stay to see your protégé shine?'

He stood absolutely still with a soft breeze blowing in his hair. Behind him, the swifts circled on the wind, getting ready to depart from Northumberland to go on their long journey back to Africa. Summer was drawing to a close as much as he might wish it to be otherwise. He'd ignored it for far too long.

'I have stayed longer than I intended.' His words sounded harsh, even to his own ears. 'I'd planned to ask you to come to London with me, but you are busy. You have made that abundantly clear today.'

Hattie bit her lip. 'But you will be back. The Lodge needs lots of work. Someone will have to supervise.'

He concentrated on doing up the buttons of his trousers and shrugging into his jacket. She wasn't even willing to make the smallest concession. It was the right thing to end it swiftly. He had lingered far too long as it was. He did have another life, even if it was less than appealing at the moment. 'Some day. It will depend on how my business goes, but we must stay in contact, Hattie.'

She picked a piece of grass from her skirt. 'You always call me Harriet.'

'Hattie, Harriet, does it really matter?' Kit slapped his hand against his forehead. She was splitting hairs. He'd offered to take her away and she'd refused. What did she expect?

'Yes, it does. It did.' Her chin was tilted upwards, not giving an inch. 'I will look forward to your return then, Sir Christopher.'

'As you wish, Mrs Wilkinson.' Kit mounted his horse and did not look back. It was always best in these circumstances not to. However, he could not stop a hollow opening up inside him.

Hattie made it to her drawing room without crying. The ride back, alone, was one that she wanted to forget. Each time Strawberry's hooves pounded the ground, she wanted to ask how long—how long had he planned this? He knew what her answer had to be.

'Hattie, what happened to your dress?' Stephanie's voice pierced through her misery. 'You look like you have gone through a hedge backwards. Hopefully no one saw you like that! People will talk, you know and it will reflect on the family. Everyone knows you are my sister.'

Hattie fumbled with the sleeve. Talk about bad luck. Why did Stephanie have to choose today to come over? And to be in such a terrible mood! Why didn't Mrs Hampstead warn her when she came through the kitchen? 'I tore it riding.'

'Riding? You tore it riding?' Stephanie came over and inspected the sleeve with a frown. 'It is the first time I have heard of riding causing such a thing.'

'I moved my arm far too quickly. The thread wasn't very stout.' Hattie shifted uneasily as Stephanie's gaze grew more piercing. 'It is the truth, Stephanie.'

'And with whom were you riding?'

'Sir Christopher,' Hattie said without thinking. 'We had a laugh about my ineptness.'

'Since when have you been riding with Sir Christopher?' Stephanie's voice rose an octave.

'We met accidentally.' Hattie kept her voice even. There was no need to panic. She'd had a slight slip of the tongue. It was not as if she'd actually confessed to the affair.

'I see…and how many times have you two met accidentally in recent weeks?'

'I fail to see why that is a concern of yours.'

'Often, I would wager. I can see it in your

face.' Stephanie collapsed down on the damask sofa and buried her face in her hands. 'You are worse than Livvy, Hattie. Clandestine. You know what a man Sir Christopher is on about. How do you think you will force a marriage if you meet secretly?'

'Is there some trouble, Stephanie?' Hattie decided to ignore the remark about forcing a marriage. 'Surely it is not against the law to go out riding. One must be civil to those one encounters.'

'There is civility and then there is *civility*. Pray tell me that you have remained sensible in all things and that you have safeguarded your reputation.'

A cold sweat pricked at the back of Hattie's neck. *She knows.* But why now when everything had ended? A sudden more horrific thought struck her. Had they been spotted? Was that why Kit had provoked the fight? 'Something is bothering you, Stephanie. You might as well come out and say it. What am I supposed to have done?'

'I heard you had gone to the Yarridge sale with Sir Christopher, but chose to overlook it.'

'To buy Strawberry. I explained about that.' Hattie leant forwards. 'Sir Christopher is an acknowledged expert in horse flesh. He wanted to thank me for assisting him during the fair. Mrs Hampstead and Harvey the groom were in attendance.'

'Hmmm, and now you just happen to be meeting him…accidentally.' Stephanie held out her hand. 'Think about what you are doing, the potential for scandal.'

'You are creating a difficulty where there is none. In any case, Sir Christopher will be departing for London soon. No more meetings.' Just saying the words out loud threatened to bring tears. Hattie blinked rapidly. 'You are worrying unnecessarily.'

Stephanie shook her head. 'You have been reckless, Hattie. I can see it in your eyes, your mouth and, yes, in your ripped jacket. Sir Christopher is an entirely different proposition to Charles Wilkinson.'

'What do you mean?'

'You have had clandestine meetings with him. Goodness knows what some farmhand or milk maid might have seen or who they might tell.' Stephanie's face became serious. 'You must not do anything that jeopardises Livvy's chances. We don't want a scandal.'

'There will be no scandal,' Hattie said tonelessly. Her entire body felt numb. Stephanie wasn't concerned about her or her reputation, but merely what it might to do to Livvy's prospects. She hadn't even asked Hattie how she was. Stephanie had to have seen that Hattie was upset. Instead she went on and on quizzing her about unimportant things.

Stephanie's gaze narrowed. 'You say this with a great deal of certainty.'

'Sir Christopher is returning to London. Directly after Mr Hook's lecture.'

'Will you continue to ride out once he is gone? Or will you start behaving normally?'

'I enjoy riding whether I encounter Sir Christopher or not. I had not really considered the proposition.' Hattie forced her voice to stay even. 'You are worse than a dog with a bone, Stephanie. What are you trying to tell me?'

'All I can say, Hattie, is that you are being selfish and extremely short-sighted.' Stephanie rose from the sofa in a huff. 'I need you now more than ever, Hattie. Stop being selfish. Livvy keeps making excuses about going to the circulating library. I can't have my eldest turning into a bluestocking. You will speak to her for me, won't you? She will never get a man that way.'

Hattie balled her fists. Stephanie wasn't really interested in her or her affair with Kit. She was simply inconvenienced. 'There is nothing wrong with the circulating library. I presume she takes

Portia. Reading is a perfectly respectable occupation.'

'There is no need to be like that. They never meet anyone of import. Portia would tell me if they did.' Stephanie put her nose in the air. 'If Sir Christopher is departing, then it is all I have to say on the matter. I look forward to having the old Hattie back. You used to be so helpful, Hattie. What happened?'

'And what if I like the new Harriet?'

'That is your choice, obviously.' Stephanie sniffed. 'But don't come crying to me when you lose everything.'

Mrs Reynaud's face was a beacon of welcome as Hattie entered Pearl Cottage, carrying a basket of various jams, jellies and tinctures, the next morning. Moth immediately jumped out of the basket and ran over to Mrs Reynaud to demand a biscuit.

'I feared you had forgotten about me, Mrs Wilkinson.' Mrs Reynaud handed Moth her treat. 'Moth has been very bad not to insist on you coming here. And here I'd thought you and I had an arrangement, young Moth. Biscuits in return for your mistress's company.'

Moth gave a sharp bark.

'Your maid said that you have been under the

weather.' Hattie kept the basket in front of her. All the way here she'd debated—did she confess to Mrs Reynaud about her relationship with Kit and ask her advice or not? Mrs Reynaud was the one person in the village who had experience with such things.

'Not so ill that I can't receive one of my favourite people. A slight chill, nothing more. My health is less robust than I might wish. The damp of this cottage does me no good. But going out is hard. I worry about people and the lecture series. How goes it this year? Still surviving, I take it.'

Hattie felt a tug of regret. Until Kit had told her this morning about his plans to leave, she'd been so wrapped up in him that she had quite forgotten her usual routine. Stephanie was right. Her behaviour was causing comment. No more. 'I've been busy. I've a new horse, the most lovely chestnut—Strawberry. Riding is a new passion of mine. I hadn't realised how enjoyable it was. The freedom it gives.'

She stopped, aware that her cheeks flamed.

'A gift from Sir Christopher, or so the gossip has it. A thank you for nursing him,' Mrs Reynaud said with a faint frown. 'His father always did have a good eye for horse flesh.'

'I bought her on favourable terms with Sir

Christopher's assistance. He rescued a little stable boy.'

Mrs Reynaud waved an impatient hand. 'You meet him on this horse of yours? Don't lie to me, Mrs Wilkinson.'

'I've discovered that I enjoy the experience far more than I thought I would.' Hattie put down the basket. She clasped her hands together to stop them from trembling. She'd thought it over last night. She had to know more about Kit. Every time they had discussed about his childhood, he'd neatly turned the conversation away. She had to know what had gone wrong yesterday. 'You said you knew something of Sir Christopher's childhood. I understand it was very unhappy.'

'A bit.' Mrs Reynaud's eyes turned wary and her hand trembled as she lifted the coffee cup to her lips. 'Is it important?'

'It was something he said, or rather didn't say. It has been nagging at me.' Hattie drew a deep breath. She had come this far. Other than Kit, Mrs Reynaud was the only person who might know. 'I wondered what happened to his mother.'

'You ought to ask Sir Christopher.'

Hattie leant forwards. 'But you know.'

Mrs Reynaud gave a sad smile. 'Yes, my dear, I know.'

'Is it breaking a confidence?'

'I doubt that. There was a criminal conversation trial which was splashed all over the papers. It became the talk of England, Europe and, I believe, America. The cartoonists had a field day with the baronet spying on his wife and her lover in the bath.'

Hattie's heart clenched. Poor Kit. No wonder he didn't want to speak of it. She could vaguely remember her mother discussing it in hushed tones when a friend of hers had run away. 'I didn't know.'

'Now you do.'

'Unfortunately Kit's mother was less than discreet, that is what you are saying.' Hattie's heart constricted. It had to be awful to have one's parents involved in such a thing and it was never the man whose name was dragged through the mud, but the woman's. And Kit had been left with his father, the man who saw no use for toys. 'What a dreadful mess. The father always gets custody in those cases and Kit's father was horrible.'

'You call him Kit now, do you?' Mrs Reynaud gave a warm laugh. 'Behold the woman who will never have a flirtation, who is one of the walking dead because her husband died. Who disapproved of such things intensely.' Her gaze became piercing. 'I trust it remains only a flirtation. Sir Christopher has a certain reputation.'

'We are friends.' Hattie waved a vague hand before leaning forwards. She'd reached the crux of the matter and only Mrs Reynaud could assist. 'He helped me when I bought my new horse, but I am interested in his mother. Do you know what became of her? Is she dead?'

'Yes, his mother was silly and naïve. She sought romance in the wrong set of arms.' Mrs Reynaud's mouth twisted. 'A hopeless romantic who didn't realise what she had lost until too late. Pray do not concern yourself with a piece of flotsam like her.'

Hattie stared at Mrs Reynaud, remembering the stories she had told and the way she had described herself. Hattie narrowed her gaze, comparing. Her stomach tightened with excitement. It made sense now. She'd wondered that she had not seen it before. Mrs Reynaud's eyes were the exact same myriad shades of grey as Kit's. Then there was the shape of their jaws. 'You're Kit's mother, the scandalous woman.'

'I have no idea what you are talking about, my dear.' Mrs Reynaud raised her teacup, hiding her expression. 'Did I ever tell you about the sheikh and me? It is a wonderful story. It is sure to entertain you immensely.'

Hattie crossed the floor and knelt at Mrs Reynaud's feet and gathered Mrs Reynaud's hand between hers. 'I should like to think we are friends, Mrs Reynaud. Why didn't you tell me that Sir Christopher Foxton was your son when he first arrived here?'

Mrs Reynaud's body vibrated with emotion. A long drawn-out sigh emerged from her throat as she bowed her head. 'Does it really matter? I gave up the right to be anyone's mother years ago. All I did was to try to play matchmaker. You are the sort of woman he should have as a bride, rather than the women he has squired throughout the years. You are beautiful and intelligent, the sort of woman I always hoped he'd marry. I may not have seen him, but I have retained an interest.'

'I shall take that for a yes.' Hattie refused to think about Mrs Reynaud's attempt at matchmaking. Her stomach churned. She'd nearly confided about her affair to Kit's mother. 'He has your eyes and your jaw. I suspect your sense of humour as well.'

'I know about the eyes and jaw, but will have to take your word for the humour. I haven't spoken to Christopher for years.' Mrs Reynaud's cheeks flushed pink.

'And the other men? Did you really lead a scandalous life?'

Mrs Reynaud lifted her head defiantly. 'I had to survive after Christopher's father ruined me. Thanks to my marriage settlement, my late husband was able to lay claim to my inheritance and use it how he pleased. He refused to divorce me in the end and kept me on pin money. The criminal conversation was proved, but my lover only had to pay a meagre fivepence for destroying my reputation. He and I parted.' Mrs Reynaud spread her gnarled hands. 'I made sure my late husband knew about each and every one of my new lovers. It served my purposes to have him suffer.'

'Your late husband. Kit's father.' The words tasted like ash.

'Yes.' The word was barely audible. 'When I left, I thought it would be only for a few weeks before I could get Christopher to join me. Christopher's father had shown no interest in the boy. But I lived in a fool's paradise. The courts look ill on fallen women who leave their husbands.'

'But he's been dead for years. Why haven't you been in touch with Kit? He must long for his mother. He is your son. I know if my mother was alive, I'd want to see her.'

Mrs Reynaud touched her pockmarked face. 'You know what I look like. I fell ill just before Christopher's father died. Divine retribution. I changed my name by deed poll as soon as I could. I didn't want to shame him.'

'You're his mother.'

'I am the woman who left him. He was only four. At first I tried to justify it. He had his nurse. He had stability and John, my brother-in-law, promised to look after him as much as he could. John desired me once, you see. The brothers were like that—rivals.' She held up her hands and turned her face away. 'When John gave me this cottage, I agreed I would never contact Christopher. My late husband spent my inheritance. I had nothing. I had no choice.'

Hattie clenched her fists. Mrs Reynaud had had a choice. She had simply chosen not to take it. 'Go on.'

'The agreement was I would let him contact me. I have stuck by the agreement. John used to share his letters with me. He'd bring them over and read them. The highlight of my existence, those letters. I used to write to him. I have packets of letters which were never sent, just waiting for the day when he did contact me.'

'Does he know you are here?'

'John promised to leave him a letter. Once,

a long time ago, I begged John for a chance to see Kit. He brought him to the Stagshaw fair. I made wild plans. John suggested we run away together and raise him. In the end I lacked the courage as I loved John like a brother, not a lover. It wouldn't be fair to him. I bought Christopher a jumping-jack and had John give it to him. Shortly afterwards, I left for the Continent.'

'Your former husband and brother-in-law are dead,' Hattie whispered. She didn't dare tell Susan Reynaud about the jumping-jack and what it had meant to Kit. She also knew the longing she had seen in his face when he spoke about his mother. She and Kit might have ended, but she cared about him. He needed to know that his mother wanted him. He needed to read those letters that his mother had saved for him. The question was how to do it. She couldn't just show up at his house and demand.

'But I'm alive and I gave my word.' Mrs Reynaud shook her head. 'Some mistakes you never recover from, my dear. I learnt that the hard way. I would like to see him just once. Not to speak to, necessarily, but to see. There is nothing I could say to him which would explain why I did what I did. Could you help me?'

Hattie hated the way her stomach trembled. Kit was leaving. He might never be returning.

It might be the only chance for Kit to learn the truth—that his mother did care about him. She hated to think about might-have-beens. She knew she'd regret it if she didn't do it. She wasn't going to think about giving him a reason to stay. They were finished. The summer was over.

'Kit's ward, Rupert Hook, is giving a lecture tomorrow,' she said, coming to a sudden decision. 'You could attend. You are one of the patrons of the lecture series. You can at least see what he looks like. You don't have to greet Kit, but you could see him.'

Mrs Reynaud's hands trembled and she set down her teacup. Her grey eyes swam. 'Yes, of course. No one would think it amiss. I just want to see what he looks like, to see if there is anything of me in him. I'm so frightened that...'

'You can sit next to me,' Hattie said.

'You are a good woman, Hattie Wilkinson.'

'I can't understand why you did what you did, Mrs Reynaud, but I do know you can only change the future. Take the first step.'

'It tore the life out of me to leave him, but my marriage was intolerable. I don't expect you to understand. I made some bad choices in my life and I have paid for them, but the one I never regretted was having Kit.' Mrs Reynaud straightened her back. 'You are right, my dear.

It is time I faced my demons. I will take your suggestion and go to the lecture. You have given me strength.'

The Corbridge Village Hall was full to bursting for Rupert's lecture. Kit regarded the various personages—the great and the good going in to hear Rupert. He had handled things badly with Hattie. The break had been too abrupt, too final. Normally he was far more civilised about such things.

Rather than going to the front and taking his seat, he waited at the back to escort Hattie to hers. He'd make one last attempt and then they'd be through.

An elderly pockmarked lady half-stumbled on the step leading to the hall. Kit put out a hand and caught her before she tumbled completely.

'The steps up can be tricky,' he said.

She gave him an odd look. 'Yes, they can.'

'You must take better care on them.'

The woman gave a small smile. 'I will.'

'Mrs Reynaud—' Hattie stopped. The colour drained from her face.

Kit froze. He stared at Mrs Reynaud and knew. She was his mother. His stomach plummeted. He moved away from the woman, from his mother. This was most definitely not where he wanted to meet her and not in front of a crowd of people.

From Hattie's reaction, he knew that she knew the truth as well. Somehow Hattie was aware of who his mother was. For how long? Had she engineered this meeting?

Deep-seated anger filled him. He disliked being manipulated. If his mother wanted to meet him, she knew where he was. He had hardly kept his whereabouts secret, but she had. He struggled to control his temper. It was wrong of Hattie to do this, particularly after their quarrel. She had set him up. It seemed everyone in the entire lecture hall had turned to look at him and his mother. It was worse than a nightmare. His first impulse was to run away, but he rejected that idea. All that would show was cowardice. He was no coward.

Whatever happened, he refused to give anyone the satisfaction of seeing his emotions. Politeness and graciousness. Nothing to show that he was hurt beyond measure by both of their behaviours. He swallowed hard and regained control of his emotions. He knew what he had to do. Hattie with her superior expression would be held to account for her behaviour.

'I wish both of you the joy of the evening. You must forgive me, but I have a lecture to attend.

I made a promise to my ward. Mrs Wilkinson, Mrs Reynaud, your servant.'

Hattie's hand flew to her mouth as she watched Kit stalk off. He had cut her and Mrs Reynaud with absolute aplomb.

She heard several shocked gasps and knew the encounter had not gone unremarked.

She had made a grave error. She had never considered Mrs Reynaud would actually encounter Kit face to face, as it were, in the lobby before everyone. The final look he gave her before he turned away had damned her for all eternity, but he seemed in control, greeting any number of people with perfect politeness as if the meeting meant nothing to him.

She went over to where Mrs Reynaud stood, clutching her reticule to her chest with a distressed look on her face. 'This is all my fault.'

'He knows?' Mrs Reynaud choked out.

'Yes, I believe he does...now.' She put an arm about Mrs Reynaud's shoulders. 'It will have been a shock for him and for you. If there is anything I can do for you...just ask.'

'I should go. It was wrong of me to come. I should have waited for him to contact me as John suggested. He looked so like his father then. It quite unnerved me.' She moved out of Hattie's embrace. 'You must allow me to depart, Mrs Wilkinson.'

'What, and miss this lecture? You can sit next to me and we shall hear this lecture. See, Livvy is signalling to us.'

Mrs Reynaud fumbled in her reticule and withdrew a battered lady jumping-jack. 'No, I won't enjoy it. Give Kit this jumping-jack from me. It is up to him then. You may tell him where to find me. Please do this for me, Mrs Wilkinson.'

Hattie closed her eyes. The last thing she wanted was to have a confrontation with Kit, but how could she refuse? She had to do something to make amends...to both of them.

Chapter Thirteen

Hattie walked into her darkened drawing room and struck a match so she could put the lamp on. She was far too keyed up to sleep. Somehow she had to find a way to deliver the jumping-jack to Kit in person. She had thought about it all during Mr Hook's lecture, but was no closer to an answer.

Despite the incident with Kit at the beginning, the lecture had been a huge success. Stephanie beamed afterwards, loudly declaring that she knew Rupert Hook had not been lying when he proclaimed he was an expert on newts. Hattie had answered vaguely, made her excuses and left.

'Don't bother to light the lamp.'

She nearly dropped the match in surprise. Kit

stood in the middle of the drawing room, lit from the back by the small fire. Tall and forbidding. Her mouth went dry. 'Kit! What are you doing here?'

He indicated the French doors. 'It is easy to get into a house when you want, and your guard dog is a friend of mine.'

Moth turned on her back and wriggled.

Hattie put a hand to her head. 'Oh, Moth.'

'I have one question for you and then I will leave you in peace.' There was no mistaking the finality to his tone. 'Why did you do it, Harriet?'

'Why did I do what?' she asked cautiously. The last thing she wanted was a confrontation.

'When did you find out? How long have you known where my mother was? Why did you set me up like that?'

Hattie's heart thudded in her ears. She knew precisely what he was speaking about. The day of reckoning had arrived, much sooner than she thought it would.

'Earlier today.' Hattie blew out the match before it burnt her fingers. She struck another one, moved over to the small table and lit a candle. 'There wasn't time to tell you.'

'You convinced her to come to the lecture expressly to see me, without consulting my feelings on the subject. Don't deny it. My mother had all summer to contact me if she desired.' Kit gave a fierce scowl. 'What did you think would happen—a joyful reunion of two people long separated? Did you even consider how I might feel about the matter? About seeing my mother suddenly after so many years?'

Hattie gave a tiny shrug as Kit's scowl increased. When he put it like that, she could see there was no defence. She should have let him know, but if she had, the situation would have remained unresolved. She bit her lip. It wasn't exactly resolved now.

'Mrs Reynaud only wanted to see you.' Hattie held out her hands, palms upwards, willing him to understand. 'I didn't plan you two meeting like that. It was supposed to be different.'

He lifted a disbelieving eyebrow. 'Was she hard to convince?'

'It only took the slightest bit of encouragement. She wanted to go. She wanted to see you, but feared something bad would happen.' Hattie willed him to understand why she had done it. 'She is unwell, Kit. It might have been her last chance to make amends. She has a stack of letters which she wrote for you. She wants you to read them. She made a promise to your uncle not to contact you.'

'My uncle has been dead for over a year.' He

slammed his fist down on the table making the china ornaments jump. 'Dead men don't know the difference between a kept promise and a broken one.'

'Like you, she believes a promise is a promise.' Hattie carefully put the china dog back in the centre of the table. Losing her temper was not going to accomplish anything.

Pure fury leapt from his eyes. 'And I was young, little more than a babe in arms. Do you think she thought about me when she turned her back on me? She never once sent me a letter. Ever.'

Hattie closed her eyes. It broke her heart. She wanted to gather him in her arms and tell him that it was not down to him that his mother had left, but she knew he'd refuse to believe it.

'I know,' she said miserably. 'Mrs Reynaud wrote you letters, but never posted them. She told me.'

'That woman...doesn't deserve to be called a mother.' His voice trembled.

'That woman gave birth to you,' Hattie said gently. She could never excuse what Mrs Reynaud had done, but she had heard Kit's stories about his father. She suspected the truth was complicated and complex and that Mrs Reynaud knew precisely what she had lost. 'Your mother wanted to see you. She wanted to gaze upon you and see the sort of man you'd become. She was not seeking any sort of grand reunion watched by all and sundry. I thought… It doesn't matter what I thought.'

'You never even considered me or what I might think. You were utterly thoughtless, Harriet Wilkinson. You abused my trust. You want the world to be the way you want it and life isn't like that.'

Hattie put her hands into the small of her back. Her heart ached like the very devil. She refused to cry. She had known what could happen, where this was leading. Somehow a little piece of her had hoped that if he saw his mother, he might have a reason to stay. Instead he would use it as a reason to go. The last thing she wanted was to seem needy. She knew the bargain they had had—a summer romance, that was all.

'Very well then. We have reached that point. Summer is ended. We knew it was coming. I wish you godspeed, Sir Christopher. Forgive me if I don't bother to see you out, but you may go the same way that you came in. I do so hate confrontations.'

She died a little as she said the words.

His jaw dropped. 'No hysterics. No pleas for forgiveness or more time?'

'Should there be? We both knew what this was—a summer affair. Nothing more, nothing less.' Hattie kept her chin up. She refused to give him the satisfaction of collapsing. What did he expect—that she'd grab his ankles and beg or plead for forgiveness? Not her. She'd acted with the purest of motives. He'd warned her what he was capable of and she'd chosen to forget it.

'You are not going to complain about being used?'

'Why should I?' She crossed her arms. 'I was never one of your women, Kit. We both knew what this little piece of play-acting was all about.'

His nostrils flared. 'Play-acting?'

'You can't stand to have a woman leave you. You leave before your emotions are engaged because you are afraid that the woman might bolt like your mother. You set rules that dictate your actions. But you are wrong about me. I would have stayed the course. And you are wrong about your mother.' She fumbled in her reticule and drew out the little jumping-jack. 'Your mother asked me to give this to you. She lacked the courage at that long-ago fair. She has letters that she wants you to read. She is dying. To forgive is divine.'

She waited for Kit to relent and to show her that he was the man she'd fallen for. That the strong principled man was not some illusion her brain had conjured up.

'Will you do it for me? This one last thing?' she whispered. 'Visit your mother? Let her know that you care about her. I know you do.'

The only sound she heard was the tick-tock of the mantelpiece clock, ticking away the precious illusions of her life. She had told herself so many lies—that she was immune from him, that their relationship was purely physical, that she was not going to get hurt. Silently she willed him to take it and prove himself. His fingers stretched out, but then his gaze hardened. His hand fell to his side.

'I'm no longer a child, Mrs Wilkinson. I've grown beyond the need for toys. Thank you all the same. Perhaps one of your nieces will have a use for it.'

He wasn't going to do it. He was going to allow Mrs Reynaud to die without acknowledging her as his mother. A great hole opened within Hattie. She had to make one final attempt to reach the man she knew he could be.

'I did it because I cared about you and what happens in your future,' she whispered. 'Why don't you care enough about me to even try?'

His mouth twisted. 'I'm not the sort of man

you should care about. I warned you of that before we began.'

Hattie balled her fists. The scene swam before her eyes and she desperately wished her heart had remembered that. Having him here, breaking all her illusions, was far worse than finding out about what Charles thought of her, but she refused to collapse in a heap. 'You are right. You did. We have nothing more to say to each other.'

'You are asking me to go.' He tilted his head to one side.

Hattie clung on to the remains of her self-control. 'I am demanding. I am sure you know the difference, Sir Christopher. Enjoy your life in London. I intend to enjoy mine here in Northumberland. Summer has ended. Irrevocably and completely.'

'Never let it be said that I don't do as a lady requests.' He gave an elaborate bow, but his expression might as well have been carved from marble. 'Your servant, Mrs Wilkinson.'

Hattie kept her body upright until she heard the front door slam. At the sound she crumpled down on the floor. Moth came over and nuzzled her shoulder. Hattie gathered the little dog to her breast and rocked back and forth.

'What have I done, Moth? Oh, what have I done?'

* * *

'I saw him,' Hattie said, coming to kneel beside Mrs Reynaud's bed early the next morning. She had called, but Mrs Reynaud's maid said that she didn't feel well enough to rise and she had refused to allow the doctor to be called. However, Hattie insisted on seeing Mrs Reynaud and was ushered up.

Mrs Reynaud's blue-veined hand grasped Hattie's as tears glimmered in her eyes. 'You saw him this morning? So early?'

'Last night. He was waiting for me when I returned from the lecture.' Hattie bit her lip, promising herself that she wouldn't burst into tears all over Mrs Reynaud. She had volunteered for this. She could hardly confess that she considered Kit to be a different sort of person. He had turned out to be made from the same cloth as her late husband—charming but unreliable, not someone to count on. 'I fulfilled your request and gave him the jumping-jack. He deserved to know that you regretted abandoning him. He reacted badly. He will be well on his way to London. He wasn't the man I thought him to be.'

'I'm sorry.' Mrs Reynaud gently placed her hand on Hattie's shoulder. 'I had such hopes. I wanted… It doesn't matter now.'

'This has nothing to do with you. I simply

had a few misconceptions.' Hattie gave a careful shrug. There was little point in recounting the precise details of what had happened. 'The scales truly fell from my eyes. I realised that I was living a life full of illusions, thinking the best of people. From now on, I shall live a life full of practicality and strict cynicism.'

Mrs Reynaud's hand dropped from her shoulder. All the vitality fell from her, leaving her an old and helpless woman. 'He isn't coming. Ever. You are trying to tell me gently. I hate gentle, Hattie. I always have.'

'I don't think he will.' Hattie forced the words from her throat.

'What sort of a child can forgive their mother for that? I was wrong to hope for understanding.' Mrs Reynaud's bottom lip quivered. Then she gave herself a shake and continued. 'There were so many things I wanted to tell him. I should have listened to John and stayed away. I ruined everything for you.'

'There was nothing to ruin,' Hattie admitted. 'You must get that idea out of your head. It was a summer flirtation and now summer is over. We both knew the rules.' Hattie forced a smile. 'Perhaps it will make for a cautionary tale to my nieces when I can bear to speak about it.'

'Last night I saw how he looked at you.'

'He has his life in London. He always did. He never made a secret of it, even if for a time I chose to forget it.' Hattie hated how the words stuck in her throat. She wasn't excusing Kit, but she had seen his unguarded expression when he realised who Mrs Reynaud was. Despite everything, her heart still bled for him and what he could be. Underneath his charm, part of him remained that little boy whose mother had rejected him. 'He has no interest in staying.'

'I understand.' Mrs Reynaud sat up straighter and tightened the shawl about her shoulders. 'He made his own fortune, you know. Far more than my unlamented husband's. He can be very single minded. Over the years, I have followed every single scrap of news.'

'I wanted you to know and I will go now, leave you to rest.' Hattie gripped her reticule. She wished she could offer Mrs Reynaud more comfort. She wanted to tell her that Kit was better than she thought and that he actually cared and would appear once his temper had cooled. 'It is not good to live a life of illusions. That lesson is now etched on my heart.'

'Mrs Wilkinson may know a lot of things, but she doesn't know everything,' a low voice said behind her. 'She remains far too quick in judging others.'

Hattie jumped. Half-afraid that somehow her fevered mind had conjured the voice, she could do nothing more than breathe. 'Kit.'

He stood in the doorway, wearing the same clothes that he'd worn last night. His eyes were sunken and his chin unshaved. Bits of bracken and twigs clung to his breeches. She had never seen him look that dishevelled or that dangerous before.

Hattie ruthlessly suppressed the leap in her pulse. After what she'd learnt about him, she refused to be attracted to him. She was not going to suffer any more lusting after someone who could never be the person she deserved. From now on, she took charge of her life. 'You should be on your way to London, Sir Christopher. You said you were going.'

'I am no apparition, Mrs Wilkinson. I am here and not on the road to London.'

'How? Why?'

Mrs Reynaud gave a little squeak and the colour drained from her face.

'Your maid let me in, Mother. I didn't mean to startle you.' Kit held out his hands. 'I am here as you requested.'

Tears flowed down Susan's face. 'You called me mother.'

'You did give birth to me.' Kit moved into the

room, filling it. 'Until Mrs Wilkinson gave me the jumping-jack, I had no idea you were dying. You should have informed me. You knew where I was.'

'Would you have read the letter?'

Kit shrugged. 'As you didn't write it, it is a moot question. But I like to think I would have without prompting. But why did you involve Mrs Wilkinson in your scheme? That was unforgivable.'

Hattie pressed her fingers together, trying to take it in. Kit remained in Northumberland, rather than departing immediately for London. And he was calling Mrs Reynaud 'Mother' as if he had been saying such a thing every day of his life. She pushed her shoulders back and lifted her chin. 'I volunteered.'

Mrs Reynaud struggled to sit and a series of violent coughs racked her.

'Are you dying?' Kit asked when the coughs subsided. 'Or has Mrs Wilkinson been exaggerating in an attempt to appeal to my better nature?'

'Kit!' Hattie cried. 'One does not ask questions like that! Particularly not to one's mother.'

He raised an eyebrow. His sardonic glance raked her. 'You are going to tell me what to say as well as what to do now?'

The heat rose on Hattie's cheeks. 'I merely meant that you should not be so direct.'

'I appreciate direct,' Mrs Reynaud cackled. 'I'm not dead yet. I hope you appreciate that Mrs Wilkinson is a good person with a sterling reputation.'

'My reputation is my concern,' Hattie said proudly, keeping her shoulders back. She was never going to ask him for anything.

'Is it really you, Kit?' The tears welled up in Mrs Reynaud's eyes. 'I've wanted to speak to you for so very long. I feared today would never come. Doctor Gormley has given me a little while yet, but my wicked past is catching up with me.'

'I have come, Mother.' He glanced about the small room. His gaze seemed to take in everything. Hattie was conscious of her old blue gown and the fact that the lace needed replacing. 'You should have let me know earlier that you were in trouble.'

'You see now why I did what I did,' Hattie said in an undertone. 'Your mother wanted to see you. It was important.'

He turned to her. His face was an imperious mask. 'I believe I have an adequate understanding of what is important.'

'I will take your word for it.'

'I'd appreciate it if you would allow me some time alone with my mother.' His face softened 'Please, Hattie.'

Hattie gave a helpless glance at Mrs Reynaud. She hated leaving her alone with Kit, knowing how cold and cutting he could be. Mrs Reynaud nodded. 'I will be fine now, Hattie. You brought my son to me.'

'You don't allow him to bully you, Mrs Reynaud.'

'Such an opinion of me,' Kit said in a low tone.

'You deserve it.' Hattie did not pause as she walked through the door.

Kit sat with his mother quietly without saying anything. He had planned several speeches out on the moor, but no words were adequate to explain the depth of emotions which coursed through his body. This crumpled bit of humanity was his mother, the woman who had given birth to him. He tried to reconcile her with his memory of the beautiful, fascinating creature who had walked away from him all those years ago. But when he looked into her eyes, he knew and he saw something akin to love and regret.

'Don't leave me, Kit,' she murmured. 'Stay. I want you here.'

'I've no intentions of going anywhere,' Kit said, watching tears slide down her crumpled face. 'I am determined to stay. You are my only living relative in the world. I wanted to know you wanted me. You are my mother.'

'Good.' She frowned slightly. 'And your intentions towards Mrs Wilkinson?'

Kit crossed over to the door and shut it firmly. 'That is my business.'

'Do you love her?'

'We are here to speak about you,' Kit said, keeping his voice calm, but making sure that his mother knew that speaking about his relationship with Harriet was forbidden. He refused to discuss his feelings for her with anyone. 'First things first.'

'She is a good woman,' his mother persisted.

'I know that!'

'You hurt her deeply. Behaving in that fashion. Everyone saw you cut her.'

Kit crossed his arms. 'I warned her. Nothing happened that Harriet did not agree to.'

'You'd be a fool to allow her to slip through your fingers. You—'

'Are you going to keep telling me the obvious?' Kit made an annoyed sound in the back of his throat.

Susan Reynaud might be his mother, but it

gave her no right to interfere in his life. His feelings for Harriet were private and very new. All he knew was that he'd never felt like this about any woman before. Harriet was more than a mistress, she was his friend. He knew he wanted her in his life.

The worst thing about last night had been the thought that he might never hold Harriet in his arms again. She had told him to go and it was as if his heart had been torn from his chest—a feeling which had only intensified throughout the night and he knew that he had thrown away something very precious.

The first step to winning back Hattie was to make peace with his mother. To see if Hattie was right and his mother did want him in her life. Out on the fell, he discovered that it was something he hardly dared hope for.

His mother gave a little laugh. 'I know that noise. It will work out. All you need to do is to go to her and explain. I believe she loves you despite your dreadful behaviour. You should marry her. I thought she might be right for you and I am never wrong in such matters.'

'And my father—was he right for you?'

'No, we should never have married,' his mother said firmly. 'My parents forced me into the marriage. I tried to run away, but they found me and dragged me to the altar. We fought worse than cats and dogs. You came along when the marriage was dead.' Her eyes filled with tears. 'I regretted many things about that time, but I never regretted having you. I naïvely thought they'd allow me to have you. The court does not look kindly on fallen women. And then later John extracted the promise in exchange for a roof over my head. All I could hope for was that, some day, you'd come and I could tell you of my love and my longing for us to be together. Today is that day.'

'You are a great believer in the power of love.'

'Sometimes, it has been all I have had to believe in.'

'I was waiting for you to come to me,' Kit explained. 'My uncle never left me any word. Until Harriet said your name at the Stagshaw fair, I had no idea what had happened to you. You vanished after my father died and that was all I knew. Then I was afraid that you'd see my father in me and would reject me.'

'Oh, Christopher.' A single tear ran down his mother's cheek.

Kit hung his head. 'I was rude to you last night. It was wrong of me. You gave me life and all I could do was to treat you badly.'

'We both made mistakes. Me more than most.' She raised her hand and stroked his cheek.

'Am I like my father?' The words slipped from his throat.

'In looks, maybe, but in temperament, no. He could never admit that he was wrong.' His mother held up her hand. 'Before you protest that I can't possibly know, John used to read me your letters and I have followed every scrap of news about you and your exploits.'

Kit regarded the woman who gave him life and knew that he wanted her in his life. He wanted her to play a part for the rest of her life. They both had wasted so many years.

'Where are those letters you wrote, Mother? I want to read them.'

Hattie sat in her drawing room, stroking Moth's head, trying to make sense of this morning. She had paused on the stairs, ready to sweep in if any pieces needed picking up, but all she had heard was the sound of silence and the click of a door.

Her heart squeezed. She should be pleased that he came back for his mother, but it caused problems. The desire she felt for him remained strong, but whatever happened, she was not going to go back to where they were before.

That much had ended. She had more respect for herself.

'Sir Christopher Foxton for you, ma'am.' Mrs Hampstead gave a loud sniff.

Hattie stood up, determined to be gracious, rather than resentful. She held out her hand and ignored the way Moth ran immediately to him. 'Sir Christopher. How good of you to call.'

'Shall I stay, ma'am?' Mrs Hampstead asked, giving Kit a fierce glare.

'I believe I can handle Sir Christopher.'

'Very well, ma'am.' Mrs Hampstead picked Moth up and tucked her under her arm.

The silence when she left threatened to suffocate Hattie. She gulped a breath of air.

'Harriet.' Kit came forwards, his arms open wide as if he was going to enfold her in his embrace.

Hattie held up her hand and he stopped immediately. Standing close enough to touch if she reached out her hand. Hattie kept her arm rigidly at her side. 'You wished to see me, Sir Christopher?'

'You are angry with me. You need to know that I did not want it to be this way. I fought against it. This thing, this connection between us, was not supposed to happen. I conduct my affairs by strict rules. Always and without exception. But with you, I find myself breaking them.' He shook his head. 'Before you become angry think about what this is doing to me. What agony it has been.'

'I have every right to be angry.' She swallowed hard and struggled to maintain control. The last thing she was going to do was to give him the satisfaction of seeing how deeply he affected her. She hated confrontations, but this time she had to do it. 'You were appalling. I never asked you to fight against anything.'

'I listened to you, Hattie.' He gave one of his smiles that had the power to turn her insides to mush. 'You see. I did as you asked. I met my mother. Surely that means something.'

She took a steadying breath. 'I'm supposed to be impressed with this sacrifice of yours?'

He tilted his head. 'You're not?'

'I am busily wondering what sort of game you are playing. You've suffered some minor inconveniences and now expect the world to bow down in gratitude.'

'I'm not playing any game. Your words reached me deep inside.' He thumped his fist against his chest. 'You made me realise the sort of man I wanted to be. Last night, I wandered the fells, unable to rest. I thought a lot about how my life was going and what I wanted from it. I most definitely didn't want my mother to die without me having taken the opportunity to meet her properly. I intend to do that. I am staying.'

'Good.' Hattie crossed her arms. What did he want—a medal for doing the right thing? 'I am sure your mother will be pleased to have you here.'

'Harriet, I'm staying. I want things to continue between us.' He put his hands on her shoulders.

Her heart thudded. He called her Harriet again.

'Are you seriously suggesting that everything is forgotten? That we go back to what we had before?' Hattie crossed her arms. 'Summer is over, Sir Christopher.'

Kit watched her much as a cat watched a mouse. 'And your objection is?'

'What we had was destroyed. I have no wish to go back to that.'

'What do you want from me, Harriet?' His voice was soft and insistent. 'Tell me and it shall be yours. I'll even marry you if it will make you happy.'

Hattie knew if he touched her again, she'd melt. And nothing would be solved. Kit might only want a physical relationship, but she wanted more. She deserved more.

'I don't want anything from you, Sir Christopher.' She hugged her arms about her waist. 'I explained why we must part. My reasoning has not changed. We agreed the rules when our affair began.'

'Rules are made to be broken.'

'Really?' She lifted an eyebrow. 'Rules should be broken only when it suits you. I don't live that way.'

Kit visibly winced.

'I was an ass. It was wrong of me. I know what is important.' He held out his hand. 'I didn't want to feel like this, Hattie. I fought against it, but it happened. I have accepted that now and stopped fighting. I want to do the right thing with your help.'

He didn't want it to happen. He accepted it. Hattie rolled her eyes. She was supposed to think this was an apology? Or, worse still, some sort of lily-livered offer? 'Fight harder and you will get over it. I promise.'

'What if I tell you that I am prepared to stay in Northumberland? For as long as you like?'

'And I am supposed to believe you? Just like that? The great Sir Christopher shows up at my house, gives a highly reluctant marriage proposal and I fall into his arms? Is that the way it works?'

A wicked glint appeared in his eyes. 'It sounds like a good scenario to me.'

'If that is all you wish to discuss, I shall bid you good day. You must leave, Sir Christopher. We have nothing further to say to each other. Ever.'

Chapter Fourteen

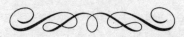

'What is going on here?' Kit asked when he arrived back at the Lodge and saw a stand off between Rupert and Johnson. Rupert physically blocked the door to his bedroom while Johnson glowered at him. Kit controlled his temper. The last thing he wanted to do was to have to deal with Rupert and Johnson. All he wanted was his bed and sleep. After he rested, he knew he'd come up with a viable plan to win Harriet.

'A slight misunderstanding, sir,' Johnson said. 'Mr Hook wishes to prevent me packing your things.'

'Returning to London would be a mistake, Kit. I beg you to reconsider.'

'Sir Christopher never reconsiders, Mr Hook. I have explained this to you several times,' Johnson said with a long-suffering sigh. 'I know my gentleman, begging your pardon. You should allow me to do my duty.'

'Unpack the bags, Johnson. I want the rose bedroom made ready as well.' Kit looked hard at his manservant. 'We are staying…for the fore-seeable future.'

Both men's jaws dropped open. Johnson re-covered himself first.

'Very good, sir. The rose bedroom will be made ready.' Johnson bustled off, shaking his head.

Kit fought hard not to laugh. He had never seen his manservant as flummoxed before. See-ing Johnson shaken out of his usual reserve was the sole moment of merriment he'd been able to derive from the catastrophe.

'We are not going to London?' Rupert squeaked.

'Are you deaf, Rupert? To repeat myself—we are staying.'

'Truly?' Rupert's voice cracked. 'We are stay-ing. Here in Northumberland? I'm about to start believing in miracles.'

Kit raised an eyebrow. Miracles? Right now he needed one, but he would not allow himself to lose hope. He intended to prove to Harriet that he was worthy and worth taking a risk on.

'I simply saw the error of my ways,' Kit said in a tone that allowed for no further questions. 'I regret that I haven't been able to speak to you about the lecture before now. Perhaps going on about the mating habits of the newt while staring directly at Miss Parteger was not the best strategy. There was rather a shocked ripple which ran through the crowd. Next time, think about your audience's sensibilities.'

Rupert had the grace to flush. 'I adore her. The words came tumbling out.' He pressed his hand to his heart. 'Kit, do you think I have a chance? Her parents want a title and I have none.'

Kit pursed his lips. Once he would have told Rupert to forget Miss Parteger and move on, but now knowing Harriet, he knew that moving on was the wrong tack. There were times in a man's life when he had to dig in and fight.

'You are determined on this course?'

Rupert gave a slow nod.

'Titles are not everything, Rupert. It is more important that you two get on. Sometimes you have to hope.'

'Without a title I am nowhere.'

'Your great-uncle might die without an heir. You'd have a title then.'

Rupert looked dubious. 'He has just married a woman young enough to be my sister.'

'It remains a distant possibility, I grant you, but it might get you a hearing.'

'How will I convince her father and, more importantly, her mother of that? Mr Parteger only found the lecture of passing interest.'

'To a truly determined man, you should see this as an opportunity rather than a door closing in your face.' Kit repeated the words he'd told himself over and over on the way back to the Lodge.

'She is an angel, Kit. I swear. Every man jack will be after her when she has her Season.'

'Then you shall go to London when she goes, but for now, you can remain here.' Kit gritted his teeth. London right now held no attraction. He had to hope that Harriet would see sense before he had to take Rupert to London. 'I promise, Rupert.'

Rupert nodded, digesting the news. 'Who is going to use the rose bedroom?'

Kit noticed the distinct change in subject. A small prickle of concern went through him. What precisely was Rupert planning? 'My mother.'

'Your mother?'

'Even I have a mother, Rupert,' Kit said drily. She was lost and now she has been found again. I intend for her to live out the remainder of her

days in comfort. And I shall be making my hom
here, for absence of doubt.'

'And Mrs Wilkinson? The way you cut her a
the lecture was the talk of the village.'

'I never discuss ladies, Rupert, you know that
Now get on with your studies. You have a repu
tation to maintain.'

Rupert's face broke into a wide smile. 'Yo
are right.'

Kit turned away. Rupert might have a repu
tation to maintain, but he had a reputation t
change. Right now, he wasn't sure which wa
the harder task.

Late the next morning, Hattie discovere
Stephanie in her drawing room, with a cloth ove
her eyes as she lay on the *chaise-longue*.

After Kit left, Hattie had been unable to sum
mon the energy to do little more than sob. Th
sobbing had given way to steely determinatio
late in the night. Going and unburdening hersel
to Mrs Reynaud was now impossible. She shud
dered at the thought of explaining the situatio
to Kit's mother.

The only real option had been to go to Steph
anie and hope she could bury herself again i
trivial tasks, anything to keep from thinking an

wishing that it could have been different, that Kit had really meant his proposal.

'You are bold coming here, Hattie,' Stephanie pronounced without removing the cloth when Hattie announced her presence. 'After what you did!'

'Is there some problem?'

'Yes, my nerves are torn to shreds.' Stephanie waved a hand. 'Yesterday, dear Mrs Hampstead informed me that Sir Christopher was at your house late on the night of Mr Hook's infamous lecture on the habits of newts. You entertained him. Goodness knows how many other people saw him go in. Your house can be seen from the road. Imagine what would happen if this news gets out! You can't claim that he was being heroic this time.'

'I'd rather not think about it.' A shiver went down Hattie's spine. Of all the times to be seen and remarked on. Right when she was finishing with Kit. She pinched her nose. It was, though, another explanation of why Kit felt the need to offer. 'It wasn't what you think, Stephanie.'

Stephanie tore the cloth from her eyes. 'You promised, Hattie. My sister! Think about what this will do to poor sweet Livvy!'

'You are not waiting to hear my side.'

'I have been comforting Mrs Hampstead, who

is in floods of tears. She told me all about how you used to go out riding and return with grass stains. She thought she knew you!'

'Mrs Hampstead should have spoken to me. I would have explained.' Hattie removed her bonnet with a trembling hand. Never had she been so angry with herself. She had been foolish in the extreme to think the affair would remain undiscovered.

'Your *lover* reappeared yesterday morning and you entertained him alone.' Stephanie's lip curled. 'Not content with the other night, was he? He had to make doubly sure that everyone knew what sort of loose woman you are. My sister! You were a widow with a spotless reputation until that man came along. One come-hither glance and you forget your principles. Everything that is important to you.'

Hattie summoned all of her dignity. Stephanie had no right to speak to her like that. Ever. But screaming at her like a fishwife wasn't going to solve anything. 'Sir Christopher made an offer of marriage.'

'And you accepted?' Stephanie clapped her hands and her entire face changed. 'You might have said, Hattie, you sly puss. I have been worrying so. I couldn't eat all yesterday and my head pains me. You were really too bad not to think about my nerves.'

Hattie waited a heartbeat. 'I refused.'

'You...*what*?' Stephanie's shriek could be heard in two counties. 'Are you destined for a room in Bedlam?'

'It was an infamous offer, made in such a way that he knew I had to refuse.' Hattie tapped her foot, feeling her hard-won self-control starting to slip. 'What sort of woman did he think I was?'

'It was an offer, an offer that could have saved your life.'

'I know the difference between a genuine offer and a pastry crust, easily made and easily broken off, Stephanie. Sir Christopher's was one of the latter.' Hattie lifted her chin proudly. 'I told you after Charles died that I had no intention of marrying anyone and I meant it.'

'I declare, Harriet Wilkinson, you carry your devotion to your dead soldier too far. I know Charles was the love of your life, but you are facing ruin. Ruin of the most public kind. You couldn't afford to turn him down. Livvy can't afford to have you turn him down.'

Hattie stared at her sister, torn between laughing and crying. What she felt for Charles was a schoolgirl crush that had long since vanished. The Kit-shaped hole in her heart would take far longer to mend. Until the night of the lecture, she'd really believed in him. But there was little point in explaining this to Stephanie. Stephanie only heard what she wanted to hear.

'He made the offer with the expectation that I'd refuse,' she said carefully. 'He knew my feelings on marrying again.'

'Was your first marriage that idyllic?' Stephanie snapped. 'People get married for reasons of duty and then make the best of it. Will you ever marry again, Hattie? Do you truly require perfection?'

Hattie regarded her hands. The old Hattie would have simply allowed the assumption to stand, but it was time she stopped hiding behind a façade. 'You were always wrong about my marriage to Charles. It was a sham from start to finish and I only found out too late.'

'Sham?' Stephanie looked perplexed. 'You were so in love with him.'

Rapidly and with as few words as possible, Hattie explained about her discovery and what she had done about it. Stephanie listened in absolute silence. Telling her proved far easier than telling Kit.

'And now you see why I can't marry Kit,' Hattie finished.

'Oh, Hattie, you should have said something!' Stephanie held out her hand. 'You are my sister.

You should have trusted me enough to explain. I want the best for you.'

'There was nothing you could do.' Hattie gave a shrug. 'And I thought if I pretended that it had never happened that it would go away.'

Stephanie rolled her eyes. 'Perhaps you were right. If I had known, maybe I would have been more determined that you marry.'

Hattie glanced at Stephanie. A huge weight fell from her shoulders. Stephanie was behaving remarkably well. And she was right. She should have had enough courage to say the words years ago. 'I most definitely wouldn't have wanted more matchmaking. You've done enough as it is.'

Stephanie tapped a finger against her lips. 'Do you love Sir Christopher?'

'Yes...or rather I thought I did. I thought he was a different man.' Hattie pressed her hands together. Her feelings for Kit were all jumbled up. She wanted to hate him, but a tiny piece of her kept trying to convince her that he was the sort of man for her. 'Don't you see, Stephanie? I have done the same thing again—fallen in love with an illusion.'

'Sometimes, Hattie, you have to take a chance. You would have done everyone a favour. Think of the doors which would have opened for Livvy.'

Hattie shook her head. Trust Stephanie to be

thinking of herself and her family's advancement. 'I refuse to marry simply to satisfy society, Stephanie.'

Stephanie pressed her lips together. 'This is the first time Sir Christopher has offered marriage?'

'To me? Yes.' Hattie pleated her skirt between her fingers. 'He only did it because of his mother, I am sure. He was adamant two days ago in his opposition to marriage. It is the only reason I can think of. Imagine being married because his mother forced the issue.'

'His mother?' Stephanie made a face. 'Surely Sir Christopher is old enough to decide what to do without his mother's input. Who is she that she commands such respect? If Sir Christopher is half the man he seems to be, he will have made the offer because he is worried about your reputation. This is typical of your excuses, Hattie. You see problems where there are none. You must trust me on this. I am your older sister.'

'Mrs Reynaud is his mother. They are no longer estranged.' Hattie clasped her hands together to stop them from trembling. Stephanie had to understand why she had refused the proposal. She was not some desperate young miss grateful for the smallest crumb to fall from his table. 'You should have heard the proposal—all about

how he didn't want this and how he was breaking all his rules. It was ungracious. He expected
me to refuse. It certainly deserved a refusal.'

Stephanie sat in silence. 'And where is Sir
Christopher now?' she asked finally. 'I would
like to speak to him.'

'Do not interfere, Stephanie. Allow me to run
my life for once. I am a grown up and fully capable of doing so.'

Stephanie opened and closed her mouth several times. 'If that is what you desire, Hattie. I
wash my hands of you. I will not interfere again,
even if you go on bended knee to me.'

'I suppose Mr Hook will go to London,' Hattie
said, trying to change the subject. 'Now that he
has given his lecture, do you think he is suitable?'

'Livvy needs a successful Season before she
thinks about marriage.' Stephanie shook her head.
'I fear Mr Hook is not for her. Did you hear what
he said in his lecture? Poor Mr Parteger was beside himself with rage.'

'I thought it was laughter,' Hattie said, remembering the snort. 'Livvy will have to choose her
husband carefully.'

'No, Livvy will marry who I tell her to. Honestly, I don't know what possesses that child
these days. She keeps going outside to think.

Portia says that she goes to the cedar of Lebanon and sits.'

'Do you want me to have a word with her... now that you are satisfied that I remain respectable in society's eyes?' Hattie asked. 'Put it in terms she might understand? Remember how you chafed when our parents forbade you meeting Mr Parteger?'

'I suppose a refused marriage offer is better than nothing.' Stephanie gave a loud sniff. 'As long as I have your word that nothing untoward like this will ever happen again, you may speak to Livvy and see if you can reason some sense into her.'

'I am through with romance and all other affairs.'

'Good to hear.' Stephanie fluffed out her skirts. 'Then we can discuss more interesting matters such as what will Livvy wear for her Season which now won't be ruined.'

Hattie's head throbbed so much by the time she left Stephanie's that she decided to walk straight home, rather than seeking out Livvy.

Later after the baby was born, Hattie decided that she would go abroad. Livvy could go with her. Between the excitement of a Season and going abroad, Mr Hook's charms didn't stand a chance. Hattie tucked her head down and started to increase her pace. She had a trip to plan.

'You need to watch where you are going, Harriet. You nearly walked straight past me without saying hello. Hopefully we are not that far out of civility.'

Hattie stumbled. Strong hands caught her. Instantly a pulse of heat coursed through her. Kit here and dressed in his day clothes with tan breeches and high-topped boots.

Her body wanted to melt against him. She kept herself perfectly rigid.

She stepped away from temptation. Kit might not have left, but things were finished between them. It bothered her that her headache melted away under the heat of his gaze.

'I thought you'd be well on your way to London,' she said around the sudden tightness in her throat.

'I told you that I was staying here, so why is it that you are so insistent on sending me to London?' Kit's mouth quirked upwards. 'One would almost consider that you wanted to be rid of me.'

Hattie clasped her hands together as the warmth of his voice flowed over her. This time, she'd be strong. She'd resist the lure of his voice.

'We have nothing more to say to each other.'

He inclined his head. 'And here I thought you

were more neighbourly than that. We are clos
neighbours after all.'

Hattie regarded him suspiciously. Neigh
bourly? Was he really staying? 'You were seriou
before and intend on living in Northumberland
What about your urgent business in London?'

He snapped his fingers, dismissing the notion
'My mother is unable to travel. She enjoys th
neighbourhood. Then there is the Lodge, which
needs fixing. Pressing matters. The business ca
wait.'

'Then I shall have to get used to seeing you a
various functions.' She tilted her head upward
so that her bonnet shielded her eyes.

'I've no plans to be a hermit.'

'The entertainment around here is a bit more
tame than you are used to.'

'I have found it adequate thus far.' He touched
his hand to his hat. 'I trust it will continue.'

'Why are you out this way? And on foot?'

His body stilled. 'Rupert is about to mee
Livvy in the woods. I came across a note from
her this morning.'

Hattie's mouth dropped opened. She should
have expected it. Livvy was headstrong, but she
also was young. 'How long has this been going
on?'

Kit carefully shrugged. His fingers itched t

straighten Hattie's bonnet. He hadn't anticipated coming on her like this. Alone. He wanted to pull her into his arms and kiss her soundly, but he'd made a mess of things yesterday. Today was about proving that he was worthy. Discovering the note had been an answer to his prayers. It was his one chance to show to her that he cared about her and her family.

'I was occupied with other things and failed to pay attention. They have been communicating by leaving notes for each other in the circulating library,' he said and watched her cheeks colour. 'These clandestine liaisons need to stop.'

'As I have discovered, clandestine does little good to anyone.'

'Has something happened?' Kit asked, every nerve on alert. She had to want him, rather than being forced into the marriage. He knew that now.

'Mrs Hampstead complained to Stephanie, but I explained your proposal and my reasons for refusal.' Her lips turned up in a mocking smile. 'All is well.'

Kit frowned. All was not well. Hattie was being utterly stubborn. She refused to hear what he had tried to say. He simply had to figure out another way. And the first piece was discovering what Rupert and Livvy were up to.

'In the note I saw, Livvy asked Rupert to meet her in the usual place. Do you have any idea where the usual place will be?'

Hattie frowned. 'What are you going to do?'

'Find out what is going on. The last thing I want to do is to panic them into taking drastic action.'

Harriet paled and he saw that she understood precisely what might be at stake. 'My sister and brother-in-law wish Livvy to marry a title. Mr Hook seems like a perfectly acceptable man, but Stephanie is immovable on this.'

'So Rupert informed me.' Kit stroked his chin. 'He might inherit a title if his great-uncle dies without an heir, but he has just married a young woman. He feels it wrong to make mention of something that might not happen.'

Harriet nodded. 'I understand the difficulty, but it might do for my brother-in-law. What is your solution?'

'A long engagement and Livvy doing a Season before the marriage,' Kit said, watching her like a hawk. He had to hope that she understood why he wanted to do this.

Harriet clapped her hands. 'Pure genius. It might work. I'm impressed.'

'I can be impressive, given the opportunity,' Kit said, making his voice become silk. 'The al-

rnative is a quick elopement. Rupert appears
ery determined. You know what young lovers
an be like when they feel thwarted.'

'Stephanie would never recover from the
hame,' Harriet retorted decisively.

'Now are you going to tell me where they
might meet?'

'By the cedar of Lebanon. It is where Livvy
oes to think. Stephanie complained about it
when I spoke to her today.'

'Now we know where they go.' He shook his
head. 'I never thought Rupert had it in him.'

'It sounds like Livvy. She loves intrigue.' Her
mouth twitched. 'You have to admit that it was a
retty good scheme. I suspect even Portia didn't
guess. She can never keep a secret.'

'Is there a vantage point where we can see
the tree?'

'Yes, up by the folly.' Harriet pointed towards
a gentle hill. 'It is a bit far away.'

'I brought a spyglass.'

Her mouth dropped open. 'You are well prepared.'

'We observe and take action as necessary,'
Kit explained. 'I've no wish to interrupt an innocent flirtation.'

'You seem to know all the tricks.'

'How do you think I learnt to avoid them?'

She laughed. The sound rushed through hir and the tight place in his heart eased a little. Th crisis had passed and he started to hope that h could triumph. 'I'm coming with you. If there i any confrontation to be done, I want to be there

'I shall be glad of the assistance.'

Hattie walked alongside Kit. Her entire bein hummed with nerves. She couldn't tell if it wa because she was apprehensive about discover ing what Livvy was up to or because Kit wa striding alongside her. She did trust Kit to pu things right.

When he reached the crest of the hill, he with drew his spyglass.

'Are they there?'

'Yes, holding hands and looking soulful.'

Her shoulders relaxed. She had feared th worst.

'Then something can be done. I blame mysel for this. I had all the clues and did nothing abou it. Livvy's sudden liking for the circulating li brary and your stories about the mountains o books that Mr Hook got out. I just don't under stand why Portia kept silent.'

'What about her parents? What will the think?'

'But I'm her aunt.' Hattie hugged her waist

anic started to claw at her stomach. A thousand what-ifs ran through her brain. 'How am I going o solve this?'

'Big gulp of air, Harriet. In and out.' Kit's alm voice penetrated through the fog.

'I am breathing.'

'Good, now trust me. You are not alone. Your iece won't be ruined. I promise you.'

Trust him? She had little choice.

'Stephanie will have a fit.'

'Better a fit now than a catastrophe later.' He erked his head. 'Run and get her. I want her to ee this while it remains innocent.'

Hattie nodded. 'You had better be right, Kit, or I will never forgive you.'

'I had better be right or I will never forgive myself.'

'What is wrong, Hattie?' Stephanie looked up rom her sewing. 'I suppose you have come to pologise for your behaviour. Very well, I will isten.'

Hattie grasped the door frame and swallowed er quick retort. 'Apologies will have to wait. Come now, Stephanie. There is something you eed to see. Livvy's happiness depends on it.'

Stephanie put down her embroidery. 'You are being awfully mysterious.'

'It has to do with Livvy and your forbidding of Mr Hook's courtship.'

Stephanie went white. 'She hasn't run away, has she? Mrs Smith's eldest did that. The shame of it. Mrs Smith had to hide her face for weeks.'

'Livvy remains at Highfield, but I hate to think what could happen. You need to come now. Simply sitting there and expecting other people to act for you won't wash this time, Stephanie.'

Stephanie opened and closed her mouth several times. 'Who alerted you to this?'

Hattie rubbed a hand across her face. 'Sir Christopher. He discovered Livvy's communication to Mr Hook. Hurry.'

'If what you say is true, then we shall be in his debt.' Stephanie grabbed her bonnet.

Kit breathed a sigh of relief when Harriet arrived back at the hill with Mrs Parteger in tow.

'They remain there.'

He silently handed the spyglass to Harriet, who took a look and passed it to her sister.

'Is all as it was?' Harriet asked. 'Hand-holding and gazing into each other's eyes?'

Kit pursed his lips. There was no need to describe the passionate embrace he'd witnessed. 'They are young and in love. And you know what can happen when love is thwarted. It is obvious that they are a resourceful pair. No one guessed until today about their little romance.'

Mrs Parteger gave a slight gasp and leant on Hattie's arm. Harriet put an arm about her. Kit suddenly understood why she had been reluctant to leave Northumberland. She had shouldered a vast amount of responsibility.

'Kit has a plan, Sister.'

Mrs Parteger wiped her eyes. 'I should like to hear it. I never considered my baby girl capable…capable of such things.'

Kit exchanged a glance with Harriet. Her eyes danced.

'A long engagement, but Miss Parteger should have her Season. I would suggest Mrs Wilkinson would be the best person to accompany her.'

'I couldn't possibly…' Mrs Parteger began.

Harriet cleared her throat and nodded towards where the couple stood.

'What I mean to say is that it is an excellent suggestion. I can't speak for my sister, but I would be honoured if she chose to serve as Livvy's chaperon.'

He watched Harriet's eyes widen. 'Of course I'd be delighted to go if the occasion arises.'

'Shall we break this embrace up?' Kit asked, giving a loud shout.

He started down the hill. Harriet's hand

touched his sleeve. Kit fought against the urge to cover it with his hand.

'Do not think this means I have forgiven you, but thank you,' she said in an undertone. 'You appear to have saved the day.'

'Only appear? I have saved the day and allowed two people to have a chance to get to know each other before they are leg-shackled.'

'And, yes, I did want to go to London with Livvy before you ask.' Her eyes twinkled with mischief. 'I hope you are not going to be insufferably smug about the whole thing.'

'You are speaking to me and that is a start,' Kit answered. He inclined his head. His fight back had started. This time he intended to leave nothing to luck. He was going to do everything in his power to show Harriet that she should take a chance on him. 'Do remember to save me a dance at the Summerfields' ball. It is all the thanks I require.'

Chapter Fifteen

The ball to mark the end of summer hummed with activity when Hattie arrived at Summerfield three days later. She hated the bitter-sweetness of attending a ball here again. It shouldn't matter that the last time she had been here, she had met Kit, but somehow it did. That evening had changed her life in more ways than she had considered possible.

Now she was committed to dancing with him again. Over the past few days as the excitement of Livvy's engagement swirled around her, she had tried to think up an excuse, but none had come.

After he had engineered the engagement between Mr Hook and Livvy, her sister felt that Kit could do no wrong. And she kept going on about how Hattie had made a mistake in refusing him.

Even now as they waited, Stephanie made several remarks about how useful Kit was. It was as if she had suddenly been re-infected with her matchmaking fever.

Hattie closed her ears.

A tingling went down her back. She glanced over her shoulder. A tall figure alighted from a carriage and then turned to help a woman down.

Kit.

As if she had spoken his name, he turned towards where she was standing, waiting to greet the hosts. A tiny smile briefly crossed his features. He nodded towards where she stood, waiting with Livvy, and then whispered something in his mother's ear.

Once she would have blushed. Now she forced herself to coolly nod, only to be greeted by an enthusiastic wave and a gesture to come over from Mrs Reynaud. To Hattie's astonishment, Mrs Reynaud was not veiled, but dressed in a sumptuous gown with a necklace of diamonds sparking at her throat.

Briefly she contemplated pretending she had not seen the wave, but she knew that would go against the fibre of her being. She did want to see her.

'I will be back.' Hattie pressed Stephanie's hand. 'This queue is taking ages. Mrs Reynaud is here. I hadn't realised that she had recovered from her chill.'

Stephanie's gaze narrowed, taking in Hattie's reaction to the latest arrivals. 'You haven't been paying attention, Hattie. I called on Mrs Reynaud with Livvy two days ago when you were indisposed. Where is your head these days?'

'I'm going to greet my friend,' Hattie declared. 'Please don't read anything more into it.'

'As if you would allow me to!'

Hattie pulled back her shoulders, suddenly glad that she had given in to temptation and had worn a new garnet-red ball gown with cream-coloured lace around the neckline. She loved the way the skirt moved about her ankles and how the garnet-studded hairnet completed the look. She was not some widow content to stay on the shelf, but a woman determined to make the most of life. She might have agreed to dance with Kit, but it didn't mean he had to be the only man she danced with.

'You look lovely, my dear,' Mrs Reynaud said with a huge smile when she reached the pair. Close up, the family resemblance was so marked that Hattie wondered how she had missed it earlier. Whatever happened, the reconciliation had done wonders for Mrs Reynaud. 'Doesn't she look lovely, Christopher?'

Hattie forced herself not to move a muscle as Kit's gaze roamed over her.

'Mrs Wilkinson looks as she always does,' Kit said, inclining his head.

Hattie dropped the barest of curtsies. As far as compliments, she could have hardly thought of one which tasted more of ash. She searched his eyes for warmth, but found his expression guarded. 'I thank you for the compliment.'

'It was sincerely given.'

'I'm pleased you brought your mother here.'

'It took some doing. Up to the last moment she kept me guessing. Apparently she has not attended such events in years. I convinced her that no one would shun her because of past notoriety.'

Hattie lowered her voice. 'Mrs Reynaud has always been sensitive about her face, but the happiness now shines from her.'

'There is more to beauty than a face. I notice other things.'

'I agree.' Hattie shifted in her slippers, aware that the receiving line was finally moving. 'I should rejoin my party.'

'You promised me a dance.' He cleared his throat. 'As payment for arranging Rupert and Miss Parteger's engagement.'

'A promise is a promise.' Hattie knew her voice sounded too bright. 'A quadrille. It is th

ast ball of the summer after all. There is no
harm in it.'

'I was hoping for a waltz, but a quadrille will
have to do.'

Hattie's heart missed a beat as the image of
them waltzing filled her brain. Her hand curled
around her fan. She was not over him and was
likely never to be over him. The knowledge
thrummed through her. 'That would not be wise.'

'Sometimes it pays to be foolish.' He caught
her hand and lifted it to his lips.

Hattie's mouth went dry. 'But not tonight.'

She hurried off before he could answer.

Kit forced himself to dance with his mother,
Livvy Parteger and her mother before he approached the orchestra with his request. Every
fibre of his being was aware precisely where
Hattie was, but the thing had to be carefully
down. He was not about to risk losing her again.

When the music stopped, he walked over to
her and bowed, stepping in front of Dr Hornby.
'Our dance, I believe.'

At his look, Dr Hornby withdrew, muttering
about his need to speak to someone. Kit waited.

'The master of ceremonies hasn't announced
it. Shouldn't we wait and find out what the figure is?'

'Why don't we take a chance? Unless you are afraid?'

She tilted her chin upwards. 'I believe I am more than equal of dancing any dance with you.'

The master of ceremonies called out a Harlequin. Kit relaxed. There were a few opportunities about her waist. She would agree to listen by the end. She had to.

'Your sister approves of the choice of dance,' Kit remarked. 'See how she smiles?'

Harriet glanced over her shoulder and her body completely stiffened. 'I can't do this. Now with everyone watching me like I'm some backward child. I'm sorry, Kit. I just can't.'

She pulled away from him and raced from the ballroom.

Kit cursed and swiftly followed her. This time, she would hear him out.

Hattie didn't stop until she reached the small card room. With a distinct sense of irony, she went in and pulled the door shut. She thought she could dance with him until she saw Mrs Reynaud's and Stephanie's faces. It was as if everyone in the ballroom was watching her and Kit with a matchmaking gleam in their eye. The last thing she wanted was for Kit to feel forced to make another proposal.

'Harriet? Open the door.' Kit's voice allowed for no refusal. 'You can't hide for ever. Do you open it or do I knock it down?'

She went over and opened the door. Kit stood completely alone in the corridor. His hair was wild and his neckcloth askew. He had never looked handsomer. She took a step backwards.

'You promised a dance and left before it began.' He gave a crooked smile. 'Are you ill? I can't know what is wrong if you refuse to tell me.'

'I'm sorry. In the circumstances…I thought it best. I saw Stephanie and your mother.' Hattie hated how ineffectual and weak it sounded. She curled her hand about her fan and straightened her shoulders. 'The music hadn't started. I felt faint.'

'It is a bad habit of yours, leaving before a promised dance has ended.' He gave a heart-stopping smile. 'We shall have to work on it. At our wedding breakfast, you will dance a full waltz with me.'

Wedding breakfast? Hattie gulped. A great black hole opened before her. She was not going back there. This time would be far worse.

'Kit…what happened back there. You don't have to feel that… I don't want you to think…'

'Hush. Listen to me. I tried being patient with you, but it hasn't worked.' He started to pull her into his arms, but she backed up against the card table. He let his hand drop to his side and came into the tiny room. 'Things need to be said between us.'

'What things?' She looked suspiciously up at him. 'We said everything we needed to that day. I refused your offer. You don't really want to marry me. You don't want to marry at all.'

'I was wrong about many things, Harriet.'

'But…' Her voice trailed away at his intense look.

'Have you examined this ring?' he asked holding out a small gold ring with an inlaid garnet. 'Can you at least do that before you dismiss me out of hand?'

'Please…' Hattie knew her heart was breaking and she wasn't sure how long her composure would remain. She could not take another half-hearted proposal. 'Please, Kit, don't make this harder for the both of us. You made your feelings or lack of them quite clear when you asked me before. Nothing has changed.'

He ran a hand through his hair. 'I've gone about this all wrong. I did mean to finish the dance before I gave you the ring.'

She shrugged, but inside she died a little. She owed him an explanation of why they could never marry, even if she was utterly cast out from society and could no longer visit her fam-

y. 'I refuse to marry because society dictates,
it. I won't have a loveless marriage. I made
ie mistake of enduring one once and I have no
itention of ever entering such a thing again.
Vhat happened was not your fault. I take full
:sponsibility for my folly. You are absolved of
ll blame. I've no idea what Stephanie has been
aying, but you must ignore her.'

'I love you, Harriet.'

'What?' Her heart did odd little flips. She had
o have heard wrong. This was Sir Christopher
oxton who was destined never to love.

'I love you with all my heart and soul.' He
vent down on one knee. 'Will you please make
ie the happiest man on earth and marry me?
lease, Harriet, say yes. Say you find a small
orner of your heart for me. Marry me and let
ie prove to you that my love is enough for the
oth of us. You won't have a loveless marriage
ith me, I promise.'

'You love me?' she asked, to control the ham-
iering of her heart. She had never expected Kit
o say those words. In her wildest imaginings
he thought perhaps he might care for her, but
eclare his love in this fashion!

'With all my heart.' He took her hand. 'I did
all wrong when I made my first proposal. I
hould have started with the obvious facts.'

'What are the obvious facts?' Hattie brace
herself for another onslaught of how he didn
want to love her and was fighting against it.

'I love you and I have no desire to live any
where in the world without you. You make m
glad that I am alive. You make me want to gree
the world with a smile, instead of hiding awa
from it. It is why I want to marry you, so I ca
know that we will be together for the rest of ou
lives. And I want everyone else in the world t
know that I have made that commitment to you

'And I am supposed to believe you were goin
say that?' Hattie hated the way she could no
allow herself to believe, but a large part of he
was afraid to believe. She had to know that thi
wasn't some great sacrifice on his part whic
he'd regret, not tomorrow or the next day bu
some day in the not-too-distant future.

'Look at the ring. I had it engraved. Afte
what we have been through, I didn't want to tak
any chances of you failing to believe my since
ity. I intend to devote my life to you. It is wh
I arranged Rupert and Miss Parteger's engage
ment. I wanted to show you that I am capabl
and reliable.'

He placed the ring in the palm of her hand
She regarded the engraving on the inside. *H., th
keeper of my heart, K.*

'You do love me,' she whispered finally.

'And you? You told me that you cared for me that night after the lecture, but when I proposed you refused. Tell me what I can do to make you care for me again.' He touched her cheek with gentle fingers. 'Have I truly destroyed all feelings you might have had for me? Tell me it isn't too late. I want to be the man you deserve to love. What are you afraid of? Tell me so I know how to reassure you.'

The naked longing in Kit's voice resounded throughout the small room. He stood there, not moving towards her, but she could sense how much he wanted to gather her in his arms.

She knew then that he'd stayed in Northumberland not for his mother, but to show her that he could try to be the man she deserved. It was the little things that counted—the way he'd shown responsibility over his mother, how he was restoring the Lodge and how he'd engineered a solution for Mr Hook and Livvy that allowed them the chance to grow up before making that ultimate commitment. And she loved him all the more for it. She had been utterly blind and she had nearly thrown away the single most-important person in her life.

'The trouble with truly loving someone is that even when your head tells you to stop, your heart keeps right on loving.' Hattie gave a smile and knew the time was right. She no longer had to hide her feelings or wish them away. The time had come to say them out loud. 'Yes, I love you, Kit, and suspect I always will.'

His smile could have lit a thousand lanterns.

'You won my heart a long time ago,' Hattie continued. 'I think it began when you fished my gloves out of the reticule, but I didn't really know how much I cared for you until that day when Strawberry and I jumped the stone wall. You taught me to face my fears. But there was one big hurdle I couldn't face—declaring my love. You were right when you said that I had to face my fear.'

'You were tardy in your love, but I shan't hold that against you. You truly won my heart when you insisted on giving me that blasted jumping-jack at the fair. You knew what I wanted—no, what I needed. You made me into a better man, even if I kicked and screamed a bit, determined to prove you wrong.'

'You were always that man, Kit,' Hattie said gently. 'You had to believe in yourself.'

'A lesson you taught me. You showed me what loving and forgiveness was truly about.' He put his arms about her and rested his forehead against hers. 'You are willing to share the rest of your life with me, then?'

She threw her arms about his neck. 'Yes, oh, yes. I will marry you.'

Kit whispered after they had soundly kissed, 'Shall we tempt fate, Mrs Wilkinson, and return to the dance floor? I've no wish to cause a scandal.'

Hattie laughed up at him. 'I will gladly dance with you.'

When they arrived back at the ballroom, the dance had finished. Hattie noticed that Kit gave a distinct nod to the master of ceremonies. As he led her out onto the floor, the man announced the next dance—a German waltz.

Her eyes flew to his. 'You are incredibly lucky.'

'I took precautions, yes.' Kit rested his hand against her waist. 'I wanted to hold you in my arms. I had anticipated moving straight on to the second dance after the quadrille, but I prefer how things worked out.'

'You bribed the orchestra?'

'It will be worth every penny if you stay with me. Will you dance?'

She gave a decisive nod of her head. 'Yes, I'm feeling brave. I can risk being in your arms.'

The music swelled up around them and he

began to move. Absolutely correctly and wit
great precision. Not even a Lady Patroness fror
Almack's or the most severe duenna could fau
him. They slowly circled the room.

'As you can see, I am being utterly trustwor
thy,' he remarked.

'It makes a change.'

'Hopefully a welcome one.'

She moved closer. 'I am not sure what to mak
of it.'

'You don't have to make anything of it. Jus
dance. Let yourself be in the moment.'

'Are you attempting to teach me something?

'I finished with lessons a long time ago.' K
concentrated on moving his feet. With each pass
ing step, the urge to crush her to him grew. '
simply wanted to hold you in my arms.'

She started to pull away, but he tightened hi
grip, making their bodies collide.

With a whoosh, she fell against him. His bod
reacted instantly. He checked his movement an
allowed her to find her feet.

'I had no plans to go.' Her voice was breath
less.

'It is good to know. Shall we continue?' H
started to move again. This time he held he
closer, enjoying the way her skirts brushe
against his legs as they moved around the ball

room. Looking down at her, he tried to make
a memory. This was how, when they were old,
he wanted to remember her—cheeks flushed,
lips full and eyes sparkling, the most beautiful
woman in his world.

'Kit,' she breathed, her lips parted slightly.

Giving in to impulse, he raised their hands to
his mouth and touched her palm with his lips.
A soft sigh emerged from her throat. She lifted
her mouth and he bent his head. The briefest of
touches.

The shocked exclamation poured ice water
over Hattie, bringing her back from the enchanted bubble she had somehow existed in.
The reality of where she was and what she had
just done closed in around her, locking her in a
prison.

'Everyone is looking at us,' Kit said in a low
undertone.

'What are we going to do?'

Hattie froze. She had done the unthinkable.
She had shown Kit affection in public, not just
affection, but a full-blown meeting of the lips!

The growing chorus of shocked gasps resounded around the ballroom, drowning out the
orchestra. All Hattie wanted to do was run and
hide. Kissing on the dance floor when one was

twenty-seven had to rank up there as one of the more foolish things she had done in her life.

'Leave this to me,' Kit rasped in her ear. 'Take off your glove.'

Hattie fumbled with the fingers. Her ring felt heavy and awkward on her hand. All the while she was conscious that everyone was watching. Even the orchestra had stopped playing. She knew that people could not see her ring. 'What do we do now?'

Kit went down on his knee, in front of everyone. 'Will you marry me, Mrs Wilkinson?' he asked in a loud voice.

Hattie nodded and answered so that everyone could hear as relief washed over her. 'Yes, of course. With all my heart.'

'Mrs Wilkinson has just done me the honour of agreeing to become my wife,' Kit announced. He held up her hand, with the ring clearly visible. 'I hope you will understand and forgive the indiscretion. In my joy I was unable to stop my baser instincts.'

A growing round of applause swelled around them. Hattie looked down at him, her heart filled to bursting. With Kit, she had found her match and she knew their life together would be filled with happiness.

* * * * *

  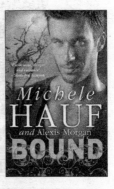

2 Free Books!

Get your free books now at
www.millsandboon.co.uk/freebookoffer

◀ in the form below and post it back to us

▐ss/Ms/Mr (please circle)
_____

▐me
_____

▐e
_____

▐s
_____

_____
Postcode

_____

▐his completed page to: Mills & Boon Book Club, Free Book
▐REEPOST NAT 10298, Richmond, Surrey, TW9 1BR

▐ out more at
▐w.millsandboon.co.uk/freebookoffer

*Visit us
Online*

0712/H2YEA